Life-Like

TOBY LITT

Life-Like

Seagull
BOOKS

LONDON NEW YORK CALCUTTA

Seagull Books, 2014

© Toby Litt, 2014

ISBN   978 0 8574 2 207 1

British Library Cataloguing-in-Publication Data
A catalogue record for this book is available from the British Library

Typeset in Adobe Garamond Pro, PT Sans, Courier, Prestige Elite, Lucida Grande and Arial
by Seagull Books, Calcutta, India

Printed and bound by Maple Press, York, Pennsylvania, USA

EPISODES

Paddy & Agatha$_{14}$

Paddy & Henry$_7$

Henry & Anyone$_{15}$

Paddy & Veronika$_3$

Veronika & Roger-Roger$_{16}$

Veronika & Alice$_8$

Alice & Rik$_{17}$

Paddy & Kavita$_1$

Kavita & Dr Anise$_{18}$

Kavita & Dr Nykvist$_9$

Dr Nykvist & Barbie$_{19}$

Kavita & Dr Mehrotra$_4$

Ghost Story$_0$

Joseph & Emmanuel$_{20}$

John & Joseph$_{10}$

John & Agatha$_{21}$

John & John$_5$

Yaminah & Yahya$_{22}$

John & Yaminah$_{11}$

John & Ophélia$_{23}$

Agatha & John$_2$

Amanyana & Bloodkill$_{12}$

May & Jesus$_{24}$

Agatha & May$_6$

Max & Dylan$_{25}$

Agatha & Max$_{13}$

Agatha & Paddy$_{26}$

FIRST PUBLICATIONS AND DETAILS

The title page appeared in *Short Fiction in Theory & Practice* 2(1–2) (December 2012). Edited by Ailsa Cox.

'Paddy & Kavita': *Short Fiction* 2 (2008). Edited by Anthony Caleshu.

'Agatha & John': *Torpedo* 7 (2010). Edited by Chris Flynn.

'Paddy & Veronika': *Horizon* (April 2011), Salt Publishing's e-mag. Edited by Clare Pollard. *The Barcelona Review* website (2013). Edited by Jill Adams.

'Kavita & Dr Mehrotra': *The Barcelona Review* website (2013). Edited by Jill Adams.

'John & John': Winner of the Manchester Fiction Prize (2009); appeared on the prize website.

'Paddy & Henry': *Mechanics' Institute Review* 5 (Autumn 2008).

'Veronika & Alice': *Fleeting Books* website (October 2013). Edited by Matt Shoard.

'Agatha & Max': University of East Anglia website (November 2011). Edited by Nathan Hamilton.

'Paddy & Agatha': Runner-up in the Ilkely Literature Festival Short Story Competition (2011); a short excerpt appeared on the festival website.

'Veronika & Roger-Roger': Shortlisted for the Willesden Herald International Short Story Competition (2010). *Willesden Herald New Short Stories*, VOL. 4 (London: Pretend Genius Press, 2010). Edited by Stephan Moran.

'Joseph & Emmanuel': *Wasafiri* 65 (Spring 2011). Edited by Nisha Jones and Sharmilla Beezmohun.

'John & Ophélia': *Tales of the DeCongested* 2 (December 2008). Edited by Rebekah Lattin-Rawstrone and Paul Blaney.

ACKNOWLEDGEMENTS

Kavita Bhanot, Tishani Doshi, Shivmeet Deol (1)

Nicholas Royle, Sarah Hall (5)

Caroline Vollans, Julian Grenier (18)

Mic Cheetham

Andrew Kidd

Russell Celyn Jones, Julia Bell

Naveen Kishore, Bishan Samaddar, Sohini Dey

Charlotte & Vaughan, Georgina, Duncan

Tev & Simone, Sally & Drew, Lisa & Steve, Alex & David, Matt & Lesley, Jenny & Andrew, John & Cathy, Zadie & Nick, Hari & Katie, Stella & Shelley, Jim, Diane, Colin, Emily

Leigh, Henry, George

PADDY & KAVITA

His bedroom door blew shut, and Max's arm—caught halfway through —was broken. He cried as if he'd just become an orphan, and knew what becoming an orphan meant. Paddy, who the moment before had opened both windows in the main bedroom, was there almost immediately. Agatha fled in from the garden; she knew these screams were different.

When Paddy picked Max up, he bent the arm back against itself. Totalled with pain, Max vomited, then fainted. He was four and a half years old and had been making a pirate ship out of black Lego.

Agatha arrived. Paddy already knew that he would be to blame. He was the one who'd been on Max duty. The open windows—a matter of airing their fusty bedroom—had created the through-draught. He was the one who had been nearest to Max, who wasn't moving.

Since his younger sister Rose died, stillborn, this was the first properly bad thing to happen to Max. He'd had chickenpox, but that had been a good thing—got it over with before he was old enough to scratch or become infertile. Generally, Max had been a protected child: stairgates on the stairs, reins when he walked down the street, shouted advice as he neared the top of the climbing frame.

Paddy felt Max's limbs, as he had done after any number of minor falls—only this time, halfway along the left forearm, he felt a queasy give.

'It's broken,' he said.

'Hospital,' Agatha said. 'Now.'

Paddy carried Max down to the car while Agatha fetched the keys. They went out, leaving the French doors to the garden open.

1

When they were halfway there, Max woke up, and it was as if his arm had been broken all over again. Agatha, in the back seat beside him, couldn't help herself—she sobbed.

'I can't drive any faster,' said Paddy.

It still took them another quarter of an hour, and then there were no parking spaces. Agatha carried Max in while Paddy drove off to find somewhere.

When he got back to A&E, the two of them were sitting together as close to the desk as they could. Max was very subdued—perhaps it was the building.

'How long?' asked Paddy. He hated returning to this place, where he had waited out his father's death.

'They don't know,' said Agatha. 'They're going to try.'

Max sat staring at the cans of soft drink in the machine. Without asking Agatha or Max, Paddy went and bought a couple.

'It's sugar,' he said. 'For the shock.'

But he had wanted a Coke for himself. He didn't know why. The taste of it was far stronger than usual—the mouthburn fiercer. It was as if someone at the factory had, along with the usual flavourings, slipped chilli powder in.

Max took a sip of the orange Tango then held it out to be taken. He was aware that one of his arms wasn't working properly. He was worried it would never work properly again.

'What happened?' asked Agatha, finally.

'Max,' called a male nurse with a clipboard.

They followed him down a corridor and round the corner where some scales stood and into a consulting room.

'He has a broken arm,' stated Agatha. 'This one.' She didn't touch.

'And so what's your name?' the nurse asked Max.

He wouldn't reply.

The nurse checked Max's eyes, his alertness, his neck and then his arm. Max tried to pull it away, which agonized.

'I just need to feel it,' said the nurse to Paddy.

'It's broken,' he said. 'Why can't you just X-ray it?'

The nurse felt along the bones, came to the jut of the break, let go immediately—too late.

Agatha had no patience with medical people. 'Why did you do that? We told you.'

'I'm sorry,' said the nurse to Max, who was beyond hearing—too loud himself. 'Did that hurt?'

'Of course you fucking hurt him,' said Agatha.

'How quickly can you X-ray him?' Paddy asked. Max had heard *fucking*.

'I'll see,' the nurse said, meaning *no queue-jumping just because I made your child cry*.

They were taken back out to the waiting room. The nurse had given Max a capful of Nurofen and another of paracetamol.

'That should help,' he said.

'Unlike you,' said Agatha, clearly.

The X-ray took two hours, then they had to wait another hour before the bone could be set.

Paddy went to buy sandwiches from a shop he knew, over the road from the hospital.

As he stepped outside, he remembered stepping outside while his father was dying. He felt a similar guilty relief.

Even as he paid for the food, he knew Agatha wouldn't eat it.

When Max, after more painkillers, and a series of extraordinary treats, had finally fallen asleep, Paddy expected the argument to begin.

'I'm going to bed,' said Agatha.

He did the washing up, then followed her, prepared to explain, but she was already asleep—a novel tented on the duvet above her belly.

That weekend, Paddy was due to go to a philosophy conference in Hull. As he anticipated, this was the ground Agatha chose, but only the following evening.

Max had been subdued all day long, still taking Nurofen, and they had allowed him as much TV as he wanted—with adverts.

'You're not intending to go, are you?'

'I have to.'

'What do you mean *have to*? Your academic career will be over if you don't?'

Paddy had anticipated this. 'No,' he said, 'but I'm due to give a paper. It's the most important forum for—'

'So it will be *good* for your reputation, if you do go.'

'I want to go,' he said. 'If Max was ill . . .'

Agatha said, 'I wouldn't go. In the same circumstances—even if I were you.'

She made it sound an absurdity. He didn't intend to intellectualize her argument: that she could never be him and yet, at the same time, him-having-been-her.

'You are going away,' said Paddy. 'Next month, on your thing.'

'I mean, I wouldn't go away right now, or if this had happened then.'

'It wasn't my fault. It was an *accident*.'

'You admitted that it happened because you opened the windows.'

'And the wind blew. And it was a very windy day. And Max was in the wrong place. And the door hit his arm at the worst possible angle— they said at the hospital. And it's a heavy door. And—'

'Any more,' said Agatha—she meant excuses.

'You know that there are millions of times you've been looking after him when something similar could have happened.'

'Are you going to Hull?'

The fact it was Hull made it seem less defensible than Glasgow or Manchester. The place didn't possess any philosophical gravitas.

'Yes,' said Paddy.

'Then there's no point talking about it.'

The following day, Agatha devoted all her attention to Max—and the day after that was Friday, which meant packing, checking and departing.

Agatha said, 'You do it.' And Paddy tried to explain to Max, who asked for some help with the pirate ship's sail.

Paddy took the train to London. He felt like crying. There was a large gap between the guilt he was meant to feel and the guilt he actually felt. *I want this*, he thought. He wanted, also, to infuriate Agatha. The trolley came past, and he bought himself a can of warm lager. He would reread his paper on the Hull train. But at Euston he was spotted by an academic he vaguely knew—Peter Bedford—who accompanied him onto the train. It wasn't crowded enough for Paddy to stick to his reserved seat, so they talked most of the way. And drank.

They were both staying in the station hotel, the Quality Royal—all the delegates were. So, once Paddy had checked in and dumped his bags in his room, he came back down for a drink at the bar. This was a very disconcerting space. The decor was hotel-usual, but when trains arrived, groups of disembarked passengers walked the length of the room pulling trolley cases.

Paddy knew everyone, apart from Kavita Singh, who was on the faculty at the University of Bombay. She was thirty-one, beautiful in a dark blue sari. He had read two of her papers on Descartes; they were interesting and, as he talked to her, became more interesting. Perhaps they even became significant.

Kavita wasn't staying at the Quality Royal. A late addition to the conference, chairing a panel for someone who'd dropped out, she was lodged at a nearby B&B. When she excused herself, Paddy offered to walk her there—surprising himself. Kavita said thank you, she would take a cab. Peter Bedford leant across to say that the rank was at the side of the building.

'See you tomorrow,' Kavita said to Paddy, who had followed her outside.

'Very gallant,' said Peter Bedford, when Paddy returned to the bar. 'And very attractive.'

'Yes,' said Paddy. He knew that to say he hadn't noticed would have been ridiculous. He was thinking about Kavita, alone, in a cab.

Back in his room, Paddy realized he had forgotten to phone Agatha to ask about Max, and about her. Slyly, he felt proud of himself. He was in so much shit anyway. Then he turned cowardly, and sent an apologetic text.

'You woke me up,' came the reply. 'Max fine. He misses you. Sleep well. Ax.'

They were still married; she could still bring herself to thumb *x*.

In the morning, to avoid a chatty breakfast with the delegates, Paddy went out looking for a greasy spoon. He found one almost immediately, just across the road, called Café M—which sounded like something from an existential novel. He had his paper with him, and wanted to work it over once more. There wouldn't be time again before the 11.15 session. He went inside and sat at a table next to the window. The place was clean and datedly modern. He ordered a full English, phoned Agatha and then Kavita came through the door. She mimed *I'll sit somewhere else*; he mimed *No, please sit here*; she mimed *Are you sure?*; he mimed *Yes, oh, yes*.

Paddy continued the conversation, aware that Kavita would now know he was married and had a son called Max. Of course, she knew he was married already—he had a wedding ring; he wore it.

Agatha was a little warmer than expected. 'Max slept through.' Paddy said he had to go—he had to register.

'That was—' he said to Kavita.

'I don't want to know,' she said. 'Subject changed. Thank you for offering to take me home last night.'

'Yes, well, Hull—'

'Maybe tonight.'

Paddy said, 'Excuse me?' and felt very English.

Kavita was wearing a pale blue sari. 'I don't want to know about your wife,' she said, 'and, if you ask to walk me home again—I mean to my bed and breakfast—I will probably say *yes*.'

Paddy didn't respond. He was hungry, and more hungover than he wanted to acknowledge.

'Depending on whether your paper is any good or not.'

'Really?' Paddy asked.

'That was a joke,' Kavita said. 'I'm usually a very direct person—not your typical Indian woman who waits for the man. The opposite cliché, that's me.'

Paddy didn't like her, her manner was already starting to annoy him, but he could—she had made clear—he could if he wanted fuck her; and in a discreet B&B no one else need know. He realized he hadn't spoken. He could fuck her. He hadn't said he wouldn't. He watched himself as he continued not to say he wouldn't.

The waitress brought Paddy's food.

Kavita ordered a poached egg on toast, and tea. Then she asked him what his paper was about. He began to explain.

'You're totally helpless,' she said, 'aren't you?'

'Yes,' said Paddy. 'I am.' And it was a relief, after all these years, to be able to admit it.

Just after they asked the waitress for the bill, Peter Bedford, the train-academic, walked past. He saw Kavita, jinked towards the door, spotted Paddy, smiled frowningly and kept walking.

'Bollocks,' said Paddy.

'Ah,' said Kavita. 'Do you think he thought . . .?'

'Of course,' said Paddy.

The conference opened at 9.30 with a plenary session of one hour. Kavita sat beside Paddy, who felt absolutely lost. His paper was the second after the coffee break—during which Kavita moved off to chat unselfconsciously with others. She was by far the most attractive person there; it was ridiculous. Paddy snuck away to the toilets where, for ten minutes, he reread his careful argument without understanding a word. Even though nothing had happened, he felt he should phone Agatha to explain.

Once on the podium for the three-paper session, Paddy looked at the hairs on his knuckles. Kavita was somewhere in the audience, but he didn't want to know where.

Afterwards, people came up to congratulate him—so he supposed he must have delivered the paper as written. More strangely yet, he must have answered some questions.

'That was very impressive,' said Kavita, who was now at his left side. 'Definitely up to scratch.'

'More than that,' said a male delegate to Paddy's right. 'I think it got us off to a flying start.'

Paddy glanced at Kavita, who gave him a smile that seemed nothing but friendly.

'There was one thing—' the male delegate said, and began to question Paddy's use of Merleau-Ponty.

'See you later,' said Kavita.

She was good at this; she could carry it off.

The first session after lunch gave delegates a choice of panels to attend. They could either go for 'Scepticism Inc.: The Self and Late-Stage Capitalism' or 'The I-Word: Linguistics and Otherness'. Paddy was just about to go into the I-Word room when Kavita approached.

'I thought the other looked more interesting,' she said. 'The *other* other.'

Paddy was ghostly in answering. 'I'll see you afterwards, then.'

To his relief, Kavita went off into the seminar room across the corridor. But, five minutes into the session, she squeezed through the door and came to join him.

During the tea break, Kavita explained that one of the capitalism papers had been cancelled—the one she had wanted to hear.

'That was a good session, though,' said Paddy. He hated his own banality. She seemed to make him hear what he was saying.

Peter Bedford came up to them both. 'So,' he said, 'how are you two enjoying the conference so far?'

Paddy thought about punching him.

The day ended with a one-hour paper given by a leading philosopher who had not attended any of the earlier sessions.

Paddy was drifting through a long trance of anxiety when he heard his name mentioned, by the voice which had just been speaking. It took him a moment to focus on what this meant: he was being cited—a previous paper of his, published last year, was being used to make a point. The words *crucial intervention* were used. People glanced towards him; Kavita, who of course was seated to his left, gave him a nudge—and not as if she'd never nudged him before; a proud, possessing nudge. In all, the leading philosopher in the field spent five minutes exploring Paddy's two-years'-previous argument about the status of the self-analytic utterances of other minds. This, he seemed to be saying, was a possible way forwards—definitely worthy of further investigation. He rounded off his paragraph by begging, humorously, a copy of the paper Paddy had delivered earlier the same day. Without thinking, Paddy went through his briefcase and pulled out the plastic folder. The philosopher was beginning his next point when Paddy said, 'Excuse me.'

Kavita began to laugh, and Paddy realized what he was doing—but by then everybody, including the speaker, was laughing, too.

On a small wave of applause, the plastic folder was washed down to the podium, where the philosopher—a practised speaker—plucked it from the outstretched hand, flicked quickly through and said, 'Ah, good, now I can finish.'

There was more laughter.

'At least in this company, no one's seriously going to accuse me of plagiarism.'

Paddy heard Kavita saying, very distinctly, 'Don't count on it, buddy.'
This time the laughter took about a minute to die down.

Paddy realized that, halfway through, he had nudged Kavita back—which seemed to mean that he was going to fuck her.

There was a meal laid on; drinking, inevitably, was to follow.

Paddy went outside to call Agatha, and was relieved and also slightly annoyed when Kavita didn't follow him.

'It went very well,' he said. 'How is Max's arm?' The conversation would not be long. 'I have to get back.' He spoke to Max, whose mouth was full of spaghetti bolognese—his favourite.

Paddy said goodbye, heard the phone in their kitchen go down and felt how far away from his family he was.

Around him, the smokers were having loud conversations. Paddy went over and cadged a cigarette, then joined the edge of the group. He was congratulated on his intervention from the floor.

'Yes, I was very flattered,' he said, to another, more serious compliment.

He had become more important. It had been worth him coming. It might have been worth the damage to his marriage. He took another gulp of bad red wine.

The cigarette allowed him, for just about the first time since finding Café M, to think. He was only in Hull for one more night. Tomorrow morning, he would check out of the hotel, and, at the end of tomorrow's sessions, he would catch an evening train back to London, then a late train home.

The filter became hot in his mouth, too hot, and he realized he still had not made a decision. More than that, aged thirty-seven, he still had not decided what sort of man he was going to be: One who did or one who didn't?

He went back inside and, as if crassly to dramatize his predicament, Kavita came across to join him. It was all too easy and obvious. Peter Bedford would be near by, watching. He was the gossiping type, as Paddy had found out on the journey up. Having seen them eating breakfast together, away from the hotel, Peter Bedford already had enough evidence to begin. It almost didn't matter whether or not Paddy slept with Kavita—people, once informed, would believe he had; even more so were he to avoid her for the remainder of the conference. Agatha probably wouldn't get to hear; she had no friends among his colleagues. But Paddy didn't like the idea of having a changed reputation. There would be future intimacy with cunts like Peter Bedford—men who believed him to be playing by the same rules as them; that the whole thing was a game, some away-from-home fun, rather than a sad attempt at self-definition through self-assertion. He could imagine what Agatha would say, if she did hear— after being furious—how it would be categorized by her as midlife crisis, clichéd, pathetic. Perhaps it was, but it was *his* life.

The meal had been extremely solid chicken in an extremely solid cream sauce.

'I'm not feeling all that well,' Paddy found himself saying. 'I think I'll just go back to my room. Get an early night.'

Kavita looked at him in a way he found almost comically suave. She was like a man—like a man was supposed to be: always assuming.

'Goodnight, then,' she said.

Paddy made a point of saying goodbye to Peter Bedford on his way out.

'Not staying?'

'No,' said Paddy. 'Bad stomach.'

'Hope you feel better soon. We'll be in the bar later, I expect—at the hotel—if you change your mind.'

Paddy didn't like the inference of this. How could someone change their mind about diarrhoea?

It took him fifteen minutes to find a taxi. The phone in his hotel room was ringing as he entered.

'You're being very cautious,' said a voice which he then recognized, by tone rather than timbre, as Kavita's.

'No, I'm being faithful. I'd like to sleep with you, but I'm not going to. It's wrong.'

'Ah,' she said, 'now we are a *moral* philosopher as well.' He'd expected some kind of outrage at his rejection of her, not jokes. She really was exceptional. She hardly cared, and that made him waver. Why wasn't he so blithe?

'I'm married,' he said. 'I feel it as a heavy burden, most of the time, but I want to stay married. And faithful. Peter Bedford already thinks we're having an affair.'

'No,' said Kavita, 'even Peter isn't that naive—or sophisticated.'

'Where are you?' Paddy asked. 'Can anyone hear you?'

'Don't worry. I'm a long way from everyone. I've taken myself off for a sad, lonely walk.'

It was her last try.

'Go back,' Paddy said. 'It isn't safe.'

'You mean, "Go back, or people will think you're with me." '

'Oh, I don't care,' said Paddy. 'This is all too complicated.'

'It isn't,' Kavita said. 'You're just making it so. Everything could have been wonderfully simple. But, alas . . . I will see you tomorrow. And don't worry, I'm going *back*.'

Half an hour later, Paddy phoned Agatha. It was a boring conversation which, for him, gave off no glow, no triumph. He hadn't been strong, only weak in a different way.

In the morning, he went down for the hotel's buffet breakfast—floppy bacon, wet scrambled eggs.

Peter Bedford was there, alone, eating the full English with toast and marmalade on the side. Paddy tried to skirt round him but was beckoned over once he'd collected his muesli.

'Pull up a pew,' Peter said. 'Feeling any better this morning?'

'Yes,' said Paddy, although he had no appetite—especially while sitting opposite Peter.

'Good. It was a shame you left so early. A real shame.'

The man seemed unusually smug. He talked about the plenary session he was due to chair at the end of the afternoon.

'It should be the high point of the whole conference,' he said. 'For most attendees.'

That morning, Kavita wore a sari of shocking pink edged with gold braid. Amid the brown pullovers and denim trousers, she couldn't have been more obvious if she'd had a spotlight trained on her. Paddy went over to say hello, just to prove that he could—that it didn't mean anything.

'Ah,' Kavita said, 'the married man.'

Paddy looked quickly around to see if anyone had heard.

'Don't worry,' said Kavita. 'Your reputation is secure.'

She was speaking too loudly.

'What do you mean?' he asked.

Just then Peter Bedford walked up.

'Good morning, Kavita,' he said. 'Slept well, I trust.'

And Paddy understood immediately.

'You look splendid in that,' continued Peter. 'Really splendid.'

Then he passed on. He was fifty-five years old, bald, tubby, married and shameless.

'Why?' asked Paddy.

'I think you know that,' Kavita replied. Her eyes were scanning the room. For the first time, Paddy felt she wasn't in complete control. It made her far more attractive.

'You wanted me to know,' he said, fumbling, 'that I was safe.'

'Oh, you're *absolutely* safe, Paddy,' Kavita said.

'But why?'

'I thought it was amusing,' she said. 'Different. I hadn't heard of anything like it.'

Paddy didn't understand where he was. There were people around him, most of them familiar, and they were talking, just as he and Kavita were talking. The room was no more exceptional than it had been the day before. But he felt completely lost there—a child among towering adults, trying to grow. He thought about Max.

'Am I supposed to thank you?' he asked.

'You could,' said Kavita. 'If you were being very old-fashioned.'

With this, she left him, and the room. It was only when she was gone that Paddy realized she must in some way have cared—more than seemed probable.

AGATHA & JOHN

Agatha began to find that Max didn't need her as much as before. First he had stopped breastfeeding. Then there was nursery in the mornings, during which she sat in a cafe with two or three of the other, non-shopping mothers, and talked only about children. And so, Agatha started to think about going away for a week, all by herself. Paddy would easily be able to cope, mornings and evenings. Any issue of coping was, she knew, hers alone. But she had no idea where she would go—a beach? an island?—until she saw a leaflet in the local library. It was about creative writing classes. When she phoned up to enquire, she found that most of them were booked up already, and the ones that weren't were the wrong dates. But she put her name down on a waiting list and, a fortnight later, they called back to ask if she was interested in a one-week residential course in Devon. It was very soon; end of the following month. The focus would be short stories. Agatha said she would call back, then immediately looked in the brochure. She hadn't heard of either of the writing tutors, a woman and a man, although the biographical notes beneath their photos showed them to have won prizes—prizes she hadn't heard of either. They were both of them, it seemed, quite important in the unim-portant world of short stories. Agatha called back and said yes.

As the month passed, Agatha became very attached to the idea of her week away. She talked about it with her friend May. 'I wonder what the other students will be like? Nightmares, I expect. Do you think they'll even call us "students"?'

'I think they'll probably call you by your first names,' said May, who had admitted to being on antidepressants.

Secretly, Agatha began to fear that Max would get ill, and she wouldn't be able to go. But come the first week of April, Max was healthy; Max was happy; Agatha was able to go; she went.

Strange things happened to time, as she took the train through westward hills. She knew she shouldn't have drunk caffeinated coffee—it always sent her straight into fractious depression. In her mind, the week was practically over already and she hadn't achieved anything. She could feel herself passing herself on the way back, sitting in an opposite-direction train on the parallel tracks. Would she be a different person then? Would she have decided to leave Paddy? Perhaps she would have fallen in love with one of the writing tutors, and the affair would have revealed to her what her life had been lacking. The woman tutor, Rachel, was famously lesbian. Maybe that was what Agatha had been wanting all along—to be taken off, plucked from the obedience of and to her chosen life. (She remembered being kissed by Sally Rogers, both aged fifteen. They had been surrounded by pink and white balloons.) Agatha bought another caff coffee from the refreshments trolley that came along but drank only half of it. She tried to write something in the black Moleskine notebook Paddy had given her as a going-away gift. Nothing came but blah. Her handwriting was shaky with caffeine, excitement and the movement of the train. So far, at home, she had written half a sludgy story about a woman going to the shops and buying fifty sausages. At one point, having lost concentration and started gazing out of the window, she announced to Max, who turned out not to be there, and to the other people in the carriage, who were, 'Look, a horse!'

One of the organizers, Beth, met them at the station with a relaxed smile and a minibus behind her.

It hadn't occurred to Agatha that other people on the train had been heading where she was heading, and she felt embarrassed that they might have seen her with an empty-paged notebook, or heard her point out the horse.

There were hellos. People shook hands as their rucksacks slipped down their arms. Everyone climbed into the minibus. Agatha remembered school hockey matches.

As she listened to the conversation, she realized that the man in the front seat—to whom she had already said hello—was one of the tutors.

John. He hadn't looked at all like his photograph. Perhaps because it was black and white and he was rudely ginger.

'It's been a bit misty, but we're hoping it will clear up this week,' said Beth.

'Good-oh,' said someone at the back.

Where they were staying turned out to be a farm with outbuildings in a gently sloped Devon valley.

Agatha was disappointed to find that she didn't have her own room. She had been looking forward to silent mornings. But her room-mate, Margaret, hardly spoke at all while unpacking. Margaret was in her fifties and took from her suitcase a woman-in-her-fifties-woman-from-the-fifties floral nightdress.

Everyone had a short while free before meeting up for dinner. Agatha walked back the way they'd driven in—along a long concrete road which passed through a field of semi-indifferent cows. It felt glorious to be alone.

Agatha stepped off the road, climbed over a gate and made her way to the highest point of a grassy hill. Here, she sat down in evening light.

'This is my springtime,' she said.

At dinner, they were repeatedly made to feel very welcome.

The redheaded male tutor, John, gave them an exercise to think about for the following day—when they would be meeting up for a class. He addressed them as writers, Agatha noticed, not students.

In the morning, Agatha took her Moleskine notebook and fountain pen along to the dining room. But before any of them had time to settle, John was handing out sheets of scrap A4 paper and asking them to write down, quickly, a pseudonym—a pseudonym for 'someone unlike you in every respect'.

Agatha wrote *Helena Mussel*, she did not know why. There had been a Helena at her school, not a girl, a drama teacher, and she had always seemed to Agatha a typical Helena: very feminine but in a muscular way, with tangy armpits and the hint of a moustache; a familiarity with horses, stables and the knack of getting on with those who spend horse-devoted lives; the sense of having access to exactly as much sex as was necessary to satisfy her lusts (Helenas had lusts), and therefore sex being no great problem or mystery. For a while, Agatha fancied being a Helena—not stupid but more robust than was perhaps honest.

Next, John asked everyone to sign the bottom of their page, with and as their pseudonym.

Agatha, as Helena Mussel, pressed down so hard that she left a small hangnail of a rip in the paper. The person sitting to her right looked across and muttered, 'Writes thrillers, no doubt.' And Agatha thought that, yes, maybe Helena had tried her hand at some shlocky erotic crime novels in the past.

Then John asked them all to write as badly as they possibly could, for three minutes.

'Badly in what way?' asked a woman called Jessica, a fairly close cousin to Helena.

'In every possible way,' John said. 'Bad grammar, bad subject, bad everything. Don't worry about it. No one's going to judge you on it. You're not *you* any more.'

Agatha had been waiting years for this command. 'I'm not quite myself,' she wrote. 'I'm not feeling myself, these days.' And suddenly, after months of clench, there came a rush of language-that-didn't-matter. Before the three minutes were up, she had one and a half sides of the paper and could have written more.

The class continued for another two hours, but they weren't again asked to write badly.

Agatha, as she walked out, wasn't herself—she didn't have to be; she was free from the effort of living up to Agatha; she no longer had to try to be as good as Agatha knew she could be.

For the rest of the day, Agatha—or, rather, Helena-Agatha—wrote badly, and knew she was writing badly, and, at a certain point, became delighted with this, because she knew it no longer mattered. She had her permission.

Before dinner, Agatha took a two-hour circular walk through cow-fields. She saw one or two of the other writers out, coming the other way, but she didn't say more than hello to them. Then she went to her room, returning to the same sentence she had left behind—and finishing it in no more accomplished fashion than if she had remained at the desk. She lay back within her badness, as if it were a hammock; it supported her: here, she knew, she could say anything she wished; no one need ever know.

Although it was melodramatic, she then went and ripped out and burnt her whole day's work in a small area of bleak, blank ground beside the pond. The ashes, a reasonable pile, were easy enough to kick beneath the leaves. Then she went into the kitchen and put on the kettle. There were two dozen organic teas from which to choose. Over the next few days, she tried all of them, and found that all of them tasted, in one way or another, like stomach bile returned to the mouth; Agatha didn't much mind. It was different to, different from—which? Start again: Being at home was different, with Paddy's normal tea and her inveterate camomile.

After washing up her mug, she allowed herself to call home, to check Max was all right. Apart from this, she had kept her mobile off—most of the time there was no signal anyway.

'He's fine,' said Paddy. 'We're having a great time, aren't we? Boys together. Come and say "hello" to Mummy.'

The line rustled.

'"Hello to Mummy",' said Max, then returned to the cartoon noises in the background.

The writing-badly class had been on the Tuesday morning. On Wednes-day, there was another two-hour session, this time with the woman,

Rachel. She was very practical and helpful about dialogue, but this had no relevance to Agatha's present monologic mood—she was in mid-splurge. Helena Mussel had overtaken her for twenty-four hours and then evaporated. Agatha could write just as badly, and fluidly, and confessionally, as herself—that much was clear. There was no need, any longer, for a pseudonym or a mask—the vomit was coming from her own mouth; indigo line of puke onto the page. Agatha felt very adolescent, and allowed herself to feel adolescent. To emphasize this, she wore her sloppiest clothes, the ones she had brought for jogging: a plain white T-shirt, a grey sweatshirt and faded blue tracksuit bottoms. She pulled her hair up into a biro-held bun. She borrowed a cigarette from Margaret, then bought a whole pack and a lighter from the village shop.

Also, along with the cigarettes, she wanked herself silly—three, four times a night and usually a couple of times during the day. Margaret liked to spend long hours talking in the kitchen but did once catch Agatha in bed. Agatha knew that Margaret knew what had really been going on beneath the sheets, but they both carried on as if Agatha's seal-like yelp had been a yawn.

Margaret was fifty-five, widowed, kind and completely without writing talent. She was the first to admit it. What she liked best was to write amusing rhymed verses about the tutors, to present to them on their departure. These usually got a laugh on the traditional last-night's reading, and that seemed to be enough for Margaret—until the next course. She had taken eleven in all and had one on soap opera booked for the autumn.

On Wednesday afternoon, some of the writers went for a swim in a nearby river. With Helena's adolescent bravado, rather than her own adolescent bashfulness, Agatha took part. What she did here didn't matter—she didn't know these people and definitely wasn't going to stay in touch with them. Neither was she going to be published and become famous, so they could hold nothing against her.

She thought about flirting with John, who swam close to her at one point. He would, she believed, have flirted back—though he seemed a little married to have gone further.

(Later that day, she found out she had been wrong. Not on this course, but a previous one. The woman in question had, however, become the wife, but only for a while—and the person telling the anecdote was the lubricated writer, divorced.)

Agatha became fond of the cows she could see from her writing window and began to imagine she could tell them apart.

After dinner on Wednesday night, a list went up on the noticeboard beside the payphone. It seemed that, if you wanted to, you could have a one-on-one meeting with whichever of the tutors you chose. And the following day, if you felt like it, you could go and see the other one as well—get a second opinion. As there was a slot free, Agatha put her name down for John, for Thursday. Mainly, she told herself, she wanted to be able to thank him in private for the writing-badly tip. After that, of course, there would be nothing more to say. 'I've been deliberately writing badly.' He wasn't likely to be very critical of this, was he?

Everyone assembled in the barn, with glasses of red wine. A guest writer had been laid on and was introduced by Beth as a *very big deal indeed*. This time, Agatha had a vague memory of his name; he wrote novels as well as short stories, and Paddy had read one of them—a thriller—a few years ago. He was dressed in jeans and a Ramones T-shirt, which Agatha realized she felt was slightly wrong. Male writers were supposed to be tweedy, elbow-patched creatures. The fact John also wore T-shirts made no difference: Agatha really didn't think of him as a writer. He was a bloke; blokes didn't write.

'I'd like to read something from my third book of short stories. And then, maybe, if I've got time, a little section from my current work-in-progress.'

A murmur passed around the ratty sofas beneath the exposed beams—*of course* there will be time. Read the whole bloody manuscript if you feel like it.

Agatha settled back, took a slug of wine and made accidental eye contact with John. He seemed to be asking her a question. It could only be to do with what had just been said. She gave a vague kind of wow-aren't-we-lucky-to-be-here smile and looked away. When she checked back, John was still watching her, but this time with a slightly puzzled expression. The guest writer had begun to read. It was a story about being in a rock band, although—as the writer later said—he'd never actually been in a rock band. At least, not since he was fourteen. But the story, although it mentioned it incidentally, wasn't really about the wild life. The main character had recently become a father to twin daughters and was worrying about what he had to pass on to them. Specifically, he was in crisis about what lullabies to sing to them. All the songs he knew seemed too inappropriate—one mentioned oral sex. Buffets of laughter came, occasionally, from the sofas all around. Agatha felt everyone was laughing more than they would have done in other circumstances. Perhaps because the writer was the guest of all of them. The room was full of a general atmosphere of warm winey encouragement.

Agatha glanced again, out of curiosity, at John—who caught the turn of her head and wanted another exchange of looks. This time, she understood him completely. He was outside the circle of well-wishing; he wanted the story to be bad, and he wanted someone else to join him in thinking so. This was a dangerous thing to do. Agatha was surprised, disappointed, thrilled. It made John seem ever-so-slightly evil and, because of that, more definitely available. He was a smoker, too, one of only four, so they would be meeting outside afterwards. Agatha realized she hadn't given him her reaction—had just glassed out and stared through him. He smiled, though, as if the unfocussing of her eyes had been intended to signify boredom. Without meaning it, she had joined him in the outer realm of mockery.

Annoyed, Agatha looked back towards the visiting writer just as he said the phrase *my daughters' cunts*. What had led up to that? She now wished she'd been listening.

A few moments later, the story was finished. Some people in the room gave sighs of demonstrated satisfaction—more encouragement.

John looked for her and, as she'd begun, however accidentally, she decided to meet him: Yes, that was a bit much, wasn't it? He smiled and took a deep gulp of wine.

'No, you're not,' she thought back to him.

The next thing the visitor read out was a chapter from the middle of a novel. Despite his introducing the characters and their situations, Agatha was unable to care much. Parts of it were funny, and she was glad to be able to do something so simple as laugh. The voice finished speaking. Applause followed, warmly. Beth, one of the smokers, suggested a fifteen-minute break before everyone returned for questions.

Outside, John, Beth, Margaret and Agatha stood talking, smoking, while people went to and fro between the barn and the kitchen. Empty bottles travelled right to left, full ones in the opposite direction.

'He was really good, wasn't he?' said Margaret.

'Oh, yes,' said Beth. 'He's always a very good guest to have. And, you'll see with the questions, very open and generous.'

'Yes,' said John. 'He writes very cleanly. What did you think?'

The question was for Agatha. 'I got a bit lost,' she said. 'I'm not all that used to listening to people read. Usually, I sit at home with a book and, if I miss something, I can always go back. I'd like to read it on the page.'

'I know exactly what you mean,' said Margaret.

'You'll be able to buy a copy afterwards,' said Beth. 'Oh, bugger, I should have mentioned that in there. Now everyone will have to go off to fetch money.' Agatha could see why this was important—they could go to their rooms and back in a couple of minutes. 'I'll just make a quick announcement now.' Beth finished her cigarette and then crushed it with a sandalled foot. Her ankles were tanned, as if it were August. 'See you inside,' she said.

Margaret, whether out of mischief or tact or a weak bladder, left a minute later, heading for the nearest loos.

'Honestly,' said John, and it was a question.

'I couldn't follow it at all. I'm sure it was very good.'

'It certainly thinks it's very good,' John said. 'But it's too show-offy, too reliant on tricks. He doesn't really know anything about life, and when he finds something out he has to go and trumpet it like it's a major revelation.'

Just that moment, the writer came out of the barn.

'Still a smoker?' he asked John.

'Luckily,' John replied.

The writer went into the house.

'I like him, though,' said John. 'He's amusing.'

'You don't—you don't like him.'

John offered Agatha a second cigarette, which she took although she was already feeling dangerously lightheaded.

'No, I don't. He pisses me off. He writes too many books. I shouldn't be telling you this.'

'It's all right,' said Agatha. 'It's not exactly anything I'm involved with. Who am I going to tell?'

'Everyone here.'

'I wouldn't do that,' she said. Then she realized she'd allowed herself to be tricked. By sharing those glances, John had put himself in an exposed position, but he'd also guaranteed she was there with him. Intimacy had been forced and that could only be for one reason.

'Phew,' John said.

'Well, not unless you gave me a very good reason.'

John looked at her directly.

'There's a challenge.'

They finished their cigarettes and went back into the barn. Agatha felt excited. John was a man she could never fall in love with, yet she hadn't refrained—she hadn't blinked.

Agatha went to see John at twenty minutes to five. He was waiting for her down by the pond, near where she performed her burnings. There was a park bench facing an oval of green water. The bench, too, was a little green with lichen. Jessica, the previous student, walked past Agatha and said, 'He's very good.'

'Oh crap,' said Agatha, to herself.

She had put her name down at the bottom of the list, hoping that exhaustion would make John cursory in his comments. Insight was the last thing she wanted—particularly on this story. It was something she'd written in a flow only that morning, and handed to him at the end of lunch.

'I very much look forward to reading it,' he had said, but he said that—she knew—to everyone.

The story was about a woman who, after suffering an undisclosed trauma, peels off her skin to become a seal. Agatha had based it on Scottish legends about selkies—where women were seals without their skins, usually women forcibly married to lonely fishermen. It was a strange story for Agatha to find herself writing—she wasn't Scottish; she hated folk tales; she had no idea where the thing had come from, and a large part of her wished it hadn't come at all. Perhaps the beginning had been the feel of swimming in wild water—tame wild water—the river. Politeness, mainly, had made her give John the printed-out manuscript. No title. No page numbers.

'It's good,' said John, while she was still settling herself on the near end of the bench. 'I like it. It's one of the most interesting things I've read in a long while. There are a few structural problems—it starts off as a story, then turns into a tale.' He explained the difference. 'But I think it could be the basis of something really worthwhile. Something publishable. Have you written much?'

'Hardly anything.'

'It doesn't read that way. But . . .'

John mused, fingers against lips, made a humming noise.

Agatha wanted him not to say anything else.

'I feel that something's been cut out of here, and it's not being acknowledged—or it wasn't in there, but it should have been, and it's trying to force its way out . . . I don't know. Do you understand?'

It seemed as if he were appealing to her; she, who had been appalled and then grief-stricken from the words *cut out*. Agatha was embarrassed to find herself crying in the hard way of three years before—when the stillbirth of her daughter Rose was the only fact. She didn't have a handkerchief; John did.

'I'm sorry,' said John, after a while. 'Sometimes I should stick to grammar and punctuation. If you don't want to talk about it, we don't have to.'

'How did you know?' Agatha asked.

'I'm a close reader,' John said. 'Especially in your case. You've been very closed off. This—,' his fingers tapped the first page of her words, '—is the first time you've let anyone in.'

'And now you're in.'

'Am I?'

'It feels like you're in.'

'In what way?'

Agatha looked him through.

'Like you're fucking me. Or like you're fucking around with me.'

'We can stop,' said John. 'If you feel this has become inappropriate.'

'Coward,' said Agatha. 'What do you think, that I'm going to say you've been sexually harrassing me?'

John hadn't liked the word *coward*; *sexually*, even in this context, seemed to delight him.

'So, I'm fucking you,' he said. 'Like I'd like to fuck you.'

'I'd like you to fuck me,' said Agatha. 'I'd like you to fuck me now. I'm ready for you to fuck me.'

'I'm ready, too.'

'But you're not going to fuck me,' said Agatha.

'Why not?'

John, she could see, was part-preparing himself for rejection. Which was when she decided not to reject him.

'Because if we fuck, *I'm* going to fuck you. Even if you're inside me, I'm going to be fucking you. That's what's going to happen.'

Now John sounded as if he was breathing through spit.

'Can I kiss you?' he asked.

'No,' said Agatha. 'But I can kiss you.' And that was what she did, and John's mouth was not Paddy's mouth, his teeth were larger, his tongue was smaller, and Agatha was excited by all these differences. She couldn't remember the last person she'd kissed, before Paddy.

When they drew apart, Agatha again tried to look at John directly. He was checking to see if they'd been seen. Then he met her stare.

'If I don't fuck you now,' he said. 'I will die.'

'I told you,' she said. 'I'm fucking you. I'm going to fuck you.'

They arranged to meet ten minutes later in the field of cows beyond the first field of cows.

'Unless anyone's there,' said John. 'Then we go further off.'

'Most of them are cooking, I think,' said Agatha.

When they got there, no one was there but themselves and the cows. They went to the far end of the field, found a small wood, got out of sight in a dell, fucked. John thought he had fucked Agatha and Agatha thought she had fucked John. They were both happy.

PADDY & VERONIKA

From the Czech Republic, her name was Veronika Markova, twenty-two years old, and she was sitting on their sofa, with Max on her lap, although the interview had only just begun.

'Do you have a first-aid qualification specific to children?' Agatha asked. She had found a list of questions for prospective nannies on a mothering website.

'Yes. I have the St John's Ambulance certificate. I have done it one year before. I can show to you.'

Veronika came with a recommendation from Sally and Drew, who were good friends of Henry and May, who Paddy and Agatha had asked for help finding a nanny; that was a couple of weeks ago—when it hadn't seemed so real.

'Max liked her a lot,' said Agatha, after Veronika had gone. 'I think that's important. He seemed to trust her.'

'Of course it's important,' said Paddy. 'But maybe he'll like someone else even more. We've only seen two people.'

Veronika was the second; the first, Sheila, had smelt strongly of cigarettes, and had said the word *fucking* twice.

Paddy was arguing against Veronika, partly because of her inexperience and partly because he already found her quite attractive. This was a situation he had hoped to avoid: at one point, he'd even suggested they go for a male nanny. Agatha had said no, although she admitted her reasons for saying no were indefensible. Of course, Paddy couldn't now say they shouldn't employ Veronika because he found her attractive. That would be to bring up the subject, and the subject was really Agatha and how attractive—or not—she felt herself to be. Since the stillbirth of Rose, Agatha had put on two stone. Some of this had gone on her stomach but the rest was in places like her upper arms and her thighs where she knew it was likely to stay—unless she did something extreme, like employing a personal trainer. Paddy still knew how to find her attractive, and not only by thinking of how she had been before. His tastes had changed: the fact that she was Agatha, his wife, was the most beautiful thing about her. He could get turned on by the idea that he was fucking *all* of that person he knew so well. But they had sex only rarely, due to exhaustion and a feeling that still hung on of inappropriateness: they were Mummy and Daddy. What Paddy, now just a couple of years short of forty, found hardest to cope with was his general desire for young women. This had changed a lot, too. As an adolescent, he had never gone for healthy types—either physically or psychologically; they had no substance to them. And he, romantic although in denial of it, had believed he might end up for ever with the first young woman that went to bed with him. In his fantasies-of-meeting, the girl was often slightly handicapped (handicapped being a useable word, back then). She wore black and walked with a limp, using an interestingly customized stick. He didn't mind. She was maybe a Goth—Goths often seemed to be lame, or have spinal difficulties. Recently, however, Paddy had begun to find the young women doing unnecessary aerobics in Europop videos extremely attractive. He saw these on screens at the gym. Since Rose's death, he was half a stone lighter, and much fitter. The Europop girls had nothing about them but their bodies—and that was now a plus. He was familiar with embedded intimacy. What he fantasized about most often was the contextless fuck. It had taken him almost twenty-five years to realize but this was what the page-three girl-type offered. *Imagine if you were fucking me now—imagine if you could step through the page, or the TV screen, and just stick it in!* Their skin was so flawlessly caramel-smooth—although he knew well enough their moles and even cellulite had been digitally airbrushed.

Veronika wasn't one of the climb-aboard girls—she was too intelligent for that. But she was closer to them than to the birds-with-broken-wings of his adolescence. Apart from being young, Veronika had blonde hair, a heart-shaped face, smooth skin and seemed very kind. This last was another quality Paddy had come to desire. Although grateful for his love, the limping Goth was also a proto-dominatrix. He didn't deserve her (he didn't deserve anyone), so she was perfectly entitled to mistreat him. Veronika, it seemed, would be the understanding sort. The subject hadn't come up during the interview, so Paddy didn't know whether she had a boyfriend. He had been waiting for Agatha to ask, but the question either wasn't on her list or she had decided against asking it.

Because Max seemed to like her so much, and because they didn't want to go through another ten interviews only to settle on Veronika, Agatha phoned up the next day to offer her the job. She would start the following month.

As it turned out, Veronika had been married at the age of nineteen and was now in the middle of a long-distance divorce. Her husband had run a nightclub in Prague and was a pimp. This they learnt from Henry and May, whom they invited round for tea as a thank-you for helping them find her.

'Apparently,' said May, 'at one point he tried to get Veronika on the game as well.'

Paddy wished he hadn't been told this. He found it disgustingly exciting. These days, the shower was just about the only place he wanked. It was possible, sometimes, to make himself come in bed, alongside sleeping-Agatha, without waking her up. Most often, though, he masturbated while the water was blasting him—and his spunk was washed away before he'd opened his eyes. It didn't take long, start to finish. He could make it happen even during a supposedly quick shower. Apart from this, he had to wait for those rare evenings when Agatha went out with May or his even-less-frequent trips away to conferences.

Veronika was in the fantasy scenario of his next shower. She was a prostitute, and she loved it. 'Give me your cock,' she said. 'I want it, your fucking cock.' Paddy had only just penetrated her, from behind, when he ejaculated—and the moment was over. Before he forgot about it, he felt some shame. But the wank had been prophylactic. He didn't censor his fantasies. They often involved degradation of women, and almost as often degradation of men by women. Sometimes quite elaborate battles of sub-and-dom developed in his head. More than once, he'd thought of May pushing him up against a wall and shoving her hand down his pants.

'Henry can't satisfy me. I need you.' Paddy was amused by the crudity of his own sexual imagination. Images from the porn mags of his youth still recurred: May had been dressed in—variously—pink brassiere and suspender set, in stripey socks and rollerskates and nothing else, in a knitted hat and stack-heeled Scholl sandals.

From her first day with Max, it was clear that Veronika would work out fine. Paddy went to work in the morning, but Agatha—who would be staying at home all that week—gave him a full report that evening.

'They played hide-and-seek. Then I let them go off together to the park. I didn't know what to do with the time.'

Agatha began to cry—something Paddy had been expecting from the moment he got back.

'I don't want him to like her *too* much,' she said.

'You're his mother,' said Paddy. 'He loves you more than anything.'

'It's you he's always talking about.'

'That's because I'm not here—I'm at work. If you weren't here, he'd talk about you. He does.'

'I really think I'd have preferred it if he'd screamed all day, and hidden behind me, and hadn't let her touch him.'

'Really?' said Paddy.

'I suppose not.'

They had some wine with their chicken-and-pea risotto, and clinked glasses to toast they weren't quite sure what.

'To work,' said Agatha.

'To two incomes,' said Paddy.

'To Max being a bit more independent.'

'He is independent. He just—'

'I suffocate him. I know. I can't help it. He has to be safe.'

'You're great with him. But I think it's good he gets to be with other people—not just your mother.'

'She's been very good.'

'Yes, but she's not exactly able to play the games Max wants to play now. He's a little boy—he wants to climb everything.'

'He was certainly climbing Veronika.'

The next evening, when Paddy came home, Veronika and Max were chasing each other around the apple tree in the garden. Max was naked. Agatha came out of the cellar behind Paddy—'He got all wet so it didn't seem worth putting on new clothes before bath time.'

Veronika picked Max up, squealing, and turned him upside down. His long hair brushed the dirt of the lawn and his penis slid from one side to the other.

'Fine,' said Paddy.

He went out to see Max.

Veronika put him down straight away, and he ran over to be hugged. But then he returned to Veronika and said, 'Again!'

There was still half an hour to go before Veronika was due to finish. She looked to Paddy, as if for permission to carry on what she'd been doing.

'He's having fun,' said Paddy. 'Isn't he?'

When Veronika bent down to grasp Max's ankles, he was able to see into her cleavage. It wasn't as deep as Agatha's; it was different.

Max swung upside down.

That night Paddy was kissing Max goodnight when he noticed something—the smell of his hair. He no longer smelt of himself. He smelt of Veronika's perfume. It was all through his hair. She must put it on the pulse point of her neck, Paddy thought. Agatha didn't wear perfume.

The next week, Agatha began work, as planned. There were more tears, and expressions of doubt, guilt and liberation.

On her first day, she said, she went out to get a coffee at lunchtime. 'I had a decaf latte,' she told Paddy, 'and I sat on a bench and drank it in the sunshine—and it was so wonderful I cried. Then a dirty old man tried to chat me up.' But even that only seemed to have added to her enjoyment of the day. 'I felt so bad leaving Max at home.'

'I'm sure he was fine. They get on very well. They're friends.'

Questions to Max before bedtime had drawn forth the information that they'd gone to the climbing frame in the park where he had been a monkey.

'Did you have fun?' Agatha had asked.

Max had nodded, definitely.

And that evening in bed, Agatha kissed Paddy with the softness that was invitation. He got up to lock the bedroom door, then rejoined her, his erection already full. This was the first time they had had sex since Christmas. Paddy did wonder whether Agatha was thinking about the dirty old man. He tried not to remember Max's inverted penis and how close it had been to Veronika's chin.

At the end of the first month, Paddy's term finished, and he only needed to spend two days a week at the department. He was approaching the deadline for a book about the philosophical problems surrounding artificial intelligence. His working title was *I Robot Therefore I Am*. The finished book would definitely *not* be called this. Sometimes he took the London train with Agatha, and went to the British Library. On other days, though, he stayed at home and worked in the attic. They had a shared desk beneath the skylight. From downstairs, he could hear Max's louder noises—bangings, wailings. Only rarely did Paddy go down to see what was going on—only when he thought Max might have suffered serious injury. Paddy didn't want to undermine Veronika's authority or confidence. He also didn't want to spend too much time with her and Max. It felt disloyal.

By now, Veronika featured in all his shower-fantasies. Max still had a one-hour nap after lunch, and Paddy imagined her coming up to the study once Max had definitely gone down. Standing in the doorway, Veronika wordlessly undressed. Her fantasy-breasts hung quite low, once released, but he didn't mind that. She crawled across the floor, got between his legs and blew him. 'I was a prostitute, you know,' she said.

In reality, Paddy was quite reserved around her. But Agatha had made proper friends.

One day, Paddy heard Veronika on the upstairs landing telling Max to stay.

'I want to see,' said Max.

'No,' she said. 'Stay there.'

A door closed—which Paddy guessed to be the bathroom door. Veronika was going to the toilet.

Max banged on the door for a while, then seemed to give up.

'I won't!' he shouted.

There was a flush, and then a long gap, then another flush and then a series of bumps followed by a squeal.

Max had fallen down the stairs. Paddy rushed to see that he was all right—though the fact he was making noise suggested he was—and Veronika, emerging from the bathroom, did too. Max cried for a while, but nothing was broken. Paddy held him, then handed him over to Veronika.

'I'm sorry,' she said.

'It wasn't your fault,' Paddy said.

'He wanted come into the bathroom.'

'I heard,' said Paddy. 'It's fine. Really.'

He went back upstairs, stopping off in the bathroom for a pee. There, in the toilet bowl, was a piece of tight brown shit—a floater. Paddy looked at it for a moment. He wasn't sure what he felt. It looked a little like a conker. Paddy took a few sheets of paper and laid them on top of the shit, then tried to flush it away. It didn't go. He needed to pee quite badly, so pissed on the floater, which danced in the pale yellow jet. Then he put more paper down and flushed again. He thought for a moment it had gone, but just as he was turning away, it bobbed up from the U-bend. Paddy got the toilet brush and, after a few goes to create corkscrew turbulence in the bowl water, managed finally to get Veronika's shit out of sight.

He spent the whole afternoon upstairs, even though Veronika took Max out when he'd woken from his nap. But when he saw the young nanny that evening, he could tell she was mortified. She knew he'd seen her shit—she had been trying to flush it away when Max fell down the stairs; then, in the panic of him perhaps being injured, she had forgotten about it, so hadn't gone back into the bathroom to get rid of it before Paddy went in. There was no way they could communicate about this, apart from both being extremely embarrassed by the other's embarrassment.

'He's okay, is he?' Paddy asked.

'He's good.'

'Probably landed on his head, then,' Paddy said.

Max was always there as a subject, luckily.

After this, Paddy was more relaxed around Veronika. He found that he liked her. His shower-fantasies became gentler. They arranged to meet in a hotel, and made proper love rather than animal sex. It was an affair, not just a fuck. She never mentioned having been a prostitute, though sometimes this was implicit in their scenario.

Then, one evening, when he'd returned late from London, Agatha told him that Veronika had a boyfriend.

'She just told me.'

'Is he Czech or English?'

'Czech,' said Agatha, excitedly. 'I can't see Veronika dating anyone English.'

'Why not?'

'I don't know. I think her sort like to have some connection with home. It must be very lonely, sometimes.'

Paddy wasn't surprised by his jealousy, but he did find it extremely grotesque—particularly how annoyed he was with Agatha saying *her sort* about Veronika.

'We should have them round to dinner.'

'Give them a chance,' said Paddy. 'It can't have been going on long.'

'Nine months,' said Agatha.

Václav was thirty-four and worked in one of the hotels on the front. Agatha waited exactly a week before inviting Veronika to bring him over for supper.

Opening the front door to them was awkward for Paddy, as was shaking hands. It was Saturday night. Veronika was dressed up in something flimsy, sparkly and short. Paddy hadn't seen it before—of course he hadn't seen it before. She wore more make-up than when working, but her perfume was the same he smelt every weekday evening in Max's hair.

Agatha led them through into the kitchen. She was worried, she said, she'd never cooked for a professional chef before.

Václav was modest and seemed very likeable. He gave them a bottle of Chilean red and some milk chocolates.

'I work on frying steaks,' he said. 'Hot plate.'

'That must be very hot,' said Agatha, then laughed at herself. Paddy saw that she was determined to find the evening delightful. He resolved to make more of an effort himself and offered Veronika and Václav a drink.

Just then, Max walked through the kitchen door. In pyjamas, he went straight to Veronika and she picked him up into a hug.

'Hello-o-o-o,' she said, then introduced Max to Václav.

Paddy wondered for a moment if this really was the first time they'd met.

'I told you about him,' Veronika said. 'He is my boyfriend.' Václav looked at Paddy, embarrassed.

'No,' said Max. 'Not your boyfriend.'

Agatha laughed. 'He is, sweetheart.'

'No,' said Max. 'He is *not*.'

'Hello, Max,' said Václav.

'Go away,' said Max.

Veronika turned him away slightly.

'Max,' said Paddy, 'that's not very nice.' He was glad to be off the subject of boyfriends.

'No,' said Max. 'No!'

'He is,' Agatha said. 'However much you might not like it.'

'Let's get you back up to bed,' said Paddy. He moved to take Max, and Veronika tried to shift Max into Paddy's arms. But he stopped halfway, still holding on to Veronika.

'Daddy boyfriend,' he said. 'And not you.'

'Oh well,' said Agatha. 'You're wrong.'

Paddy tried to pull Max off Veronika, but the boy had tight hold of her collar.

'Come on, Monster,' said Paddy. He reached for Max's wrist.

'No!' shouted Max, and yanked hard to stay with Veronika.

A seam gave. Veronika's dress was torn at the shoulder.

When Agatha gave a shout of annoyance, Max let go and began to cry.

A flap of fabric fell down, exposing Veronika's right breast. For a moment everyone was looking at it. Then Max started to point.

'Nipple! Nipple!' he shrieked. It was the funniest thing ever in the world.

Veronika covered herself up.

'I'm so sorry,' said Agatha. 'Max, you've ripped Veronika's lovely dress.'

Václav was standing between Veronika and Max, as if the boy might try to attack her again.

'I didn't,' said Max, back to tears.

'We'll pay for it,' said Paddy, then realized this was exactly the wrong thing to say.

'I'll get you a safety pin,' said Agatha. 'Or would you like to borrow one of my dresses? I can easily lend you. It might be a bit big.'

Veronika stood without moving. Paddy was worried that she was about to have hysterics. He heard a trickling sound from the floor. When he looked down, he saw pee dripping out of Max's pyjama bottoms.

'Oh, Max,' he said.

Then he looked across to Veronika's shoes, and saw that they were a little splashed, too.

'Come on,' Paddy said. 'I think that's enough damage for one evening. Say goodnight.'

Max said nothing.

As Paddy carried him upstairs, he heard Agatha in the kitchen saying, 'I really am terribly sorry.'

Once changed and in bed, Max went to sleep almost immediately.

Paddy came downstairs to find Agatha alone in the kitchen.

'They left,' she said. 'They decided to leave. After you took Max, she became really distressed—went into some kind of shock. It was quite scary. They spoke in Czech.'

'Little bastard,' said Paddy.

'Did he say anything?'

'No.'

The food was ready, so they sat down to eat it.

'It wasn't a very nice dress,' said Agatha.

'I thought she looked lovely in it.'

'Well, yes,' said Agatha. 'Of course you did.'

Paddy didn't start the fake conversation he might have done.

'Nothing was ever going to happen.'

'But you wanted it to,' Agatha said.

'Not really. Not as a practical thing.'

'How's that supposed to make me feel?'

'Better.'

'You haven't even noticed—I wore a new dress, too.'

Paddy saw no way out but apology.

'It's ridiculous. She's a girl.'

'Would it be better if something had happened?'

'Yes,' said Agatha. 'Then at least it would have happened, and I could stop waiting for it to happen.'

KAVITA & DR MEHROTRA

She might have saved money by opting for the usual Bombay taxi: cramped, fumy, with no air conditioning and a few gods on the dashboard. Instead, Kavita waited an extra fifteen minutes and took a limousine, a silver Mercedes, from the airport to her parents' apartment on the top of Malabar Hill. She was exhausted, wanted to get home as soon as possible, felt icky and snuffly from the flight, ached sharply—whether truly or out of terror—in her left breast.

'So I hope your philosophical conference was really worth it,' said her mother, coming to greet her in the hall. 'Was it?'

Normally, Kavita would have insisted on unpacking her own luggage, just as she had insisted on packing her own, but this time there seemed no point in, again, making her point; she left it beside the front door—the maid, Francesca, would deal with it: send the saris to be dry-cleaned, have her reputable cousin launder the underwear. There were no secrets in there to be found. Kavita had brought no scribbled telephone number away with her: that would already have been emptied from the wicker wastepaper basket, lined with a clear plastic bag, back in the B&B in Hull. Hull which surely no longer existed, so impossibly other did it seem.

'I am fine,' said Kavita. 'I would just like to go straight to bed, without a long discussion of my failures.'

'It made you exhausted. I can see how exhausted you are. I told you the whole episode was a bad mistake.'

'Goodnight,' said Kavita.

'It is eleven o'clock in the morning,' said her mother. 'I do not want you to die—and I especially don't want you to die as a result of your own arrogance and stupidity.'

Kavita had hoped she would be out. This morning, though, her mother had stayed away from the art gallery, specializing in photographs, which bore their shared surname, Oberoi, just as did her father's import–export business.

The apartment was chilly, even compared to the limousine—which had to be cool, as part of the service it offered. Her father didn't see the point of air conditioning unless it was merciless.

As soon as she entered her room, Kavita opened two windows. Her parents had repeatedly forbidden this. They were worried that Kavita's much younger brother, Sunil, would be fool enough to climb out—fall the thirteen floors to the dusty concrete car park below. Kavita told them, every time, that Sunil was *banned absolutely* from entering her room, and that if he died because of doing so then it was his own silly fault. They did not allow her a proper lock on the door, to keep him out; the place needed to be cleaned every day, they said. All those books to dust; that was her life, for them, all those too-many too-complicated sterile dirty books.

Kavita let down the venetian blinds, drew the indigo silk curtains—these, she had been able to choose for herself, the only unpatterned fabric in the apartment—and lay down, still clothed, on the bed.

It was mid-August. Her chemotherapy and then her convalescence would take place during the worst of the summer. Perhaps her father's had been the best idea after all: go to Sweden, where there were world experts. Then the whole thing would have been done within the cool comfort of minimalism. The clinic he suggested had won international awards for its therapeutic architecture. To have had a reason to go there could almost be made to seem a boon. Kavita liked Sweden and, even more, the concept of Sweden.

Her father had not stepped out of his office—the Home Office, as Kavita had once jokingly nicknamed it—to see her. She had not really expected him to. It was her duty to pay him a visit, and by avoiding this she was adding to the uncountable ways in which she had already insulted him this past week.

When she left on Thursday, her father had told her never to come back, and her mother had told her to ignore her father.

'He is too angry to do what is his proper thinking.'

On top of her silk-sheeted bed, Kavita fell asleep and dreamt immediately of Delhi, which was where she had grown up. Her body had come home and now her spirit—call it that—wanted to go home. The family had been forced to move to Bombay when her father reached the level of being both too rich and not quite rich enough for Delhi society. He needed to be in Bombay to be close to his money, to make sure that his money continued to grow and, more importantly still, that it continued to be his.

Bombay, except in sought-out detail, remained for her an inelegant city, unclassical. But her judgement, as she knew, was prompted by homesickness for Delhi: she wanted dry heat, not humidity; history, not industry. Nothing in Bombay satisfied her—apart, perhaps, from the night-spangling parabola of the Queen's Necklace—which was the view from her room and the family's dining balcony. During the day, though, Marine Drive formed a sea frontage that might almost have been Marbella, and no one with any sense of self-preservation used the beach. Bombay had other qualities than the classical—qualities commonly associated with vulgarity: it was frantic with energy both useful and useless, it was the undoubted centre, it was full of people who worked very hard at being fascinating, it was inconvenient but deep with possibility, it was less judgemental than Delhi—although that wasn't saying all that much.

Kavita was back inside the house of her birth and of the first twenty-six years of her life. It was the only real and right place in the world—everywhere else, judged in comparison, was lacking. The house was where most of Kavita's dreams took place; her nightmares were far more widely travelled. If she hated her father for anything, it was because he had sold the house when he might just as easily have kept it. What made this even worse was that her Auntie lived in the next-door villa, and so whenever Kavita went to visit she was given an update—sometimes even a tour—of the latest renovations. She could not refuse; the owners were very keen to get her approval. Somehow she always managed to give them the impression that she had bestowed it. In reality, she spent much of her life secretly in mourning for her house. It would, she knew, have been *her* house. Sunil, aged eight, was already a Bombay boy. If only they hadn't moved, Kavita felt, she would not have got cancer, for nothing bad could ever have happened to her, guarded by the magic of the tessellated floors and the wisdom of the pot plants, within that turreted palace of tumbledown survival.

In her dreams, as in her past, Kavita had another mother, mischievous, confiding, flirty, brave, and an entirely absent father. They lived together, she and her better-*ma*, in their three great projects: to avoid unwanted invitations, to understand the England of Queen Victoria and, above all, to civilize Sunil. The only person whose opinion mattered was her maternal grandmother, the Tigress, and most things modern were too trivial for her even to form an opinion of. She sat all day upon piled plush cushions, drinking espressos from an imported machine, smoking a pipe and writing letters to her five sisters. They were, self-consciously, the Hindu Mitfords. Kavita had loved to sit enveloped by her *nani*'s smoke and swathed in her *nani*'s smell—mostly a special hair lacquer that she had made up biannually by a shoeshop in the Burlington Arcade, Mayfair.

'You will come through,' her grandmother had once told her, as if life were a matter of always returning from the trenches. (For the Tigress' father, this was exactly how it had been.) And so, despite her diagnosis, Kavita never suspected Nani's tobacco clouds of causing her cancer; she knew for a fact that, had the Tigress still been alive, immersion in that aromatic haze would have been an instant cure. But her grandmother had decided to follow her daughter and her beloved granddaughter to the hated city—and had died three months after the move. Bombay, which she only ever saw through the window of the new limousine taking her to her new home—Bombay had surely killed her.

Nothing happened in Kavita's dream; it was a long safe stasis. She woke up at six in the evening, feeling dehydrated, feeling worse. A glass of water (Evian ice cubes in Evian) had been placed on her bedside table some time ago—the base of it was ringed by condensation. Kavita was more than used to people entering her room as she slept but, for some reason, she resented this particular intrusion. It had been Francesca, she knew, because the books and papers from her luggage were placed on the edge of her desk, visible from where she lay on her right side. Francesca always did this, as if to put anything in the middle of the desk would have made Kavita angry, and in this Francesca was right, it would have been an attack.

Kavita undressed, showered in her bathroom, put on a sports bra, grey sweatshirt and faded blue tracksuit bottoms. She could smell food, and knew she should eat some, although the airline food still seemed to be keeping its shape in her stomach. Barefoot, she entered the dining room.

'Your appointment is tomorrow, 10.30 a.m.,' said her mother, as Kavita sat down. 'It is important that you are there on time. Dr Mehrotra has made an exception of himself to see you.'

'Hello, Papa,' Kavita said.

'Good evening,' he replied. 'Are you rested from your flight?'

'I am.'

Her mother continued, 'Dr Mehrotra cured Mrs Vishnu, and without removing the bulk of her breast tissue. They have a new treatment which sucks—'

Kavita's father looked at her mother, who shut up.

'I am going to the club tonight, to play snooker,' he said, after which they ate in silence.

Francesca, under orders from Kavita's mother, knocked upon the door to Kavita's room just as the alarm on Kavita's cellphone started to trill.

Kavita showered and put on an outfit which would be easy to take off again, at least partially: white bra and knickers, white blouse and black skirt-suit by Armani. This was her businesswoman costume. She wore it, satirically, whenever she was called upon to deal with the family fortune. Most often, this involved trips to the firm of lawyers who administrated her and Sunil's trust funds. (Hers would pay out on the day of her marriage, otherwise on her fortieth birthday; Sunil's would pay out on his twenty-first.) To wear these Manhattan-bought clothes now, apart from being practical, made her feel slightly more in control as well as slightly further distanced.

As Kavita came out of her room, her mother shouted across, 'Sajjan with the car is waiting for you outside. It is nine o'clock. Don't leave after quarter past. There will be traffic, like all the Tuesdays.'

'Good morning,' said Kavita.

Once seated at the table, Marco, Francesca's husband, brought her a glass of water and two small plain dosas.

'Signora,' he said. Kavita had ceased to be *Signorina* the day of the diagnosis.

Her mother came and sat beside her, in her father's chair.

'Your father is upset. He will not show it, but he is, deeply upset. He did not return from the club until after eleven last night. That is a bad sign.'

For some reason, Kavita's father punished his wife for the sins of their grown-up daughter. Perhaps because he had no way, beyond violence— which he had only rarely used—of punishing Kavita directly.

'From now on,' said Kavita, 'I will devote myself to getting better.'

This satisfied her mother, who seemed to interpret it as meaning not only *I am trying to avoid death* but *I am trying to avoid causing you any unnecessary bother.*

'Dr Mehrotra is the best breast-cancer specialist in India. What he cannot cure cannot be cured—even by men in Sweden.'

Kavita left at sixteen minutes past nine, her mother making flutterings behind her.

The car—a seven-seater Volkswagen people carrier in Indian blue— was parked in the shadow of a wall, its engine idling. Kavita waited for the driver, Sajjan, to bring it round. She liked Sajjan. He was sixty-four and had driven the Tigress (who owned a Bentley) for the last fifteen years of her life. When prompted, he would talk about her—and the Bentley—with genuine adoration. Otherwise, he would speak only of the inferiority of Bombay traffic to Delhi traffic, both in terms of driving and the quality of the vehicles on display. His life, too, had been ruined by the move.

Sajjan got out of the stopped car and came round to open the door for Kavita. He was dressed, as always, in a dark blue uniform modelled on one the Tigress had once seen in an article on the Tyrol. Sajjan continued to wear it, out of loyalty to her, insisting that the lederhosen-style shorts were more comfortable even than a cotton kurta-pyjama. He had a new pair made twice a year.

Sajjan did not say anything as Kavita climbed into the backseats, for which she was grateful. He knew where they were going, and why. But when he had started the engine and driven out onto the highway, he said, 'You should have let me collect you from the airport, Baby. There was no need for you to take another car. If you had let me know the flight number and arrival time.'

'That would have meant speaking to my mother,' said Kavita, meaning the both of them.

Sajjan nodded, as if he knew the impossibility of this.

'I would have driven you to the airport, too,' he said.

'They would have fired you, Sajjan. You would have been assisting in my suicide.'

'I would have done it,' he repeated.

Kavita had always hoped that, in some way, she might remind Sajjan of her grandmother—and these words of his suggested that just possibly she was starting to.

'Thank you,' she said.

'Now I will be quiet,' Sajjan said.

Kavita nodded at the two eyes squinting into the rear-view mirror.

There had been an accident involving two auto-rickshaws, a motorbike and a child at the bottom of Walkeshwar Road, and two lanes of traffic were forced down to one.

It took them twenty minutes to get past the snarl; they were nearly late.

Sajjan took them through the backstreets and played the horn with the callused nub of his wrist. Like Francesca, he had his orders from Kavita's mother.

The car drew into Dr E. Borges Road at twenty-five past nine.

'I will wait for you, Baby,' said Sajjan.

Kavita tried not to hurry as she walked into the hospital, a tall, white building that looked like stacked shoeboxes. She did not want to be out of breath when she met Dr Mehrotra for the first time. Today, they would be discussing her treatment programme. She was going to have some of her remaining eggs removed, in case she changed her mind about children in the four or five years left to her. (Her mind was not going to change, but her mother had insisted upon this.)

Dr Mehrotra was head of the department of breast surgery at the hospital. It had taken the intervention of Mrs J. Vishnu to get Kavita an early appointment—for the Friday afternoon. When Kavita had said she would be on a flight to Heathrow at that time, and had refused to alter her plans, Dr Mehrotra had graciously suggested another time. He was very young to have reached such an important position—only just forty. Kavita knew this because her mother had told her, while also telling her how unreasonable she was being by not taking the earliest opportunity for seeing him.

'He is at the height of his profession,' her mother had said, and although Kavita knew this was an implicit declaration of her love, she was still annoyed by it. What her mother also meant was that Dr Mehrotra was the kind of son she herself would have wanted—instead of her philosophical daughter, instead of her sport-obsessed son. And son-in-law would have been almost as acceptable.

Kavita knew from the way her mother spoke about him that Dr Mehrotra was a good-looking man: there was a certain neon glow to her voice, again to say *if only . . .*

Unable to resist curiosity, Kavita had googled Dr Mehrotra and found out that he was married with two children, both boys, nine and six. His wife owned a boutique in Raguvamshi Mills which imported Scandinavian furniture and rugs. Dr Mehrotra's profile on the social-networking site was very pleasant and open. Apart from chess, he listed his interests as 'Classical Music. Ballet. Tai Chi. Tennis (from the spectator's point of view, alas). French Cookery.'

Chess was an understatement. Other websites revealed that as well as being a surgeon, Dr Mehrotra played chess to international-master level. A child prodigy, he had made a decision during his brief and untroubled adolescence to devote himself to the healing arts rather than sport. He still kept up his game, however, and blitzed occasionally with Humpy Koneru or whoever was in town. On one occasion, he had drawn a tournament game against his near-contemporary Viswanathan Anand —they had been fourteen years old.

The hospital complex was vast. Kavita had twice to ask directions to Dr Mehrotra's office. His name was on the door and his secretary was behind her desk.

'Good morning. I am Dr Kavita Oberoi. I have an appointment at 10.30 to see Dr Mehrotra.'

'I'm afraid Dr Mehrotra is running a little late today. He has yet to arrive. If you would be so kind as to take a seat, he will see you the moment he arrives.'

The secretary, while young and pretty, was extremely flat-chested, and Kavita wondered whether this might be considered tasteful.

Kavita seated herself in a very comfortable leather chair that she more than suspected was Scandinavian in origin. Upon a low glass table there were fashion magazines and also leaflets about breast cancer, but she could not force herself to read either kind of literature. She wanted something in-between them, neither insulting nor patronizing—a magazine about fashionable cancers.

Her gaze went round the room. Dr Mehrotra's certificates were up on the ivory-painted wall behind his secretary's head. Also, there were two framed photos of him. In one, he faced Viswanathan Anand across a chess board and a complicated endgame; in the other, he shook the hand of someone Kavita didn't recognize. It looked like someone important in the BJP.

To pass the time, Kavita thought about her failure with Patrick. She had gone over everything more than once during the flight, and had in the end decided she was glad her seduction had been resistible. It would have been painful to think of his betrayed wife and children. Now, though, she wished—for herself—that she had succeeded. It would have given her a feeling of greater strength.

Half an hour went past. The secretary apologized three times for Dr Mehrotra's lateness—every ten minutes, exactly. 'This really isn't like the doctor at all. He is an extremely punctual man at all times.'

Another patient arrived, a brightly dressed woman in her late fifties. 'My name is Batliwalla, Mrs.' She, too, was asked to sit down and wait.

Mrs Batliwalla nodded at Kavita, smiled sadly and then dived straight for the fashion magazines.

'I will call his home,' said the secretary, after another ten minutes had passed. 'Perhaps he has been unavoidably detained.'

Kavita and Mrs Batliwalla listened as the young woman dialled Dr Mehrotra's number, fingernails scratching on the keypad.

'Hello,' she said, then louder, 'Hello? I'm sorry, I can't quite understand you. Is something the matter? Who am I talking to? Yes. What are you doing there?' There was a dropping pause. 'He is? Yes. She did. Yes. I understand. Thank you.'

They looked up at the secretary.

'I am very sorry but Dr Mehrotra is dead. Apparently, his wife stabbed him more than several times. The children, she spared. I can't understand. Dr Mehrotra was a good man. We were not having an affair. You will both have to see another specialist. Please go to your homes, and the hospital will contact you there within the coming days. This is a great upset. I must type up a notice. Excuse me.'

Kavita and Mrs Batliwalla looked at each other, briefly.

'Are you sure he's dead?' Mrs Batliwalla asked. A stupid question, but Kavita had wanted to ask it, too.

'Absolutely sure,' said the secretary, then turned away. She opened a new file in Word—Kavita could see this on her screen.

Standing, Kavita said, 'I am very sorry. Please pass on my condolences to his family.'

'Yes,' said Mrs Batliwalla. 'Please also pass on my sincere condolences at this difficult time. But not to his wife.'

They went out of the waiting-room door. As soon as it was closed, a choking could be heard. Kavita thought about going back in. But the young secretary had been so brave, staying professional until they had gone.

Mrs Batliwalla realized she was still holding a copy of *Vogue*. Sombrely, as if it were a wreath, she placed it on the floor beside the door to Dr Mehrotra's office.

'Which breast?' Mrs Batliwalla asked Kavita.

JOHN & JOHN

. . . allowing your eyes gently to close, said the soft voice in John's head, *and then now starting to bring your awareness into this present moment,* the voice which was coming into his head through the white bud-earphones, *because we're going to centre this first meditation upon the breath,* a male voice, Californian, he thought, probably Californian, a slightly gay, droopy, insinuating voice, but only mildly gay and only vaguely insinuating—after all, the voice telling him what to do was telling him what to do for his own good, he had chosen to listen to it, and the pillows and cushions under his bum weren't giving quite enough support, his double-backed legs tucked to either side weren't getting quite enough blood and there was the spot on his back that needed squeezing. John began to wonder how some men ended up with gay voices—even men who weren't gay, or, quite often, who didn't think themselves gay even though everybody but their mothers knew they were gay as gay could be. His left knee was going to start to ache and then to stab—he knew that, he knew it for certain. The instructor or meditation guide or guru had already counselled his listeners, both present at the original recording session and anticipated through tape and compact disc and podcast—had already advised them to *find some comfortable and stable position in which to sit, either cross-legged or squatting down, on a cushion* (as John was, on a pile of cushions on a bed) *or on a chair* (as John might have found more comfortable, though more humiliating, with his going-to-be-arthritic-one-day going-to-be-really-painful-today knee). The easy, relaxed, trademark competence of the calm gay voice annoyed John, and made him want to open his eyes, twirl his finger around the off-white doughnut-shape of the iPod click wheel and then push the central select button for AC/DC or the Ramones or Napalm Death—anything to fuck up this false striving for a calm he would probably never achieve, and did he really want it anyway? Calm was uncreative. Writers who went Zen all went gooey and

rubbish—look at Christopher Isherwood—so why did he think calm was something he needed? The calm gay meditation voice was bringing him back, reminding him not to let himself *be distracted by stray or irrelevant thoughts.* The breath—*stay with the breath.* He always thought of the owner of the calm gay voice as Christopher—partly because of Christopher Isherwood and partly because of Christopher Street in New York. He tried to stay simply with the breath, but whenever he started a meditation, he always envisaged one after the other several things: the Edinburgh Book Festival, the white tents in which the Edinburgh Book Festival was held, the square within which the tents were pitched, Henri Bergson, Henri Bergson's concept of duration (which he had been reading about the last time he attended the Edinburgh Book Festival) and the hotel room in which he had sat on the bed, during that last Edinburgh Book Festival, not quite as he was kneeling on this hotel bed now, and had first listened to the newly bought compact disc of *A Beginner's Introduction to Meditation.* These thoughtforms always broke up his first few moments of strived-for serenity, even though he shouldn't be striving. And then always followed the image of the young woman he'd almost not slept with after his event that year at the Edinburgh Book Festival—how close he'd come to missing out on that dip in the back above the bum, those shifting-lifting haunches, that sweet introductory blow-job, those droop-free breasts—after which, until his second climax, all the sex had been anticlimax. The whole passage of these images—from tents to breasts— took only a few seconds, and then John was back in the ambience of the faraway recording session, listening to Christopher's voice of gay calm. Back, because this was one of his favourite bits, if he could be said to have favourite bits—when Christopher referred to *thoughts and memories and plans* going on in the mind, and then said, matter-of-fact, gay or not gay, *this is the stuff of your life.* John liked that phrase so much that he always intended to remember it so that he could write it down after finishing meditating. But he always forgot, distracted by his subsequent distractions—of which there were always many. He wanted to steal that phrase, *the stuff of your life,* use it as a title for a story or a chapter. Stuff suggested stuffing, of sofas, of chickens, of women. There was something satisfactory and true in the dismissiveness of the phrase. Your life—

Christopher seemed to be saying—is not the stuff in it but your life is largely comprised of stuff. And stuff can be dealt with—taped up in cardboard boxes and sent off for storage. John was aware of his thoughts as being thoughts, and of them being intrusive to the point of ruining the meditation. But he was vain of them, too. There was a conceit of intellect, like the stylistic conceit of leaving a Latinate word in a written sentence even though the Anglo-Saxon is more direct and more subtle. But John preferred his prose a little conceited. Flaubert, James, Joyce, Nabokov. Self-admirers. Fingernail-gazers. Christopher the Californian now told John to *become aware of what is going on all around you*, particularly the sounds. He said to *accept them with attention, patience and loving kindness* —not to *attempt to challenge or oppose them*, but *merely to let them figure in your consciousness until your consciousness becomes bored of them and lets them drop. Which it will.* And suddenly there was a white woman, a redhead, on her knees, sucking a long black cock—it was an image from the interracial porn film he had watched on the hotel television, half an hour ago, after checking in, before showering. He had masturbated for the five minutes it took until ejaculation. As always, he had swallowed his come. It was a trick he'd learnt in boarding school, after lights out, when gentle slappings and squishings could be heard from many of the surrounding beds. Catch the spunk in the foreskin—a bit might go on the sheets if you weren't quick enough, but that didn't matter, it wasn't their mothers who were going to be washing them. Then, ease the off-white goo into the cleft between thumb and clenched forefinger. Hope there wasn't too much, or it wasn't too runny with pre-come. Knock it back as, years later, he would swallow his first raw oyster—and realize the sensation was entirely bizarrely familiar. A very big black cock, uncircumcised, with a pink bell-end that—when exposed—looked the colour black flesh does when third-degree-burnt or napalmed. As the porn actress mock-lovingly tugged the foreskin along the shaft, the pink appeared and disappeared— then it disappeared into her by-contrast dully pink-grey mouth, only to reappear and disappear, slippery, slimy. John came long before the black porn actor—in fact, he'd turned the television off before that moment of no doubt humiliatingly extravagant gush. As if the size of the black cock itself hadn't been humiliating enough. The black cock must have been eight or nine inches long, and wide, too—although slightly flaccid-looking at times. An entirely stereotypical, racist version of a black cock—long, thick. John was not meditating. He was failing comprehensively to meditate. He was not planning or thinking, but instead he was remembering a thick black cock being fellated. He listened to the next words of Christopher's calm gay voice, which were *letting the awareness gently rest on the breath*. Always the breath, always the fucking breath. But now another thing happened which always happened when John was meditating, or trying to meditate, or trying and failing to meditate: the mention of the breath made him realize he was breathing—that he had a body, with lungs and other squishy internal organs—organs that could be damaged or become cancerous—and that his breathing-body would, one day, perhaps today, perhaps right now this moment, die and be dead not stop being dead. Breath meant death, like any boy or master at his school with halitosis—death-breath. John felt his heart start to beat more intensely, and this reminder of the fact that one of his internal organs was something as fragile and long-suffering, long-serving as a meaty muscular heart was added to the breath-of-death thought. Far from calming him, the injunction *to rest gently on the breath* was making him believe he was about to start having a heart attack—he couldn't rest on the breath, the breath wouldn't support him, it was breath, he wasn't a fucking feather, he wouldn't float, he would fall, and land, *hard*, spilling his internal organs sideways, and die, and be and remain dead. If he stopped breathing, he would die. And if he lived, he would grow old and get arthritis, especially in his left knee—probably first of all in his left knee, because that's what was starting to really hurt now, ignore it as he tried. And although Buddhism wasn't mentioned any more than passingly on this tape, John now thought the words *The Buddha The Buddha*. This was a non-denominational, secular meditation tape—probably so as not to offend, or so as to be purchasable by American Christians, stressed ones, stressed about Jesus sending them to hell on Judgement Day because they'd done something evil that no one had ever flagged up to them as evil. *The Buddha The Buddha*—and John thought about the Buddha himself, and the Buddha was two Buddhas simultaneously: the thin youngish Buddha achieving enlightenment beneath a tree in Northern

India or Southern Nepal and also the fat laughing Buddha that a friend of John's had once had, when they were ten years old, the Buddha as garden statuary, a little green with lichen, brought inside and established on an altar on a bedside cabinet from MFI. The Buddha knew that minds were full of obscene crap, and that the way to discipline them was to meditate, by staying with the breath-that-meant-death but death wasn't so bad for the Buddha because, fat and thin, he realized that there's no such thing as actual death, although hearts stop and lungs turn black and hard and stop working, and John—who hadn't smoked for five years, apart from occasionally, when in pursuit of a woman—suddenly thought of a cigarette in his mouth, cushioned against his top and bottom lip, and how perfect it would feel, the smoke tubing out of it, far better than this attempt at being a Buddha in a hotel room. What had reminded him of cigarettes was cancer and the idea of death through the lungs. And again John panicked because what if every time he meditated from now on he not only thought of the Edinburgh Book Festival and tents and Natalie-the-girl-he'd-almost-missed-fucking and Henri Bergson's concept of duration but also thought of wanting a cigarette? He would never be able to meditate again. This was becoming his worst meditation, ever. It couldn't go any worse than it was. He shouldn't have watched the porn. He shouldn't have watched the television. Watching television always fragmented his mind, ruined his concentration. And had he said yes to a coffee on the plane on the way over? No, he hadn't. But he had thought about sex with the air hostess who had served him. Which reminded John of the receptionist downstairs. And his wife. He *was* married. Not that they lived together any more. Or spoke. He reminded himself he was still technically married. He remembered the wedding and the church and his father's smile and the tits of the receptionist downstairs. He wanted to fuck the receptionist downstairs, to bring the receptionist downstairs upstairs, in the lift, and fuck her, just as he'd wanted to fuck the air hostess who had served him, although her calves had been rather solid from so many hours standing, just as the receptionist downstairs probably had solid calves. He imagined her, the air hostess who had served him, with her skirt up in the toilet cubicle, riding the length of his cock—which wasn't his cock any more but a long thick black cock, *the* long thick black cock. And the air hostess who had served him became the receptionist downstairs, whose uniform was navy blue and of a horribly ridgy corporate fabric. John thought of the woman who was still his wife, and of his many unfaithfulnesses, both before and after the separation, and the receptionist downstairs riding his long thick black cock, and lying on top of him on the covers of this bed, the pillows around him, her on top because his left knee—the bastard—would give him so much pain if he tried the missionary position, after this meditation, even in his fantasies. Why hadn't he sat in the chair rather than knelt on the bed with all the hotel room's pillows and cushions beneath his arse? Now, he would have to ask the receptionist downstairs to go on top when he brought her upstairs, in the lift, to fuck her as he'd imagined fucking the air hostess who'd served him and as he'd once fucked Natalie in the hotel after his event at the Edinburgh Book Festival. He needed to return to the breath. He was trying to control his sexual urges, to use his sexual energy for something productive, not just getting himself perpetually into shit, like with Yaminah, the mad bitch, and this was the reason he had watched the interracial porn on the hotel television— because if he did that, and wanked, he was less likely to troll downstairs later on, after the minibar, in search of the receptionist downstairs, who would probably have gone off shift by then anyway, but who had definitely held eye contact longer than necessary while he was checking in, and if he didn't check downstairs soon she would almost certainly have gone off shift by the time he did check, and he was only in this hotel for one night. John went back to the breath, for a series of breaths—forcing himself to listen to it as it went in and out, in and out, although he knew that having to force himself to listen was entirely counter to the spirit of this meditation. He should simply be letting his thoughts come and go, watching them with kindness and loving attention, but they didn't come and go, they came and didn't go. He thought about how rarely he thought about his wife, Ophélia. In the past half hour, he'd thought about very little beyond the receptionist downstairs. She was brunette and had a tan that suggested she'd just come back from holiday—which in turn suggested a boyfriend. Perhaps a black boyfriend with a long thick black cock, so she wouldn't be interested in white-guy guests who, from the computer screen in front of her, she could probably tell had paid for the porn channel only to turn his television off after watching and wanking for only five minutes. But if he left it another half an hour, although she might have gone off shift, he would know he was definitely ready to go again, should sex occur, with the receptionist downstairs upstairs on top. The pain in his left knee reminded him he was supposed to be meditating, and not thinking about sex or cigarettes. John became aware of the calm gay voice—aware of it because it wasn't speaking and hadn't been speaking for some time. He was in the middle of one of the gaps left for the listener just to get on with meditating. But he could hardly be said to be doing that, could he? He was just pinballing from sexual fantasy to sexual fantasy, as usual. It was useless—he should open his eyes and give up. Turn the television back on. Go and see if he could get chatting to the receptionist downstairs at Reception. Ask her if there were any decent restaurants near by, money no object—and whether she might be free to accompany him, seeing how he was at a loose end, new in town, unmarried. At the Edinburgh Festival, it had rained the whole time he was there—it had rained the whole time he was fucking Natalie on the same bedcover where, two hours earlier, he had listened to the gay Californian meditation voice for the first time. And in two hours' time, he could be pounding his long thick black cock into the receptionist. The Buddha. An aeroplane came into earshot somewhere overhead, bringing back an image of the now-partly-imaginary air hostess who had served him by being fucked by him in the tight, efficient toilet cubicle, with a whine as the wheels came out of the bottom of her plane and the fast air rushed around them, beginning her descent to orgasm, but not too loudly in case the other passengers were to hear, though it was hard to keep quiet with the pounding of his long thick black cock, and he heard the hiss of her breath far up over his hotel room as the whine of her pleasure lowered its note as she headed down towards the runway with her wheels now out and his long thick black cock that slurped in and out of her, like the toilet flushing behind her when it came to the end of its cycle, after the terrifying prolapse-causing suck when he flushed sitting down and it took his cock out as a bloody slug and his bowels as a brown rope through the side of the plane and out into the fast clear air over Edinburgh as the plane flew down in-between the raised high buttocks of the imaginary air hostess who had served him and who was now bent over the sink of the cubicle as the aeroplane now whistled out of earshot or below the height where its climax could be heard from his hotel room where he had a knee and the knee was telling him not to kneel on his knee any longer or he would feel more and more pain in his knee, and where Christopher wasn't speaking now but only a memory of what Christopher would say were he to be addressing this issue, which he did in another of his five meditations, by saying that you should give the pain in your meditating body your full, compassionate, loving-kindness-feeling attention for as long as it took for your mind to lose interest in it. But the knee was a knee, and wasn't listening to Christopher—or letting John listen to Christopher, who was now really speaking in his recording into John's head about *letting the breath find its own pace*, not trying to control it in any way. And Christopher's calm gay voice continued, as if in reply, *whenever you find yourself distracted by thoughts, just gently bring yourself back to the breath* (of death, thought John) *and let your awareness rest gently upon it* (I can't rest, thought John), *examining it closely, the sound of it, the feel of it, the swirls around your nose, the coolness, the itching, the tingling.* He made it sound so easy, so possible. Had Christopher killed his desires with breathing? Or was Christopher fallible as anyone, going off into fantasties of long hard black cock in the locker room, gang rape in the prison showers. And now John was the one being fucked. First by the receptionist downstairs, who came unexpectedly but delightfully equipped with a strap-on, and then by the black porn actor with the long thick black cock. Fucked up the arse, that was what would be on the hotel television right now. Anal. Hard anal. The breath. *The Buddha The Buddha.* But now the long thick black cock was pounding into Christopher, who had given up to it without resistance among the meditation cushions on the floor in California, surrounded by the devotees present at the recording session for this tape, and the fat garden Buddha was looking on and laughing, alongside the air hostess who had served him, whose hand was reaching over into the Buddha's lap, finding something there to palp amid the flab, and the Buddha seemed to be enjoying it, because it meant nothing. And then, from nowhere, from somewhere,

Natalie joined in with Christopher and the black porn actor—taking Christopher's dangling long thin white cock in her smooth-backed hand, much as she had taken John's smaller cock in her hand in the hotel room in Edinburgh, after his event in the Festival, which, in his head, she was doing now simultaneously—her hand was in both places, fantasy and memory, her smooth knuckles clasped around Christopher's made-up long thin white cock and his own present-but-in-the-past cock. This was, literally, a headfuck. Especially as Natalie was simultaneously herself, John's wife, his girlfriends, his ex-girlfriends and every woman who had ever touched his cock—and his cock was the long thick black cock of the black porn actor, and Christopher's long thick white cock, the Buddha's flesh-buried cock, and every cock that had ever been. *See if you can feel every breath for one minute more.* The meditation had almost finished, but he hadn't been able to hold to the breath for more than— what?—two, three breaths in a row. But to try was to fail. To try was to exert oneself, and one shouldn't have a self to be conscious of to exert. John imagined the calm gay voice telling him, calmly, that with meditation there was no such thing as success or failure. But John knew there was, because he'd already failed to stay with the breath for the first ten seconds of this last minute. And then an image came to him, not porn: his breath was a flannel-like creature, underwater, a strange fish from the depths which swam by going from roughly concave to roughly convex. As he breathed in, the thing-fish covered his face and as he breathed out it flanged away—though adhering still to his mouth, where it did not stop but helped with his breathing. The image of the flap-fish made it easier to concentrate on his breath, though he knew the vivid visuality of it was a distraction from the pure no-mind that is the ultimate end point of meditation. But fuck that. John stayed with the breath for three, four, five breaths. The fish was now less a fish and more a cloth of muslin, underwater, shaping one way and the other, without texture. And then a light bell rang three times in his head to signal the end of the twelve minutes of the first meditation of *A Beginner's Introduction to Meditation.* John had forgotten his knee, and the long thick black cock. Pure mind. It was possible.

AGATHA & MAY

An email arrived while Agatha was checking her email—*tink*—for aggie1970. It was From: maydaymayday, with the Subject: Fwd: Oldfriendd.

Agatha knew the sender, her friend May—but May usually phoned when it was urgent, or dropped an envelope round if it was embarrassing. Emails she used exclusively for arranging meetings. And her subject lines were always also the first line of her message: How about this Wednesday for . . . or Henry wants to know if Paddy . . .

Oldfriendd. This might be Viagra spam, or fake-Rolex spam. But there was no attachment, so as long as Agatha didn't follow a link she wasn't in danger of giving her new laptop a deadly virus.

Agatha pressed the up arrow on her keyboard, which took her past a couple of emails she would soon be avoiding answering. One of them was from John, the creative writing tutor. It was the third he'd sent and she expected it to be the last. The darkened grey line reached mayday-mayday:

'Ag,' wrote May. 'Not sure if you will want to see this. Bit funny hearing from her after this time. Let me know if you hear more. Mx'

There was a gap, then a line detailing that On Tue such-and-such a date <Sallyupthealley> wrote:

Immediately below, this information was repeated, in blue type, with the additional information that Sallyupthealley was Sally Rogers.

Sally Rogers was a girl Agatha hadn't thought about for at least six months—a girl from Agatha's secondary school. Sally Rogers would now be a woman, roughly the same age as Agatha. Sally Rogers was the second girl Agatha had kissed on the lips, but the first to put her tongue all the way into Agatha's mouth. It was at a party, in the conservatory. On the sofa next to them were pink and white balloons. Agatha could see them

59

now, over Sally Rogers' shoulder, where the pink bra strap poked out from beneath a half-moon of red and white polka dot. It was at Helena Mussel's fourteenth birthday party.

'Hi May,' she said, 'Sally here! I hope you remember me . . . you do don't you? How are you? I'm well . . . well not really, but that's another thing. Thing is do you have email contact for Aggie from school? I know you know her. I need to contact her urgently. I hope you're very well. You have kid too don't you? I hope theyre well. Thanx for doing this. Luv n kisses, Sallyxxx.'

Sally Rogers' mouth had tasted of gin, which is what she'd been drinking, neat, just to show everyone that she could—gin and cigarettes, Sobranie, black with gold filters.

'I like it like this,' she said. 'I'm *very* unconventional.'

When she finished kissing Agatha, and rubbed her cheek on Agatha's cheek, Agatha could feel the stiffness of the hairspray in Sally's pulled-pointy sideburn. Her hair was backcombed to look like Robert Smith's in the video for 'Just Like Heaven'.

'That was nice,' whispered Sally. 'Shall we do it again?'

'No,' said Agatha.

There was a signature at the bottom of Sally Rogers' email. The first line was a Facebook address, the second a MySpace and the third was a stand-alone website. All three were hypertext links.

Agatha tried the Facebook. It told her what she already sort of knew, that it was a 'social utility that connects you with the people around you'. In order to look at Sally Rogers' page, she had first to Sign Up. This took a few minutes, as she entered a false name and false details—sex, birthday. She chose Andy Wallace, seventeen years old. Andy Wallace had also been at the party. He and Sally had gone out together for a while.

Sally Rogers, when her Facebook page came up, had—at some point between the mid-eighties and now—dyed her hair black. But Sally Rogers was a blonde. Sally Rogers *had* to be a blonde—the universe was gone slightly wrong if she wasn't. Sally Rogers was looking like her mother, and although Agatha had never seen Sally Rogers' mother, she just knew *that's* what she'd looked like.

'Sally Rogers,' it said, to the right of her photo, 'is in a better place than she was.' Her Relationship Status was Married to—oh God!—Andrew Wallace, with a link to his Facebook page. Her birthday, as Agatha now remembered, was 25 December. So, she'd ended up marrying Andy Wallace. Her Political Views were Monster Raving Loony Party. Her Religious Views, I believe in God but not as a bloke with a big white beard.

Agatha was offered the opportunity to View Photos of Sally (413) or to View Sally's Friends (374). She could also Send Sally a Gift, See Sally's FunWall, Send Sally a Message or Poke Sally.

The Mini-Feed box showed what Sally Rogers had been up to, online, recently. But Agatha had already clicked on Andrew Wallace.

He was still good-looking—at least his profile photo was good-looking—he had spiky dark hair, cheekbones. His newest status update said Andy Wallace is having a Wire-a-thon.

Agatha hit the back button on her browser, then went straight for Sally Rogers' thumbnail photos.

There she was, not always with short black hair. Sally Rogers lifting a champagne glass second from left in a row of five middle-aged women. Sally Rogers wearing half-ironic leopardskin. Sally Rogers dancing in a rooftop garden with a black sky behind her. Sally Rogers dancing on the same rooftop making a face that made her look like a chimpanzee. Sally Rogers in a plain white T-shirt overexposed against black. Sally Rogers with vomit down her white vest. Sally Rogers holding up her hand to try to avoid being photographed. Sally Rogers asleep with a white cat in front of her. Sally Rogers flicking a V-sign at the camera. Sally Rogers pouting at the person she'd just flicked a V-sign towards, or was just about to flick a V-sign towards. Sally Rogers on a boat on a blue sea. Sally Rogers—almost certainly Sally Rogers—wearing a Catwoman mask. Sally Rogers drinking tea, looking hungover, in a kitchen with a photograph behind her on the corkboard of her asleep with a black-and-white cat in front of her.

Agatha clicked on the kitchen photo, to make it bigger. Sally Rogers had a kitchen with chessboard pattern vinyl on the floor and a bright red

SMEG fridge. One of her mugs had an Andy Warhol Marilyn Monroe on it. This photo was from the album 'Selected Hangovers volume 3'. Agatha had a quick look at some of Sally Rogers' earlier hangovers. The floor was always the same. The mug sometimes changed.

Going back to the previous page of photos, Agatha selected the one with the boat. This was from the album 'Larging it old school ha-ha in Ibiza'. There were another two photos of Sally Rogers against the blue sea. For the second of them, she had taken off her bikini top and was grabbing her own breasts and pouting like a topless model.

Agatha went back to Sally's homepage. Today, Sally is in a better place. Yesterday, Sally was taking it one day at a time, like everyone says I should. On 25 August she was in a million little pieces. On 22 August she was just out of hospital. On 18 August she was really very worried. On 17 August she was still overjoyed. On 17 August she was overjoyed. On 16 August she was back, back, back. On 8 August she was going for a well-deserved holiday. On 7 August she was in a state of disbelief. And on 5 August she was eleven weeks pregnant!!!

Agatha went back to the photos of Sally larging it in Ibiza. They were, she was glad to see, from the previous year. Next, she looked for the most recent photos. There was an album called 'Crying', posted the day before. It contained two photos of Sally, unmadeup, the bottom half of her face pale with screenglow and slick with tears.

The previous album contained a sequence of photos of Sally's tummy, one taken every day for a week.

The one before that showed her holding up a pregnancy tester. Camera flash had turned the little window white, but the way Sally was pointing to it and her beamy smiling left no doubt that there had been a blue cross or a blue line.

Back on Sally's homepage, Agatha scrolled down to Sally's posts. The messages were all from people she didn't know. 'Look after yourself.' 'Just take it one day at a time, babes.' 'Hold on and stay strong—things'll get brighter eventually.' She felt bad about reading them, and wondered why they hadn't spoken to Sally on the phone, or gone round to see her. Probably they were living in different cities, or abroad. In their profile photos, all of them smiled and goofed. They looked the sort of friends Sally would have.

Agatha brought May's email back to the front. She hit reply and typed, 'Take a look at Sally's Facebook page. She had a miscarriage. Ax'

Typing it made Agatha feel it.

After crying for a couple of minutes, Agatha decided to look at Sally's MySpace. This, she didn't have to join because she was already signed up—although she'd never done anything with her page. Tom was still her only friend.

On MySpace, Sally was sallyupthebackalley. It looked as if she hadn't done much on her homepage since the miscarriage. Sally's profile photo still showed her dressed as a sexy chambermaid, posing on four-inch stilettos, with her bottom towards the camera. She was pouting and pretending to spank herself.

'Rehab' by Amy Winehouse started playing, making Agatha jump.

Agatha clicked on the edge of the window displaying Sally's Facebook page. Then she followed the Andy Wallace link again. This time, though, she read his Status Updates closely. Today. Andy Wallace is having a Wire-a-thon. Yesterday Andy Wallace was just keeping busy, you know? Before that he was grateful for the much love and support, really questioning like everything and still coming to terms with the whole deal.

Agatha viewed some of Andy's photos. There were only five added by him. Four of these showed him with his arm around Sally, her hair a different colour every time. Andy always stood to the left, Sally to the right. Agatha wondered if they did this deliberately.

The phone by the bed rang. Agatha knew it was May.

'Hiya,' Agatha said, picking up.

'Hello,' said Paddy. He wanted to know if he should buy any food for supper.

'No,' Agatha said. 'I'll get it.'

She wouldn't tell him about Sally Rogers now—better to wait until this evening. Otherwise he'd go off on one worrying about her.

'Bye,' said Agatha.

The phone started ringing again before she put it back in the cradle.

'Hello,' she said.

'It's May. Look, I knew before I emailed you. I'm really sorry. Should I have warned you?'

'You looked too?'

'Her Facebook. Isn't it awful? How can anyone put that stuff up? It's indecent.'

'She's a different kind of person to us,' Agatha said, although she'd felt similarly appalled. 'Sally always was different.'

Andy Wallace's best mate Richard Havelock had caught her and Sally Rogers kissing on the sofa with the balloons, and had immediately told everyone. For the rest of her time at secondary school, Agatha was called *lezza*. Sally wasn't. Sally was just Sally. She wasn't even *slag*, even though she was.

'Are you going to email back?'

'I never liked her. We were friends but we weren't friends, not like *we* were. I always felt she was punishing me for something.'

'For being prettier,' said May.

'Boys always liked her better,' said Agatha.

'They didn't like her. They got off with her.'

'That was the same thing, back then. We didn't really talk to them, did we?'

'All I ever did was talk to them,' said May, mock-sad but also sad.

'Well, you made up for time at university.'

May laughed.

'I suppose I did. Sally was the one you kissed, wasn't she?'

'*She* kissed *me*,' said Agatha.

'That's not what I heard.'

'We kissed each other, then. What difference does it make?'

Agatha could hear children in the background, behind May's breathing.

'I thought you two were serious,' said May. 'I was really jealous when I heard.'

'Jealous of her?'

'I wanted to be your best friend. I didn't want her to do things with you that I hadn't.'

Agatha asked, 'So we never kissed, you mean?'

'Proper kissing?' said May. 'No, we didn't.'

'Not even later, when we were drunk at uni?'

'No. It never happened.'

'I'm sorry. You're more my friend than she ever was.'

'I don't mind now,' said May. 'Don't be silly.'

The offer was waiting to be made.

'If you ever want to kiss me, properly, you can,' said Agatha, with deliberation. 'You can just come round and do it and go away again. We don't have to speak.'

'Oh,' said May.

'If that will make up for anything.'

'What a strange conversation to have,' said May. 'As if it means anything now.'

'It seems to,' said Agatha. 'Anyway, I think I have to reply, don't you?'

'I *would* like to kiss you,' said May. 'Just the once.'

Only now did Agatha feel embarrassed.

'I'm thirty-eight,' she said. 'I haven't shaved my legs since—'

'You're Agatha,' May said.

'Today?' asked Agatha. 'Do you want to come round straight away?'

'No,' said May. 'Another time. I'll surprise you.'

Agatha felt delighted. May was suddenly vivid again—she could see her down to the eyelashes.

'Fine,' she said. 'I mean, good.'

'Now I feel silly,' said May.

'Well, I'll be disappointed if you don't,' said Agatha.

'Bye,' said May.

'See you,' said Agatha.

Agatha decided not to respond to Sally's email, then pressed function-N. She copy-pasted Sallyupthealley's address into the To: box. As a subject she put Sympathy, deleted this, put Your email, deleted this and put Old Friend.

'Dear Sally,' she typed. 'I had a look at your Facebook page before writing this. I am so sorry that you and Andrew lost your baby. Paddy and I went through something similar, and I know how terribly painful it can be.' This she changed to 'how terribly painful it is'. Then she added, 'If you feel like talking about it, now or later, please give me a call.' Agatha typed in her number, then deleted it, then put it back in. 'Love, Agatha.'

She clicked the Send button, and regretted including her number. The phone seemed alive. It would be impossible to relax until Sally had called.

Agatha went back to Sally's MySpace page, intending to close it. A little icon beside her sexy-maid photo showed that Sally was Online Now! Agatha felt nauseous. Sally was probably reading the email.

In the box below the photo, Agatha clicked Send Message.

'Hello,' she said. 'It's Agatha. I've sent you an email. Call straight away if you want to talk. Love, Agatha.'

Agatha picked up the receiver and waited for it to ring. It still made her jump when it did.

'Hello?' she said.

'Oh Aggie,' said Sally. 'Thank you for getting back to me. Thank you. Wow. You see, I knew you and May were still friends because I heard from a friend of hers, Lucy, not from school, I don't know if you know her, I heard about what you'd been through. I mean, when you lost your baby, and it was so much later than us, and I've been thinking about you ever since we lost ours, which wasn't hardly a baby at all by then, not like yours must have been. Lucy said you had to give birth, not a Caesarean or anything to make it better. And I've been feeling really guilty because I heard about it when it happened but I didn't send you a card or get in touch or anything, but now I know what you must've been going through—or I know a little bit of what it's like. I didn't understand before. I thought until babies were born you didn't really love them, you just waited for them to happen. I'm really, really sorry. I should have written you a letter. I'm sorry—'

PADDY & HENRY

Paddy was in the pub with Henry.

Henry had just bought a third round. Paddy was on Guinness, because it was Agatha's turn to get up with Max the next morning; Henry was on bitter, London Pride, with a whisky chaser, Bushmills, because he no longer gave a fuck—or wanted to give the impression he no longer gave a fuck.

'We're getting divorced,' Henry said. 'May and I—of course May and I, how stupid? Who else could I say that about? We're getting divorced, and it's my fault. I'm the one, if you're looking for the one. It's because I *want* to. We shouldn't be getting divorced—the kids—we still love each other, as far as that goes. But I'm insisting we get divorced— I'm following through—as a necessity, as a matter of urgency.'

Outside, the early May afternoon, Saturday, was beautifully, astonishingly warm—it had been hot for two weeks and everyone was acclimatized. The country, particularly the seaside, had done its moodswing: women were sexier; men were stronger; children were more easily entertained. England was semi-Californian, at least in its clammy dreams.

'So,' said Paddy, 'you had an affair and May found out?'

'Yes, but that has nothing to do with it.' Henry picked up the whisky and downed half.

'Does May think it has nothing to do with it?'

'No,' said Henry, blinking. 'She would stick with me, despite that. So it *is* irrelevant because it's not the reason I want out. I wanted out a long time before I met Philippa.'

'Do we know Philippa?' asked Paddy.

'From work. No, you don't. She's not relevant.'

'How old is she?'

'What does that matter?' asked Henry, looking at Paddy for the first time since saying the word *divorced*.

'She's not forty, is she?'

'No. Of course not.'

'So, she's—what?—twenty-nine?'

'Four. Twenty-four,' said Henry. There was part of a smile.

'That would be why May thinks it's relevant, then.'

'Look, I expect you to give me a hard time—don't think I don't.'

'This isn't a hard time,' said Paddy. 'What Agatha will give you is a hard time.'

'Philippa being young wasn't the reason I had an affair with her,' said Henry.

'But if she hadn't been young you wouldn't have had an affair with her.'

Paddy, inevitably, was thinking of Kavita—although that wouldn't have been an affair, and he hadn't ever seriously considered a divorce.

'Look, we're getting off the point. I have something very specific to say. Philosophical, almost—not to want to trespass on your territory, being merely a humble journalist.' Paddy was bored with dealing with Henry's professional insecurities, and had, a while ago, stopped responding to negative set-ups like this. Henry, who had been expecting the politeness of an interruption, found his rhythm off-put. 'What it is is, we've looked up, our generation, up and back, and seen all those divorces among our parents' generation, and we're so determined not to repeat their failures— repeat their crapness, that we're killing ourselves, literally killing ourselves. With suppressed desire, as you ask. Those poor kids, we think—meaning us in the seventies, but also meaning our own kids, in anticipation. So we never grow up. We avoid pursuing our desires. And I can't help but feel this is going to hurt our kids even more. All this coveredness. Because we're going to blame them and secretly hate them, without being able to admit we hate them. It's unnatural to be perfect parents. It's unnatural to *want* to be perfect parents. Our kids will see that, and they'll be traumatized by it.'

Paddy took a moment to sip his pint; it was an obvious prop, but it gave him the time he needed: that's what it was there for, in the absence of a cigarette.

'I don't think,' he said, 'there's any danger of me being perfect.'

'And me, too, you mean,' said Henry, with anger.

'Were you trying to be perfect?'

'Yes, I think I was. I think I've always tried to be something inhuman, even though I knew it was impossible. I loved robots, when I was growing up. Loved doing robotics dancing. I always wanted to be a robot—even in *Star Wars*.'

'R2-D2 or C-3PO?' asked Paddy.

'R2-D2, of course. I'm not that much of a freak.'

'Of course,' said Paddy.

'Kids need to be secure about their mother and their father,' said Henry. 'They need a good home. But they also need to be able at some point to see round them, see beyond them—see through them, I suppose. Otherwise they're—we're Gods they'll never be able to bring down. Not without a catastrophic loss of faith. Is that what you want to set Max up for?'

'Max doesn't believe in God. He told me that the other day—out of nowhere. I didn't bring it up.'

'What does he believe in?' asked Henry.

'Firemanland,' said Paddy. 'It's a place. He made it up when he was about three. I think it's a little like Heaven but without God—just lots of firemen.'

'No fires, then,' Henry said.

'Oh, lots of fires. But they're all put out before anyone gets harmed. Max puts them out. He's the fire chief. It says so on his yellow hat. That's important to him.'

'Did your parents get divorced?'

Paddy shook his head.

'Didn't think so.'

'I wanted them to,' said Paddy. 'At times, I even prayed for it. All my friends' parents were getting divorced. And my friends got two of everything—two bedrooms, two bikes. They could get more of whatever they wanted. I liked the girlfriends better than the mothers. It seemed ideal.'

Paddy wore flip-flops, blue cotton trousers and a plain white T-shirt. He was aware of his belly, but it wasn't embarassingly big; his height disguised it. Henry was in blue-and-white deck shoes, khaki shorts and a pink polo shirt, brand new.

'I don't like us, as a generation,' said Henry, returning to theme. 'We've got computers—they define us—but we haven't gone far enough with them. They just break down all the time and we spend most of our time dealing with that. We haven't gone far enough with them to be able to reject them, when we need to. We're still madly incorporating them into every aspect of our lives.'

'R2-D2 speaking?'

'I don't like digital. All this copying—one-to-one faithful copies, copies the same as the original, but no soul. No soul at all. A digital generation. Compressed. Repressed. Unoriginal. We're not allowing ourselves—we're not letting ourselves live. We need the freedom of moments when we're not in control.'

'I'm never in control.'

'Aesthetically in control.'

'What about raves? All that drug-communal stuff that was meant to last. We got out of it en masse.'

'Perhaps,' said Henry, who was nostalgic for ecstasy, and had dropped it a couple of times with Philippa, who was already losing interest in it. 'Did you do all that?'

'No,' said Paddy. 'Or only once. Somewhere in Oxfordshire. I was too worried about messing up my brain. Agatha was more into all that. She loves dancing.'

Without announcing it, Henry left for the loos. Paddy drank up, then looked around. He felt comfortable in this pub; its demographic was his own. He wasn't a regular, but the bar staff smiled at him whenever he came in. It didn't matter if they recognized him; they recognized and accepted his type. At the stage of life he was at, that seemed to be enough. Henry was demanding more: he was talking as if it still all mattered, and could be altered. Paddy felt disturbed by this. He wondered how much of what Henry was saying he really disagreed with. Little.

Henry returned, with drinks. He had switched to lager but the chaser remained.

'You can get the next lot,' he said. 'And the lot after that.'

'Okay,' said Paddy.

'The story of my childhood is the story of a divorce. Not my parents' divorce. That, fortunately—for the most part fortunately—never happened. No, it was the divorce of my best friend's parents. She was a witch, you know. A proper one. Wiccan. I only learnt that recently. White-robes-at-midnight kind of thing. She was having an affair with my uncle Ian, who was living with us, and that's why my best friend from when I was five moved away, aged fourteen, and I hardly saw him after that. And before that we'd been like that.'

Having hit a wall of *that*s, Henry paused to look around him. Paddy decided a silence was better than a response.

'I never understood that until now,' said Henry. 'My father mentioned it at Christmas—as if it were something I already knew. He was talking about my best friend's mother Penny. She still lives in their village. He was saying he wondered how anyone would go for her. I could see exactly. She had that witchy thing. May doesn't have enough of it. I think that's why she bores me. In bed, she bores me. In conversation. I don't like her any more. I blame her for being who she is, which is unfair.'

'It is,' said Paddy. 'You knew who she was when you got married.'

'I did. And I haven't found out any more. I think that's it. I expected some revelation—as if wives were made of different stuff than other women.'

'They are, I think.'

'Really?'

'They're more solid,' said Paddy.

'They become more solid, yes—after children.'

'No. They have more density. They exist in a more certain way.'

'I feel the opposite,' said Henry. 'May has evaporated. She's gone—all that's left is kids and clothes.'

'She works,' Paddy said.

'Kids, clothes and bitching about the local education authority. It's not much.'

Henry drank for a while, and Paddy watched to see how he was doing it—to see how good at it he was. There was a lot of acting, still. Bravado of consumption. All drunks had that, though. Paddy felt he might need to start being responsible, which would alienate Henry instantly.

'Have you slept with anyone but Agatha?'

'No,' said Paddy, immediately.

'Have you wanted to?'

'Yes,' said Paddy, as immediately as he could.

'At least you're honest,' said Henry, and returned to drinking.

'Don't you want to ask me any more?' Paddy said.

'No,' said Henry. 'If you'd slept with someone I would. But otherwise it's just more digital repression.' He looked at Paddy with a woozy intensity, as if from six inches underwater. 'We're a generation that hasn't made any mistakes, and *that's* our mistake.'

Paddy nodded, smiled. 'I think you might be right.'

'Do you think I'm fucking right or not?'

'It's a good working hypothesis.'

'Is it true?' asked Henry.

'We're careful for a reason. We're trying not to hurt things.'

'If you don't hurt things, you don't respect them—because you don't really acknowledge their existence.'

'And that's why you want to hurt May, to acknowledge her existence?'

'No—to make her exist. To make her sweaty and alive—force her back into analogue and the seventies. It can always be the seventies. We can reinvent it.'

'That doesn't really make any sense,' said Paddy.

'Fleetwood Mac, *Rumours*. You know exactly what I mean. Cocaine. California. Misery. Sunshine. Misery in the sunshine. Great tunes. Sweat. Divorce. Real women with real armpits.' Henry lifted his glass and, for a moment, Paddy thought he was about to propose a toast, loudly. There were quite a few other people around.

'Is Philippa real?' Paddy asked.

'Of course not. She never existed.'

'You mean you made her up?'

'I might as well have. It didn't matter that it was Philippa rather than Rachel or Natascha or God help me Belinda. She had no real existence. She was too young.'

'Did you hurt her?' asked Paddy.

'I tried to. She wouldn't let me. That generation are very tough. They don't allow it. They just tell you to fuck off, and they mean it. She wrote a blog about me, which caused a whole lot of trouble before my boss persuaded her to take it down. Everyone had read it by then. Everyone had read it within the afternoon. That's how May found out.'

'Did she read it?'

'A fucking blog.'

'Did she?'

'No,' said Henry. 'She confronted me with her knowledge of the fact of its existence.'

'So, you didn't tell her any of this until you were forced to.'

'I wanted to get caught. Can't you see? I chose Philippa because she's the world's least discrete woman. She's all celebrity culture. Nothing but. If it isn't public, it doesn't exist.'

'When did this happen?'

'A month ago,' said Henry.

'Before or after you came round for dinner.'

'Day before. We were barely speaking, otherwise.'

'You put on a good act,' said Paddy.

'Oh, we're very good. The best.'

'I don't think Agatha noticed anything. She didn't say she did.'

'I like Agatha. Agatha exists.'

'She does,' said Paddy.

Henry finished both drinks, working up to—'I wish I were married to Agatha, not May.'

'No, you don't,' said Paddy.

'Maybe not. May is better, now she's miserable. I can feel things happening inside her, developments—it's exciting. A bit like when she was pregnant, the first time.'

Paddy was sure he didn't want to know this. He would have to decide how much to tell Agatha. It would be a relief if Henry asked him not to say anything. There was no sign of that; the opposite.

Outside, it was still light and still warm.

'Are you seeking my approval?' asked Paddy. 'I think that kind of cruelty is disgusting and immature.'

'Don't go all formal on me,' said Henry.

'It's not original. You're not innovating. The same argument could be made for wife-beating.'

'I've thought about it,' said Henry.

'What have you thought?' asked Paddy.

'I think it might help, with communication.'

'Henry, you're not that stupid.'

'I am.'

Paddy knew he had to be responsible.

'Let's go home.'

'You owe me two drinks—four drinks,' said Henry.

'Another time.'

'Excuse me,' said a young woman who'd been sitting with another young woman at the next table. 'Is that all you're going to say?'

Paddy realized after a moment that she was talking to him and not Henry.

'You're not just gonna leave it like that, after all what he fucking said?'

'Which part?' asked Paddy, who wasn't sure when they'd started listening.

'The part,' said the other young woman, 'about wanting to hit his fucking wife.'

'What a wanker,' said the first woman.

Paddy knew this meant him.

'Why are you attacking me?' he asked.

'Look, this one's just a cunt, but you're a fucking wanker. Why are you still even friends with him?'

Both the young women had long straight hair, patterned tops, short skirts, bare brown legs. Paddy was finding it hard to tell them apart. They were in their mid-twenties.

'Let's go,' he said to Henry.

'No,' Henry replied. 'I'm staying.'

Paddy was aware that many people in the pub were listening. He'd stood up, at some point, and his height had drawn further attention.

'Okay,' he said. 'I'll see you later.'

'See you, mate,' said Henry, and held out his hand. 'Thanks for listening.'

Paddy shook hands.

'I can't believe that,' said one of the young women. 'I can't believe he's just fucking leaving.'

'I'm just fucking leaving,' said Paddy. 'Goodbye.'

Walking home, he decided not to mention the divorce to Agatha—not until he'd had another chance to talk to Henry. On the phone, preferably.

'How was he?' Agatha asked, in the kitchen.

'Fine,' said Paddy. 'Work's a bit manic, you know.'

'How's May?'

'She's fine.'

'What did you talk about?'

'His job. Politics. My work.'

Agatha seemed satisfied.

'How was Max, going to bed?' asked Paddy.

At ten o'clock, Paddy received a text from Henry: 'I went to her place and fucked her. The fit one. Amazing fuck. Don't tell Agatha.'

Paddy owned *Rumours* on vinyl. He eased it out of his dusty, alphabetized record collection, put it on.

'Why are you playing that?' asked Agatha, coming into the living room.

'Henry mentioned it. I wanted to hear it again.'

Agatha smiled and said, 'I love this record.'

VERONIKA & ALICE

Veronika finishes vomiting, stands up and inspects her skirt. Relieved, satisfied, she flushes the lavatory. The cubicle she has chosen is last on the left. When she steps out of it, a woman of near fifty turns and gives her a sympathetic frown.

The woman looks like she's had several children, she has the right kind of fat.

'It's terrible, isn't it?' the fat woman says—her accent from outside London but still probably England. 'Aeroplanes. Flying.'

Veronika nods, safe. The fat woman does not mean what she might have meant, before she said *Aeroplanes*.

'Thank you,' says Veronika. 'I am fine.'

'Is Prague where you live?' asks the fat woman.

'Yes,' says Veronika, pretending her English is worse than it is. 'Thank you, I am pretty fine.'

The fat woman smiles, hand-dries, smiles and leaves.

Veronika stands.

The fat woman has made big splashes round the bowl.

Veronika gets ready to move.

Outside the washroom is the long, wide corridor and off to one side of the long, wide corridor is the departure lounge and beyond the departure lounge is the plastic tunnel thing and after the plastic tunnel thing is the tight seat on the plane—the plane back to Prague.

Veronika's mother has promised to collect her from the airport.

Veronika waits in Arrivals for ten minutes.

The taxi driver smiles as she approaches. 'Dobry den,' he says, then hefts her suitcase round to the trunk. He is perhaps forty and very bald, but he is being friendly. Veronika tells him the address.

As they drive off the taxi driver says, 'Good visit?'

'I live there,' Veronika says. 'I like it better than here.'

'Then why'd you come back?' He isn't offended. He seems glad she is talking. She is glad she is talking.

'An engagement party.'

'Who? Not you?'

'A sister.'

'Younger sister or older?'

'Younger,' says Veronika.

The taxi driver looks at her in the rear-view mirror.

'Lucky man, if you ask me.'

They are on the highway now.

'You don't know my sister.'

'But I see you.' He looks at her again. 'Yes, very lucky.'

They are going quite fast now. He is probably trying to impress her with his driving, with his car—a Mercedes.

'My sister is not like me.'

'No?' he asks. 'She's ugly?'

'She's like my mother.'

'So what's your mother like?'

'A bitch,' says Veronika. 'Just a total bitch.'

The car slows down a little.

'No one should speak like that about their mother.'

'But it's true. Some women are bitches and some women are mothers, so there must be mothers who are bitches.'

'Perhaps she's had a hard life. Things weren't so easy—'

'She was born a bitch. Her mother told me. She never slept. She always cried. She bit when she fed.'

'Your grandmother is still alive?'

'My grandmother is wonderful. And, yes, she lives in Strahov.'

'We are going to your mother's, then—Hodonínska?'

'Yes. Home to mother.'

There is a pause while the driver passes a goods truck.

'When's the wedding?' he asks.

'Early next year,' says Veronika. 'I am bridesmaid.'

'Are they getting married here?'

'In the Town Hall, I think.'

'I got married there,' says the taxi driver. 'And I got divorced there, too.' He seems very pleased with this and chuckles to himself for a while. 'The divorce was even better than the wedding,' he says. 'Almost worth getting married for the feeling after the divorce. *She* was a bitch. My God.'

Veronika asks, 'And did you have children?'

'Thank Christ, no.'

'But if you'd had children, she'd still have been a bitch.'

The taxi driver thinks about this. He slumps into a new mood. 'I hoped maybe it would change her.'

'What I mean is, she'd have been a mother and also a bitch.'

'But children should never say that about their mothers. If they do—' He raises his hand. 'Bam!'

'You think you should hit me for saying it?'

'Your father should.'

'My father can't hit anyone any more. He's dead.'

'I'm sorry,' says the taxi driver.

It is Veronika's turn to laugh.

'He was a *cunt*.'

She still has a key, and finds her mother—Jitka—at the dressing table, asleep. The bottle dropped to the carpet when her mother let it go, but there isn't any spill.

Veronika puts her ear to her mother's lips, then tiptoes into the kitchen. She opens the window and breathes.

By the time her mother comes through, Veronika is into her second pot of coffee and her fifth cigarette—from one of the packs on the table.

'Would you like some?' Veronika asks, touching the rim of her cup.

'Well,' says her mother, 'you look better than last time.'

'You don't,' says Veronika.

Her mother had fallen asleep on her eyeliner, and the indent stripe runs pink up her cheek, skips her eye and resumes on her forehead. She is even thinner than before.

Veronika says, 'I thought you were coming to collect me.'

Her mother zones out and then in. 'Well,' she says, 'you're here now.'

'You *cannot* be drunk at the party,' says Veronika.

'But I was drunk at *my* engagement,' says Jitka. 'And my wedding.'

'I know,' Veronika says. 'Your eyes are horrible in the photos—when they are open.'

'Yes, some coffee,' Jitka says. 'Please.'

Veronika stands up, fetches a cup and saucer from the display cabinet, pours out from the Italian coffee pot.

Jitka waits until it is in her hand. 'Don't speak to me like I'm a child. You spend too much time with children.'

'I'd like to go see Grandma,' says Veronika. 'May I borrow the car?'

'There isn't a car,' says Jitka.

Veronika looks at her, at her meaning.

'It wasn't a very *strong* car,' says Jitka. 'Not as strong as me.'

'When?'

'I don't know,' Jitka says. 'Last month.'

81

'Why didn't you tell me?'

'I forgot. When did we speak? I speak with Alice all the time.'

'And you were going to pick me up from the airport in . . .?'

The taxi collects Veronika outside her mother's apartment block fifteen minutes after Veronika dials the company. During this time, she and Jitka sit and smoke.

Veronika does not talk to this driver because she is so angry—also, his car is a Skoda and smells sweetly of unwashed penis.

Veronika's grandmother—Marta—can't get out of bed to answer the door, so Veronika buzzes number 12.

Mrs Wiszczorova is waiting for her as the lift doors open. She wants to talk about the wedding. The Wiszczors are invited, all eight of them. Everybody will be invited; nobody will want to miss it.

'Can I pop back later?' Veronika asks. 'I want to see my grandmother.'

'Of course,' says Mrs Wiszczorova, and lays the key out on Veronika's palm. 'She is just the same.'

Veronika waits for Mrs Wiszczorova to re-enter her flat before unlocking the door to number 14.

'Grandma!' she calls. 'It's Veronika!'

By the time she enters the room, both of them are crying.

They embrace.

'I did not expect you until this evening,' says Grandma, as soon as she can speak. Her voice comes through half a day's silent phlegm. 'You look beautiful.'

'Why didn't you tell me about the car smash?'

'Which—?' Grandma quickly understands. 'She didn't tell me.'

'But she still comes?'

'Every afternoon. But every afternoon, I expect her not to come. She's getting very bad. You can smell it.'

'She promised to collect me from the airport. I had to take a taxi.'

Grandma says, 'I hope that this wedding will recall some important things to her mind.'

'We went straight into arguing.'

'It is so good to see you.'

Veronika leans across to kiss her grandmother. The mattress feels as soft as ever, and the air around her grandmother's face blurs with cheap perfume. Nothing in the tiny yellow room has changed, and it must never change. Veronika wishes death away from her grandmother, who will be seventy in December.

'How is Alice?' Veronika asks.

'She is ready,' Grandma says. 'But I think she was always ready. But there are no arrangements.'

'We used to have weddings with our dolls. You made us a special white dress.'

'I remember,' says Grandma. 'With pink cross-stitching on the bodice.'

'How is your chest?' Veronika asks.

'Up and down. Let's talk about something else. It is lovely to see you again. Did I say that?'

They hug again.

'We will need a car for the wedding,' says Veronika. 'To collect you and bring you back.'

'Perhaps Wladislaw . . .' Wladislaw is the Wiszczorova husband. He touches bottoms and is forgiven because he can't help it and is otherwise charming.

'Mother has enough money,' says Veronika. 'We'll hire something. I'll do the driving.'

'You can't drive in a dress like that! I will ask Wladislaw.'

'Has *he* been to visit?' Veronika doesn't have to say Rik—she knows Grandma will know exactly who she means.

'Alice brought him, once. They asked your mother's permission, then they came and asked my blessing. Since then, he speaks to me by telephone. They say they are busy.'

'But Alice has come?'

'She showed me small images of the dress she wants, last week. You will not like it, but you must say that you do. I said that I did. It is too old-fashioned? If she's not careful with her make-up, she'll look just like her mother.'

'Mother wanted to do all the make-up herself.'

'No!' says Grandma. 'Then Alice would look like a bad circus clown.'

'Alice has a friend who is a beautician,' says Veronika.

'Alice has lots of friends who are beauticians,' says Grandma. 'Too many. But, tell me, how are you?'

Veronika's fingers are caught up in her grandmother's hands, jiggled softly.

'I quit my job with Max,' says Veronika, and tells the story.

In the small lobby, Veronika drops her grandmother's key into the Wiszczors' postbox.

When Veronika arrives back, around seven, Jitka has gone out. There is no note, but Veronika knows not to expect her. In the kitchen cupboard there is a half of black bread that might be edible if toasted. Veronika decides to go to sleep. She will put a clean sheet over the couch. First, though, she texts her sister and confirms their meeting, tomorrow at ten o'clock.

Veronika wakes up because her hair feels like it's burning. Her mother has it in two handfuls and is yanking Veronika's head from side to side.

'The Queen of England!' Jitka screams. 'The Queen of England!'

Veronika's head is pushed into the cushion then lifted into the air. There is lots of pain, although most of it hasn't reached her yet—she's still a little asleep.

'Stop,' she says. 'Stop it.'

'Don't judge me,' shrieks her mother. 'Don't you dare judge me. You don't know.'

The yanking doesn't stop, and Veronika—starting to feel dizzy—knows she has to do something. One hand takes hold of her mother's neck, the other moves way out to the side. Then, hard as she can, Veronika slaps Jitka's face. Even in doing so, she tries to avoid giving her mother a black eye.

The grip on Veronika's hair gets tighter, and she is forced down into the cushion.

She can't do much else except grab her mother's hair—only, it isn't her mother's hair, it's her wig, and it slides over her face with small tearing sounds.

'Shit!' shouts her mother, and lets go.

There's some space now between them, and Veronika uses it to bring up her feet and kick her mother in the belly. Jitka slides off the edge of the couch and starts to scream. Without giving her the chance to attack again, Veronika quickly stands up and pushes her screaming mother to the floor. Then she gets on top of her, calves pressing down on Jitka's elbows. This is the safest position; Veronika was around fifteen when she found this out.

'Let me go,' says Jitka.

'Calm down, Mother.'

'Let me free.'

'In a minute.'

'I have dangerous friends. They won't let this happen. Rik is dangerous. Who do you think you are?'

Veronika thinks of Max. He used to love playfighting. Both sides of her head are stinging.

'If I let you go, you must promise to be calm.'

'I am calm! I am calm!'

'You must promise to be calm.'

Her mother sulks. 'You think you are the Queen of England,' she says. 'Everybody hates you.'

Veronika thinks about slapping her mother again, but it would be a different kind of slap—one she has only rarely allowed herself. 'Be calm,' she says.

'Let me go,' says Jitka.

A minute later Veronika stands up. Immediately her mother pivots round and grabs Veronika's leg and bites her ankle.

Veronika kicks her mother in the face. She can feel the loose skin tearing beneath her toenail. She thinks it's one of her mother's cheeks.

Jitka screams again, drags herself up and runs for the bathroom. Veronika follows her and when her mother is safely inside she pulls shut the door.

'You've ruined me! Look at that! You've ruined everything!'

It takes half an hour before Jitka stops raging and Veronika lets her out. Jitka spits in her face and heads for the fridge.

Veronika goes into the lounge and phones for a taxi and begins to pack.

Half an hour later Veronika leaves. Her mother is snoring.

This time Mr Wiszczor stands there with the key.

'Hello, Veronika,' he says. 'How are you?'

'I'm sorry,' she says. 'I couldn't stay at my mother's.'

'Do you need anything?'

'I will come round tomorrow.'

Veronika drags a seat cushion through from the lounge and lets it fall at the foot of her grandmother's bed.

In the morning Veronika makes honey porridge for the two of them, and they don't talk about why she is there.

Alice takes Veronika to the best Starbucks in town. She is friendly, so Veronika feels sure their mother hasn't woken up yet. Alice has photos on her BlackBerry.

'What do you think?' she says. 'Isn't it the most beautiful . . .'

'It's lovely,' says Veronika. 'You will look beautiful.'

'This is the back, with the full train for you to hold.'

'Wonderful.'

'And this is the tiara.'

'Yes,' Veronika says.

'And these are the shoes. I'm borrowing them from Lenka.'

'Amazing.'

'And this,' she watches Veronika's face, 'is for you.'

'Oh, wow,' says Veronika. 'That's superb. Really, I can't wait to try it on.'

'I will order it soon,' says Alice. 'And this is what the cake will look like, only the icing will be blue not pink. Blue is so much nicer.'

Her BlackBerry ringtones Mendelssohn.

'Mum?' says Alice, and listens.

Veronika can hear, too.

'But she says,' says Alice.

They are approaching the Charles Bridge, a little way along from Starbucks.

'Why would I do that?' Veronika says. 'Why would I want to do that?'

'Because you want to destroy everything, like always. Because you are jealous. Because you are evil in our family.'

'*She* attacked *me*.'

'So?'

Veronika is aware of passers-by.

'I didn't mean to cut her face.'

Passers-by who overhear.

'Then why did you?'

An old man carrying a box of apples.

'She bit my leg,' says Veronia.

'Show me,' says Alice.

A very thin young woman talking on a cellphone.

Veronika pulls up the bottom of her jeans. There are a few small red marks.

'Where?' says Alice.

Veronika points—one, two, three.

A tall man who glances down.

Alice leans back against the window display of a shoe shop and crosses her arms. She is hugging her BlackBerry.

'I'm not evil,' says Veronika.

A large Gypsy woman with a baby in a sling.

'I don't believe you,' Alice says. 'My engagement was going to be so perfect.' Alice sobs and begins to cry. 'You—'

'Alice,' says Veronika, and tries to put her arms around her sister's shoulders.

'Get off!' Alice shrieks. 'Get away!'

A quite thin young woman talking on a cellphone.

Veronika doesn't press. 'I will see you later,' she says.

It takes a minute for Alice to form words. 'You will not be my brides-maid.' Breath. 'I will have Lenka.' Breath. 'She is your size. Lenka can do your job.'

'But she's lying!' Veronika says. 'I was asleep.'

'I will go and see her,' says Alice.

'I will come with you,' says Veronika.

An old woman carrying a skateboard.

Jitka stands in the doorway, refusing to let Veronika enter.

'She will kill me,' Jitka says.

The cut doesn't look so bad, Veronika thinks. It's only as wide as a toenail. The bruising is minimal.

'Let's go to the hospital,' says Alice. 'You might need an injection.'

'Tell her to go away,' says Jitka.

'Come with me,' says Alice.

'I want to stay here.'

They stand for a while, then Alice says, 'Lenka is going to be my bridesmaid. Veronika will just be a guest.'

'No! No!' Jitka shouts. 'Don't be so stupid. Veronika must be the bridesmaid.'

'But we hate her,' says Alice.

'Veronika has to be bridesmaid—she's your sister. Don't you understand?'

'She attacked you.'

'Unless Veronika is bridesmaid, I will not be there.'

'Fine,' says Alice. 'Whatever. Now I'm taking you to the hospital.'

'Wait one minute,' says Jitka. 'I will get my bag.'

'I don't want to be bridesmaid,' says Veronika. 'I don't want to be a guest. I don't want to be your sister and I don't want to be your daughter. I'm leaving.'

A moment.

'That's your choice,' says Alice.

'Veronko, no,' says her mother. 'Come here. Come here.' She makes to hug her.

'This isn't a family,' says Veronika, stepping back. 'This is just pain and more pain. Why do we do it? You hate her even more than I do.' Veronika is talking to Alice. 'Because you're the same person she is. And you're going to marry to same man she did. Can't you even see that?'

Jitka has started to laugh. Alice begins to smirk.

'You're so fucking jealous,' says Alice. 'Just because your own marriage only lasted three weeks.'

'I hope you're enjoying this!' Jitka shouts, to the neighbours behind their doors. She hoots.

Veronika says, 'I would like one picture of my father, before I go. The photograph by the pool. It's in the box.'

Jitka stares at Veronika.

'Please let me get it,' says Veronika.

'What?' says Alice.

'Please,' says Veronika.

Jitka laughs. Jitka smiles. Jitka steps aside and Veronika walks past her into the flat.

KAVITA & DR NYKVIST

STATEMENT

DATE OF SERVICE	DESCRIPTION OF SERVICE	CHARGES	CREDITS	BALANCE
▮▮▮▮	DNA Screening			
	Pathologist			
	Lab Services			
	Preoperative work-up: Diagnostic mammogram bilateral	▮▮▮▮		
▮▮▮▮	Preoperative work-up: Blood work			
	Preoperative work-up: EKG			
	Preoperative work-up: Urine Pregnancy test	▮▮▮▮		
	Dr Nykvist, physician: Consultation after-care			
▮▮▮▮▮▮	Dr Nykvist's insurance			
	Mr Marc Lyth, breast surgeon			
	Mr Marc Lyth's insurance	▮▮▮▮▮▮		
	Mrs Hildegaard Wang, plastic surgeon			
	Mrs Hildegaard Wang's insurance			
	Oxygen			
	Operating Room anaesthesia			

DATE OF SERVICE	DESCRIPTION OF SERVICE	CHARGES	CREDITS	BALANCE
▮	General anaesthesia	▮		
▮	Operating Room Time: 180 minutes	▮		
▮	Operating Room Central Supplies	▮		
▮	Med/Surg Supplies	▮		
▮	Implant charge, left breast	▮		
▮	Implant charge, right breast	▮		
▮	Venipuncture routine	▮		
▮	Incentive Spriometer	▮		
▮	90 minutes in Post-Op room	▮		
▮	Hydromorphome HCl	▮		
▮	Pharmacy	▮		
▮	Semi-private room	▮		
▮	Breakfast	▮		
▮	Laundry	▮		
▮	Chemotherapy x 20	▮		
▮	Ms Heather Large, nutritionist	▮		
▮	Yoga instruction, late-cancellation fee	▮		
▮	Full cranial prosthesis (wig)	▮		

ACCOUNT TOTAL	CURRENT	30 DAYS	60 DAYS	90 DAYS	OVER 120 DAYS
151,177.05					

DATE	PATIENT NAME	ACCOUNT NO.	PAY THIS AMOUNT
	KAVITA		151,177.05

MAKE CHEQUE PAYABLE TO: ██████

PHONE #: ██████

MESSAGE:

IF YOU HAVE ANY QUERIES OR QUESTIONS PLEASE CONTACT OUR RAPID RESOLUTIONS DEPARTMENT

JOHN & JOSEPH

It was John's minimum requirement—not to have to write *and* sleep and, for that matter, fuck in the same room. When the laptop went off at the end of the day, he needed to be able to close the door on it and walk away— usually towards another screen; otherwise, work continued; otherwise, he would keep returning and returning for another peek. And so, when renting, he always went for two-bed flats. In this latest flat, though, John had almost immediately found he couldn't be doing with either of the bedrooms. One was at the front of the house, and had a window with people's ankles and calves and dogs walking past; the other was to the side and lacked natural light. After a week of angry oscillating, John had decamped to the kitchen table—and now, as much as anywhere in the world, not excluding his parents' post-divorce houses, it was his home.

John's laptop was set up so that behind it lay the garden. The other way round, with back towards the French doors, the light over his shoulders made of the screen a grey-white fog. Even without this, eye strain was his main occupational hazard—apart from RSI. He had to wear specially articulated gloves whenever he typed; really, he should get a desktop computer, and arrange the screen at the right height. But he needed to be mobile, and not just within wherever he happened to be living.

Sometimes he went back and worked in the cafe near last month's flat, where the Armenian had been. It was safe now; she'd given notice and moved on to Uruguay. He'd managed to wangle one night with her— through bad jokes, large tips and the promise of a drive to Hastings in a friend's black Karmann Ghia (a car she thought belonged to him, having once seen him drive up in it). A very lonely, very hairy girl, especially the armpits—that was his memory. He wasn't even disappointed by her disappointing breasts, because, after months of hot-weather fantasies, he had expected them to be disappointing, and was even rather pleased they were. These weren't breasts he would ever have to live with or try to be faithful to.

John knew that when he started to think about sex, it was time to stand up, turn round three times, sit back down and start again. This he did.

It wasn't a yard—John refused to call it a yard—*yard* was too American, and he wasn't American or even in America, unfortunately; he would continue to call it a garden, although, because it was mostly paved and completely without grass, it should probably actually be called a yard. The paving stones were odd: square, alternately pinkish and yellowy—leaving the tall-wall-surrounded place looking as if it were founded upon adjacent slices of Battenberg, without the marzipan. For no good reason John could see, there was a proper garden shed in the right-rear of the garden; a shed fitting for a much larger place, and, more bizarrely still, inside the shed—because he'd checked, curious, the first day he moved in with the keys—was a huge lawnmower of the sort with a heavy steel roller, in green paint of the respectable past. John then was only able to pull it around within the shed, a couple of feet towards the door—that was enough to see the thing wouldn't fit through, unless disassembled. For a mad moment, John had imagined the lawnmower's being placed on the wooden floor first of all and the shed raised around it. That would have made the whole garden a worthwhile artwork, though without a worthwhile audience. More conventionally, the shed housed a spade, a rake, a pitchfork—none of which were required for cultivating the half-metre wide flowerbeds; a trowel and a handfork would be more than enough for that. Apart from art, the only other explanation was that this shed had been storage space for a larger garden near by. John's garden had no doorway, however, and no sign of one's having been there before. To get the lawnmower anywhere near grass, it would have to be carried by probably three strong men through the house, in parts. This had made John think about the landlord; perhaps they were a very suspicious person, wary of theft. But then why leave the lawnmower there at all?

One previous tenant had put some flowers out in pots, and a few of them had survived to this summer. John believed the gardener to have been a woman in her mid-thirties. The pots weren't terracotta but the rich blue of Moroccan tile-work. They were too expensive and taste-particular for someone to leave behind without good reason. She could always have repotted them—that was the kind of thing gardeners did, move things from one place to another, and then back, and then back again, and again. It was turning oneself into a manual labourer, but because convention called it 'gardening', people were prepared to waste their lives doing it. John felt this way about golf, too. Put it down as a job description: tiny ball, small hole, 550 yards intervening, odd-shaped tools, long walks, wind, rain. No one would do this, day after day, if you paid them a low hourly rate. Or they would, of course; people filleted fish and cleaned toilets and sucked the cocks of total strangers (potentially diseased strangers). But they wouldn't *enjoy* it.

John realized he wasn't thinking about what he should be thinking about: the script. It was the third episode of a sitcom set in an aquarium. Working title: *Something Fishy*. His film agent had got him it, bitch. It was really a rewrite, a salvage job, from some notes bequeathed him by the last-but-one producer's assistant—who had been present at the original pitch meeting, scribbling, and then, along with the producer, had abandoned the project. They were now a couple, in Hollywood, helping to remake a Portuguese slasher movie. John was envious. He hated all the characters in *Something Fishy*, wanted to kill them extravagantly—so that people in the fifteenth row ducked, and some macho types puked or left the cinema. He imagined a peacock's tail of blood as the neurotic aquarium manager, Clive, was decapitated by a Great White. He imagined the horn of a narwhal plunging into the belly of Nancy, the ditzy secretary.

John stood up, turned round three times, sat back down and started again.

It was two minutes to four and something was vaguely wrong in the garden—he looked up from the screen—something was wrong with the garden, with the proportions of it; a new something was there, an area of darkness, a column. (All this in less than a second.) Someone had put something tall in the garden—a figure of a statue carved out of something that was too dark to be marble. No, wrong: someone tall and dark was in the garden. John looked harder. His eyes focussed after a moment. There was a black man—a black man dressed in black skin; that is, naked—a naked black man, big, in the garden, tall, with the shed behind and to one side of him. This was exciting. That was John's first thought. Something was happening, which was better than nothing happening. Then fear that was a physiological reaction hit him, a jump inside himself, a trying-to-get-out—and, along with this, a massive adrenalin kick. He could see the cock of the black man who was very tall, around six foot four, and was black in the way of American or Caribbean but not Nigerian or Congolese blacks; there was bronze and yellow within the black. His hair was cropped very close but without any lines or design in it. His lips were large—of course his lips were large, and presumably his teeth were very white, at least in contrast with his skin, but he wasn't smiling or snarling.

John sat very still but was aware that the black had seen him, was looking at him now, and that the light of the screen would make his white face bright within the dark of the room. The black man's face was expressionless, his full lips set firm. John wanted to move. The keys to the French doors were in a kitchen drawer over to the right. The doors needed to be unlocked at top and bottom with one key, then in the middle—beneath the doorhandle—with another. Which would take perhaps a minute, if done as fast as he could. The black man would be able to see it all. John might also, before he opened the door, arm himself with a carving knife. This could be enough to make the black man run off, as could simply standing up.

John looked again; the black man hadn't moved—he appeared to be posing, very calm, very statue-like. He had the kind of black pubic hairs that John recognized from interracial porn films—the ones which go into little bunches, leaving exposed skin all around. The black man's chest hair, too, was a series of dark dots against the brown. His penis was large, larger than John's, even though flaccid, and it hung with the curve of a banana. The glans, a circle of it, stuck out through the smooth foreskin. John realized he was thinking things he shouldn't think. The black man's face was a little like that of a monkey. You weren't allowed to think black men looked like monkeys, even when they did—even when, like with this one, their stubby nose looked quite similar to a monkey's nose. Most of the things John thought about black men he knew he wasn't allowed to think.

John remembered anthropological photographs from the start of the last century. *This is primitive man*, they said. *Admire his innate nobility.* Digital porn couldn't catch the colours of this kind of black skin as sepia did.

What was this man-who-wasn't-a-monkey doing in the garden? What did he want? He didn't look angry. He looked as if he didn't want anything at all, just to be able to stand there for a while and be admired. There was vanity in his pose, John felt; strut, and a sense of his own beauty. He *was* beautiful, although his monkeyish face wasn't particularly handsome. The nostrils were very wide. His body wasn't perfect. There was a slight scar, which might have been an operation scar, running diagonally across his abdomen. He was without fat. Was he gay? Was this a come-on? John wanted a closer look at his cock—to see it in real life and not on a screen. What must it feel like to have a cock like that? To look like that? It must feel good, just to want to stand naked in front of another man, be admired and envied by him. But did the black man know the person inside this house was a man? Was his kick exposing himself to men specifically?

John thought about the police. Should he call the police? Before he'd even tried to speak to the man. The man was trespassing—that was against the law. Did it make any difference he was naked? That made it indecent exposure, though John would have been embarrassed going to court over something so feeble. He didn't care that he'd seen the man's cock. Not as a matter of law, he didn't care. And he didn't want to go to court and have people think he cared one way or the other about seeing another man's cock, black or not, big or not. And people would think he had more of a problem because the cock was bigger than his own. And the black man's lawyer would probably make that point—and both men might be required to put their penis size down as a matter of public record. And you could bet they wouldn't be allowed to do the measuring themselves. It would be someone very intimidating with very cold hands, in a very cold room. John decided not to call the police. But maybe he should be doing something to warn the man off.

They had been looking at each other for about four minutes now. But John didn't want to warn the man off. John wanted him to stay—he wanted him to feel comfortable standing there, as long as he meant no harm. And what clearer way was there of declaring his harmlessness than appearing naked? If not vanity or something sexual, it might be some religious thing; the black man was mad, thought he was Jesus. But the pose was African, didn't have even a hint of the crucifixion. And he wasn't giving off mad vibes. The black man was standing as if to attention; no body twist, quite up and down—like, now John saw it, like one of those African statues where everything goes straightforward, as if the statue were a figurehead on the prow of a ship, a mothership. John wanted to know how this was going to end. It might almost be a political protest. If the shed was art, this too could be intended just for him. Perhaps this was a sign of some sort. *The* sign. Or was he hallucinating? A naked black man had nothing to do with what he was writing. He had eaten recently, not taken drugs, not even too much caffeine.

The black man shivered, and John realized he had stopped thinking of him as capable of movement, capable of speech, capable of reasons. John knew the black man would speak English. If he had been even taller, nomadic-looking, any question might have been answered with incomprehensible clicks. But he looked as if he'd been here for a while. Britain if not Brighton. It occurred to John that he had been racist all along: he had no reason whatsoever for believing himself to be more intelligent than this man. Which of them was the subject and which the object? Just because the black man was standing there, posing, didn't mean that he himself was any the less looked-at, examined, estimated, anthropologized.

They had now reached a recognized, negotiated status quo: I won't move if you won't move. Others of his racisms came clear to John. That he had, first of all, assumed a threat. But fear hadn't been his first reaction; shock, incredulity, wonder, envy—all had come before. He felt he should, when he spoke to the man, as he surely had to, begin with an apology— and not just for his own racisms but for all the racisms of those like him, before him. I did assume you were planning to burgle or assault me. That was the first thing I thought. Just as, when I see a hooded black boy coming towards me in the street, I think of how much money there is in my wallet. You know that, don't you? You sense it when people walk towards you. I rehearse the arguments for just handing it over, not putting up a fight. 'Every black boy?' he might ask. No, just the dangerous-looking ones. 'Which ones are those?' The ones older than about seven—seven or eight. 'And do you think about the size of their penises, too?' Of course I do. Everyone does. And they spend a lot of time touching them, from what I've seen. That's one stereotype they're not afraid to live up to. John realized that thinking this dialogue, he had been staring through and not at the black man. The black man, though, had continued to watch him—and seemed to be annoyed by his failure of attention.

How *had* he got into the garden? He must have climbed over one of the walls. John's house was in the middle of a long street of terraced houses backing on to another identical street. To come from either end of either street, the black man would have to have clambered through eight or ten other gardens—this made it more likely he'd come from one of the gardens backing directly on to John's. But what did that matter? That he might see him again in the corner shop?

It was time to stand up. John delayed for another minute. Could the black man see where he was looking? Was he conscious when his cock in particular was being examined?

John stood up and went across to the drawer containing the key. He was out of sight of the black man, unless the black man decided to move to the side. The key was towards the front of the drawer, just where John had left it. Otherwise, the drawer was empty, apart from papers relating to the oven and microwave. John moved to the French doors, aware from the first glimpse that the composition of the garden-image had changed: the area of darkness was missing, and would—from now on—always be expected and always be missing. The black man was gone, and John wished more than anything that he'd had a chance to speak to him before he went. We could have made friends, thought John. I need some black friends. Don't *need* them but it would be good to have some, seeing how I don't have any at the moment. It would be hard to explain how we met. But no one asks that old-fashioned kind of question any more, not unless you're going out with someone. Everyone's met everyone, and if they haven't already they soon will.

John unlocked the door and opened it, half expecting the man to leap out at him from left or right. The garden was empty, though. Perhaps the man had used the shed to climb up to the top of the wall, then over. John waited for the laughter, but none came. He walked to the exact spot where the man had stood. He went back to the glass doors and pushed them shut. Then he went back to the spot. To see what the man had seen he needed someone to be sitting in his chair. Someone white. Still expecting laughter, perhaps to encourage laughter, John dropped the keys on the paving stones and began to undress.

JOHN & YAMINAH

John wrote:

I was very aware of being back in my boyhood bed, lights out, sheets smelling (as sheets always had) of 100 per cent pure home, and Persil Automatic. ~~Safety.~~

After Mum and Dad had trogged upstairs, I stayed in the lounge to watch the end of some action movie—I can't remember what. But I hadn't really been watching, and I got bored, gave up on the bloody thing, and switched off halfway through the big climactic Hero vs Villain clifftop fistfight. I'd seen it before, even though I hadn't seen it before. Perhaps it was one of the *Missions Impossible*. I've never understood how, after all those nosediving helicopters and fuel-depot shootouts—how a punch in the guts counts as any kind of escalation. (This is my problem, I know. This is why I'm stuck writing shitty TV.)

To rise from the brown sofa was a considerable challenge, made somehow yet greater by the fact that the sofa was brown. I felt very forty-one years old. Also, for dinner we had eaten most of the seventies: prawn and avocado, grilled lambchops with new pots and buttered French beans, and for afters banana splits. These details. Between us, we put away five bottles of Riesling, and Mum hardly drinks at all. It was *Mission Impossible 3*, I think.

The food was my belated birthday treat. I'd driven up the weekend after my party, to which my parents had been invited but didn't come because it was too far and too late.

In the upstairs bathroom, avocado, I used my own toothbrush but, for some reason I don't understand, my Dad's denture-related toothpaste. It tasted of chewing gum that's lost its taste.

And the next thing, I put on my pyjamas and got into that bed, where I lay looking at the yellow streetlight coming through and even more brightly *around* the Spiderman curtains, ninth birthday. I remember gazing up at them for a good long while, thinking of how angry they used to make me when I began to fantasize about bringing Toyah Willcox back for a snog. (I win a competition on Swap Shop to go and see *Top of the Pops* being recorded, and Toyah—performing her latest hit, 'I Want to Be Free'—plucks me from the crowd to dance with her and finds herself unable and unwilling to resist my pizza-faced charms. Toyah was by far my most elaborate snog scenario. Siouxsie Sioux just barged straight into my bedroom with her tits out.) Mum and Dad refused to change the curtains while they were still what they called *good*. 'What's wrong with Spiderman?' Mum used to ask, in a tone that suggested the correct answer was some disease I'd never heard of. And now I dozily started arguing with her again, the issue becoming fuzzier and more passionate. 'What's wrong with Spiderman is what's wrong with this whole house, with your whole lives—'

An incoming text buzzed me back awake.

My cellphone displays the sender's name in a boxy white font through the black top of the clamshell. (I like this detail; it's the reason I chose this handset.)

Yammy, it said—meaning Yaminah.

At first I thought it was a mistake, a pocket-dial. By this time of night, Yammy was always off her head, unless she was in detox. I was amazed she still had my number: I hadn't seen her for six months, and on average she lost her phone every fortnight (usually stolen by some druggie). Our break-up had been ugly and long and had happened several times. Yaminah was in love with me, and didn't want to let me go. But the yummy Iranian fruitcake was too much of a mess even for my cynical exploitation—

John got out his phone, laid it alongside his notebook, and began to copy out the text:

> Hey john hey sorry i
> do this to you this
> way but right now i
> just can't speak to
> no one but you need
> to know so i have to

After the first page, I scrolled down, and continued to do so—line by line—as I read the rest of her message.

> tell you this way.
> You know my bad
> habits. You know
> what i mean. They
> are now on me in
> punishment come
> back. I had lots of
> lovers after the
> first time we broke
> up. One of them was

I tried to remember the first time. Was it outside the ICA bar, shouting, or was it outside Soho House, screaming?

> the worst. I did it
> because i hated my
> life. Allah is just. My
> body has the hiv
> virus. Im sorry
> john. You must get a
> test before you
> give it to another if
> you have it. I pray
> you dont have it. I
> was not in love with

you. This should not
be happening to us.
I have not told my
parents. I am so
shamed. Y x x x

I reached over to turn the bedside lamp on, then didn't.

The phone in my hand vibrated. I knew it was her, and when I pressed to answer, the sound of her came to me—out of her lungs and through the wide opening of her mouth. I knew what she was saying almost immediately, even though not a word was clear. She was saying, *I'm sorry. I'm so sorry. John, I'm so sorry.*

'Okay.'

'Don't shout at me. I'm going to die.'

I made himself ask, 'How many others have you had to tell?'

'Oh God,' she said. 'Two.'

'You told them today?'

'I told them yesterday.'

'And what if I'd fucked someone yesterday night?'

'I know. I know. But Imran said he was gonna kill me. And probably he hasn't even got it.' She sniffed, liquid. 'We always used protection, innit.'

'I don't know Imran. Who else?'

'Benny. He's a mate of Bazza.'

'So how did he react?'

'He said he thought he'd probably got it anyway.'

'But he didn't give it to you.'

'Lesley did.'

'Lesley, that's a man's name?'

'He comes to Bazza to get his. I shoulda known. God, you must really hate me.'

'I do,' I said. 'I thought I hated you before, but . . .'

'You're probably okay. We hardly—It was more drugs than fucking, wasn't it? But you should get yourself tested.'

'Don't ever tell me what I should fucking do, okay? Ever. You stupid fucking bitch.'

'I'm sorry. Look, I'm paying for it.'

'Well, I'm sorry about that.'

'Let me know, John, when you get your result. Text me. I need to know, to know what I've done, like. Or else I'll just have to call you again. Where are you?'

'That's none of your business.'

Her asking made him aware, even more, that this shouldn't be possible. He was in a safe place—the safest place—a place he had once fled because it was too safe. The blankets had bobbles on them that had bobbled up in the early eighties. Spiderman was webbing his way from skyscraper to skyscraper.

'I will let you know,' he said, then shut the phone. It had ActiveFlip, so cut her off straight away.

John got up out of bed, brought his old skateboard down from on top of the wardrobe. Still in pyjamas, he carried the board quietly downstairs—Mum was snoring—and out through the kitchen door. He didn't start to ride it until he was on the once-black-now-grey-but-right-now-yellow-under-halogen tarmac of the street. The first push-off felt good, already consolatory; the night air was warm past his temples, through the gap between pyjama-top and pyjama bottoms. He could feel it, too, on his cock—there was a slit with a button, hard to keep closed.

The close where his parents live swoops down and leftwards, reverse cambered, to some garages. He bent his knees a little and clacked off the pavement onto the road, then made S-shapes as he sped up. He felt extremely American, which was also comforting. Garaaahdjes not garridges, sidewalk not pavement. The slope got steeper; he hadn't been this fast in a while—the line he should take was clear, it was the line he'd always taken: cut in tight round the garages, almost clipping the first corner, then he'd be able to make the bend and not hit one of the flat metal doors with T-shaped handles opposite. But a motorbike, parked where it shouldn't be. But the handlebars catching the (avoiding) inside of John's left elbow and tugging him all off-balance. But the skateboard keeping going into the bottom of a mustard-coloured door, pushed on by John's falling backwards off it.

They landed the same time, he and his old board, and he was on his bare feet and limping before he had realized he couldn't walk without limping. A Neil Young song started playing in his head as he scooped up the skateboard, which had lost a good inch-wide chunk from the right corner.

'Fucker,' said John.

John limped back to the motorbike, took the board's side-edges in both hands and smashed the stupid fucking front headlight. Then, feeling the need, he pulled out his cock and pissed in an arc over the shiny back seat and the dull engine. It was a Yamaha.

Dropping the skateboard end-first to the tarmac, John pushed his left foot through it, tipping it forwards until the front wheels landed with him already riding, right foot—luckily the ankle he hadn't twisted—now pushing and pushing as he began to climb back up the slope. This time, though, he leant left and took a slow turn out of the close and along the middle of the wide road. Detached houses in red brick were set back behind small, dry, unfenced lawns. This here was the one he'd gone to for remedial maths lessons before O levels. That there was where Sam had lived with his scary blond-haired older brothers, Michael and Andrew, who had turned into punks and become even scarier.

As he went gliding, the pain beginning to ripen in his left thigh, John noticed the light get brighter as he approached each streetlight and then start to fade away as he reached the midpoint. The light also got yellower and greyer. He hoped he might see a cat or a fox, a significant animal, but there were only hidden people—the sound of theme music from a television, bedroom lights, another television.

John did not yet know where he was going but he knew he was going somewhere, so he kept going, down to the left at the T-junction where a bigger road dropped away and he no longer had to scoot. This momentum took him halfway up to a right turn, beneath beech trees, and this road—with more uphill effort than before—took him past his primary school. This might have been his destination, but clearly it wasn't, because he was still going—past where the library he'd borrowed sci-fi from had been, past where the sweet shop he'd stolen from had been. He listened for cars as he approached the next T-junction, but the village was quiet; he could have heard an engine five streets away. Left, then right, then straight up towards the Albion pub, where the door abruptly opened and yet no one came out. He was on Unstable Street now, and it became clear to him—still skateboarding down the middle of the road—slaloming the long bumps of the painted stitch-lines—where he was approaching: Pippa's house.

Before he got there, there was a mini-roundabout and three kids sitting on the benches outside the council offices, who shouted something predictable beginning with *c*. John was aware how he must look, he just didn't give a damn. He stopped and skated back towards the kids, but they ran off shouting *pervert*. So he did a powerslide and then went back the way he'd been going.

Pippa's house in the soft air, rounded-off gingerbread-coloured bricks on the turn down towards his middle school, a lovely swoop, but here was the place, and here he coasted to a stop. Cool. She had been so beautiful, at middle school, Pippa Maynard, and he had no idea what had happened to her. He kicked the tail of the skateboard and the nose flew satisfyingly up into his hand. He was cool. He wished Pippa had been there to look out her bedroom window and see that. Pippa had looked like she could be from California or off the television. Her limbs were slim in a way other girls' weren't—they fit themselves all the way along, eight years old, nine and a quarter, ten. At eleven, he had started at a different school from her, and that was it. He couldn't remember seeing her again. He couldn't remember ever speaking to her. He had certainly never thought of asking her out. It was adoration merely; looking across the playground at a thing that was right in every way, and that didn't need him in any way. There were no lights on in Pippa's house—which somehow made America turn back into England again.

He realized, from the temperature difference, and then from looking down, that he had come all this way with his cock showing.

Most of the way back home would be downhill, if he took a slightly different route. He had known the pavements so well, once. Where you needed to jump because a tree-root was starting to poke out. Where it was so skin-smooth that even if you fell off your jeans wouldn't rip.

But there was somewhere else he had to go. The hill down towards his middle school, Station Road, was steeper even than his parents' close down to the garages. He started on the pavement, but it was too granular, and when a gap came up between parked cars he popped the kerb and was onto a black slope that was the pure dream of smooth. He was crossing to the left side of the road when he saw a car coming the other way. The faces inside were mildly astonished as he went past, going into a crouch to impress the driver in the rear-view mirror. At this pace, the air began to feel colder—and, coming through the thin cloth pressed to him, he felt more naked.

The road had one or two turnings into it before it crossed a small river, not bumping up into a bridge, and bottomed out. John wondered if there was anyone living in the village who would recognize him, at this speed.

The low buildings of the middle school came into view on his right. He turned in at the entrance gate and made his way, in a long tracking shot, past the tennis courts and temporary classrooms up to the main building.

Kick, and the board was once again in his hand. He walked parallel rows of paving stones round the edge of the building, then stepped onto lawn where they ran out. These bricks were yellowish, darker than when he'd attended. A new building had become a not-new building.

Round the side and twenty yards along brought him to a classroom that he seemed to remember sitting in, learning French. He looked in at the small tables and chairs. Already he felt disappointed. The coming down the hill had been more important than this. Pippa's house had been the place, and this wasn't.

He ran carrying the board across the lawn and up into the heathy land beyond the sandy path. Here, he was halted by the crying of his eyes. He had been a boy. He had stopped being a boy. Why couldn't he go back? He wanted to unsmash the lights on the motorbike. The blankets on his old bed would heal him, even if he did have the virus. He lay back on a grey-sandy patch between heather clumps and looked up at a liquid-distorted sky. She should have phoned him straight away. Perhaps those people in the car had seen his cock, and would report him to the police. He didn't have his mobile phone with him, which felt bizarre. You could live a whole normal life with HIV now. There wasn't any need to go cobwebby thin and stretched-skinny and die. But he wouldn't be able to give his parents grandchildren. And all those people he still wanted to fuck, he'd either have to lie to them or risk their lives. Who should he tell? He thought about who he should call, in case they met someone tomorrow—it was, in a way, disappointing there weren't that many. Was it worth calling until he knew? He would go tomorrow, in London. There were places in railway stations, weren't there? He considered a wank. The stars were shaped like white starfish in his eyes. He couldn't see them accurately, through the wetness. I'm not ready to think about this, he thought. I should skateboard some more. As long as I'm moving, then I'm okay. Perhaps he could get back to being American, if he went fast enough—if he went to the top of Station Road and took a run-up and came down again.

John stopped writing and looked up through the window right in front of him.

AMANYANA & BLOODKILL

As ancient chronicles do tell, the Great Breaking entered its most critical phase when the Ram-Warrior Bloodkill challenged Amanyana the High Sorceress to a duel.

They stood facing each other, in the middle of the main thoroughfare of Anthill Castle. It was raining torrentially, white lines streaking downwards to splash briefly on their heads and shoulders. Around them, the diverse citizens of this embattled outpost went about their common business—bartering goods, buying weapons, boasting of quests past, present and yet to come; above them towered three- and four-storey buildings, rickety with age and rancid with neglect.

Amanyana looked Bloodkill over, assessing what he displayed of both strengths and weaknesses—she felt frizzy with excitement but around an inner core of calm. Duels were nothing new to her, they were a hazard one had to face every day in this harsh world. The more martial races—Hammerheads, Spine-Giants, both breeds of Nazgong—often picked on Sorceresses, mistaking them for easy meat.

Amanyana had only two courses of action: she could either accept or reject Bloodkill's challenge. If she rejected it, she could go upon her way untroubled—except, perhaps, by the creeping suspicion of her own cowardice. But if she accepted, she must battle him until one of them had lost all Strength and Soul.

Bloodkill would be the highest-ranking opponent she had ever faced—although she had encountered three Ram-Warriors before. Like each of them, Bloodkill was possessed of the curly-horned head of a billy goat jutting out of the pumped-up body of Mr Universe in a Universe with deeply psychotic physics. His heavy armour, covering all but his long white face, was lapis blue ornately embellished with the yellow that stood for gold. Snug in the Ram-Warrior's cloven right hoof sat a double-edged battleaxe, a single accurate blow from which would end their contest instantly.

Bloodkill spake. '**yo**,' he said. '**u wanna or not?**'

'**kk**,' said Amanyana.

And as she accepted the challenge—to the sound of trumpets and drums—a tall flagpole magically planted itself betwixt her and her opponent.

The countdown seconds began to seep away, Amanyana using them to cast powerful spells of protection upon herself; being a twenty-fifth rank Sorceress, she had plenty—and she selected the three which experience had taught her were most useful against Ram-Warriors: Willow Breeze-Bend, Slippery Sideways Crown and 50/50 Bifurcation-Heal.

With these in place, Amanyana backed away from Bloodkill. There was a limit to how far from the duelling flag she could stray, but she wanted to maximize the distance between herself and that fell battleaxe.

The final second evaporated. Bloodkill put his head down and hypercharged.

Having anticipated this, Amanyana teleported herself twenty yards forwards, spun round 180 degrees, targeted the Ram-Warrior and fired off her Total Chill spell.

To her astonishment, it did nothing—no frost block appeared round Bloodkill's legs, no ice-paralysis set in. There could only be one explanation: somewhere, somehow, Bloodkill must have picked up the Total Chill counterspell, and also managed to acquire a Spectral Shield, so as to keep this fact hidden from opponents.

Amanyana immediately knew she was in profound trouble. Without being able to immobilize her far stronger adversary, she would have far less time to fire off her attacking enchantments. Reflexively, she was already sending a sequence of these his way: a Snowblinder, to dazzle him for five to seven seconds; a Fire Imp, to creep up behind him and drain a quarter of his Strength; an Insta-Rink, to make the ground between them treacherously slippy.

Yet still the dread Bloodkill advanced defiantly towards Amanyana. His hoof-boots were proof against Enchanted Ice; they had not lost one iota of grip. (Amanyana knew a more skilled Sorceress would have noticed the boots, and not wasted precious Soul casting the Insta-Rink spell.) At the flash of the Snowblinder, a visor appeared to protect the

Ram-Warrior's eyes—looking a lot like 1980s ski-goggles. To cap it all, Bloodkill struck his axe blade with a Rare Flint to create his own Spark Imp, which quickly bested Amanyana's Fire Imp.

Becoming more frantic, the Sorceress created a Total Whiteout for ten seconds and tried to work her way around to Bloodkill's weaker left flank. But he wasn't fooled—through his Fight Visor, he was clearly still able to heat-detect her, something no mere Ram-Warrior should have been capable of. Why did he have so much magic? His race usually spent all their gold on weapons, armour and mead.

Suddenly Bloodkill was looming over her, raising his battleaxe for the deathstroke. Amanyana knew she only had two or three chances left to stop him. She tried a Forced Hilarity, which was a low-level enchantment but had no possible counter—and this halted Bloodkill for five precious seconds, as he laughed manically. The Teleport Spell was still recharging, so she backed further off as she beamed Hairy Hail towards the caprine face. This stuff clung to a character for up to three minutes, slowing their movements down by 15 to 20 per cent—not nearly as effective as the Total Chill would have been.

Bloodkill finished laughing, then threw his head back and roared to the Goat Gods. It took a confident player to spend time and keystrokes expressing during a duel. Amanyana knew she was almost certainly toast.

As Bloodkill closed the final few yards upon her, Amanyana in desperation turned herself into a mouse and ran between his legs. Small-Rodent-Becoming was a new spell—she'd only acquired it on level 24 —and she wasn't really sure how to get the best out of it. She also hadn't studied any of the counterspells. Could Bloodkill, perhaps, suddenly turn into a Vicious-Goat-Cat?

There was a dreadful pause. Then, with growing horror, Amanyana-mouse saw the great Ram-Warrior shoulder his axe, conjure up an ornate golden cage and bend down to entrap her.

In rodent form, Amanyana was unable to use any of her usual spells and enchantments. All that she had were four possibilities: Squeak, Jump, Bite, Pee. She waited until Bloodkill's hoof was around her midriff, and she was being lifted off the ground, then she jumped and bit in quick succession.

The next thing Amanyana knew, Bloodkill had fallen to the ground in agony as her tiny sharp teeth sunk into his sensitive pink nose. She bit and bit again, watching the Ram-Warrior's Strength and Soul melt away. When she tried peeing, it went in the Ram-Warrior's eyes, blinding him.

The moment she reverted to her customary female form, Amanyana tried the Total Chill again. This time it wasn't countered. Bloodkill lay at her feet, ice-caught.

She finished him off with her favourite spell, which could only be cast on an immobile opponent: Mummification.

Instantly, Bloodkill was enwrapped head to hoof in spirit-bandages which sucked from him what little Strength he had left.

A message came up: 'Amanyana has bested Bloodkill in a duel!'

May sat back from the computer and let out a quiet whoop.

'**good fight**,' said Bloodkill, as the bandages fell away. '**much respect.**'

Once upright, his character made a low bow to Amanyana.

'**choose something**,' Bloodkill said, and opened his Jewel Box to her. Many of the quests required of Ram-Warriors involved quarrying trips deep into the bowels of the earth, so these were rare stones indeed. A Sorceress might play for months without ever getting her hands on one.

'**r u sure?**' May typed.

'**u deserve it**,' Bloodkill replied, and laughed heartily.

A delighted May took her time, eventually choosing a diamond diadem which had the property of enhancing all Amanyana's freeze-spells by three per cent.

'**many thnx**,' May typed. '**u r supergenerous.**'

'I said, "I'm back,"' came a shout from downstairs. Henry was back.

'**must go**,' May typed. '**spouse-aggro. but brb**'

'**friend u?**' asked Bloodkill.

'**with pleasure, noble one**,' May typed, then logged off from The Waste Lands: Demented Zones of Torment—more commonly known as Waladezo or Wala3.

May went down to the kitchen to see if she still hated Henry. He was peanut-buttering some sliced white. Since the day she found out about his affair with the girl at the office, she hadn't cooked for him once. A Pot Noodle steamed on the countertop. Yes, she still hated Henry.

'And now you ask how my day was,' said Henry, after some time had passed. 'And I tell you.'

'"How was your day?"'

'Shit,' said Henry. 'Extremely shit.'

'I'm glad to hear it.'

'Everyone's being so hypocritical.'

'I suppose that means they're on my side.'

Henry scooped another lumpy gloop out of the jar. May felt a little sick—non-smooth peanut butter was wrong.

'They're just pretending they haven't done any of the things they've done.'

'Maybe some of them haven't,' said May. 'I hope *most* of them haven't,' said May.

She watched Henry spread the peanut butter; too thick, too much salt; not her problem, or was it? He was the father of her children, and a lying cunt.

'Look,' said Henry, 'are we trying at this or not?'

'Trying doesn't mean just letting you breeze through.'

'No,' said Henry. 'Clearly there's no danger of that.' The top slice went on the sandwich. 'How are the kids?'

'They're fine. Hope did a drawing for you. It's either me or a hippo. And Felix has an FT.'

FT meant the *Financial Times* meant the Pink One meant Felix had a very nappy-rashy bottom. May hated that she was still using the code they'd developed in Hope's early babyhood.

'Why?' asked Henry, not accusing.

'He did a nuclear-pooclear,' said May.

'What did he eat? Strawberries?'

'Nothing unusual.'

Henry swallowed, with difficulty. 'And how are you?'

May knew the FT was her fault. She had forgotten to change Felix's nappy before taking him and Hope out to the playground. While the children were having their afternoon nap, she had entered a particularly intense dungeon: The Caverns of Carnage. But, what with being repeatedly killed, and repeatedly having to resurrect, it became clear that she couldn't complete the quest solo. The monsters—Shriekbats and Chthonics—were too numerous and too powerful.

'I'm fine,' said May. She was thinking of Bloodkill, and whether he would agree to journey with her to the Caverns of Carnage.

'Have you thought any more?' asked Henry.

'I don't want to talk to you right now,' said May. 'I have too much to say.'

'Look—'

'I'm going to do some emailing.'

She was back in the game within five minutes. Bloodkill was there on her friends list. She spirit-messaged him, '**Hi.**'

'**yo**,' he replied. '**thort u gone.**'

So far, Amanyana had done most of her questing alone. May preferred it that way; in her current mood, she didn't want to interact with anyone, not even through the chatboxes that appeared above characters' heads. Amanyana was a solitary type, Sorceresses usually were. May had begun playing the game a couple of days after Henry suggested their marriage might not *necessarily* be over. (He had, she knew, spoken to—been spoken to by—Paddy, his parents, Agatha.) The germ had been an article in the *Observer* about virtual worlds, and how more and more women were escaping into them. At the bottom of the page was a list of URLs: World of Warcraft, Second Life, Anarchy Online; Waladezo hadn't been mentioned. May had come across her first hint of it while reading up on World of Warcraft, which was the game that initially attracted her. She enjoyed fantasy films—well, she had enjoyed *The Lord of the Rings*. The *Wikipedia* entry on WoW mentioned as an aside that Waladezo was a darker and more violent MMORPG—Massively Multiplayer Online

Role-Playing Game. This was what May wanted. Not Anarchy Online, which sounded naff. And not Second Life, because that didn't involve any killing. May wanted killing. Lots and lots of killing. She'd had quite enough of birthing, mothering, caring, loving. It had done nothing but make her unattractive and unloveable. It had reduced her to nothing.

May's first few visits to the Waladezo site were confusing. She created Amanyana almost at random. There were three main classes of characters, Quick, Undead and Ghost. May knew straight away she wanted to be Undead. Of the list of races, Sorceress sounded the most evil. The name Amanyana happened because May had been reading about Mahayana Buddhism, and wanted something similar-sounding. As for her appearance, May tried to make her character as vampy as possible. Amanyana's raven-black hair hung all the way down her sinuous spine; at the front, she had a crisp widow's peak. Her face was extremely angular, with high cheekbones denoting nobility and dark shadows about the eyes suggesting long nights conning the occult arts. Her breasts were fantastically proud, her waist impossibly slim, her legs ludicrously long. Amanyana was apparelled in a dark green cloak trimmed about the hood with rarest Zagmink fur. Beneath the cloak she wore a dress of black satin, tight about the bust and hips, loose about the wrists and ankles. As it moved, the inky fabric sparkled with blessings.

Amanyana enquired of Bloodkill whether he had ever ventured into the famed Caverns of Carnage.

'**not as me**,' Bloodkill said. '**but did it b4 as spiner**.'

'**want to go now?**' Amanyana said.

'**can stay 10 mins max**,' Bloodkill replied. '**shuldnt b on now**.'

'**lead on**,' said Amanyana.

Henry entered the attic room with sounds of breath.

'That doesn't look like email to me,' he said.

'What do you want?'

Henry said, 'I really think we should talk.'

May said, 'I really think we shouldn't.'

Amanyana ran out beneath the guard's tower and across the drawbridge of Anthill Castle.

'Is that a goat?' asked Henry.

'It's a Ram-Warrior,' said May, before she could stop herself.

'And that one's you?'

'That's me. Please go.'

'You look sexy,' said Henry, then corrected himself. 'You look sexy too, of course.'

May was wearing a white nursing bra and black panties beneath too-tight black jogging bottoms, a plain white T-shirt and a ragged scarf that had comforted her ever since GCSEs.

Fzz—Amanyana teleported twenty feet forwards, aiming to get to the Caverns as soon as possible.

Henry left.

Amanyana loped dolefully across the grey deserted plateau of the Specular Wastes. Bloodkill matched her pace quite easily.

An arrow on the map told May which direction the next quest was in, and that they were two minutes twenty seconds away. Keeping one finger on the forward arrow to keep Amanyana moving, May typed: '**what lvl is yr spiner now?**'

'**70.**'

'**wow! u spend much time questing?**'

'**i live 2 play**,' Bloodkill replied.

May very rarely thought about whom she might be encountering online. The monsters were all controlled by some central computer, but she didn't make much distinction between them and the characters controlled by real people.

'**so do i**,' typed May, then felt guilt about Hope and Felix. But it was probably true, right now. They were her duty not her choice. If she could have redesigned her life, from scratch, they wouldn't ever have existed. She had wanted a stable nuclear family, not to bring up two post-divorce children in a small flat on her own.

They arrived at the tall, lowering entrance to the Caverns.

'**let me tank**,' said Bloodkill. '**spell me if I need a heal.**'

Together they plunged into the ghoul-infested underworld. Bloodkill fought valiantly from the first. Amanyana had never encountered a combatant so quick, so alert. When a pair of Shriekbats flew down at her from the ceiling, and her Strength was reduced almost to nothing, the Ram-Warrior first of all dispatched them with two flicks of his battleaxe, then healed her with powerful herbs.

Further they advanced, deeper they plunged, closer and closer to the object of their quest—a small casket containing a human skull, stolen a hundred years previously from the Lord of Anthill Castle by the ancestors of these cave-dwelling ghouls. The Lord's great-great-grandson wanted the skull returned, so that it could be properly interred, and the Lord's tormented spirit laid to rest.

Amanyana felt exhilarated. She was progressing much faster and less cautiously than she would have done on her own. Three more Chthonics came round the corner. Bloodkill took out the first, but then stopped moving. He was no longer being controlled. Amanyana did her best against the remaining pair—exhausting her Soul; one of them died, but the effort left her unable to cast any more spells.

'Amanyana cries out for help,' said the words.

The Shriekbat struck once more, and Amanyana was instantly transported to the Bonefield Outside Anthill Castle.

With resignation, her disembodied spirit began to make its way back to the Caverns of Carnage.

'what happened?' she spirit-messaged.

'gotta go,' said Bloodkill. 'my mum cort me. soz.'

'Bloodkill has departed this world,' said the words.

Amanyana turned around. Even though she dearly wanted revenge against those blood-sucking Cthonics, there was no point going back into the Carverns without the Ram-Warrior to assist her.

As she crossed the Specular Wastes, she saw a rabbit lolloping in front of her. Although she would gain nothing by it, Amanyana shot off a powerful spell, and nuked the white-tailed little innocent.

'What do you want to talk about?' May asked Henry, when she got to the bedroom. Henry was under the duvet, naked.

She was already wondering whether Bloodaxe might sneakily log back on a little later.

'How can we make our marriage work again?' said Henry. 'I sincerely want it to work. What can I do?'

'Oh,' she said, the list ready, 'the washing. The washing-up. Buy shoes for Hope. Know what Hope's shoe size is. Get a plumber who actually turns up. Get the showerhead fixed. Change all Felix's nappies whenever you're here. Get up in the night when he wakes up. Tell your parents not to come next weekend. Take me away. Buy me lots of large diamonds. And be someone I can trust again.'

'Okay. I will try.'

Henry was too rabbit-like.

May asked, 'Have you seen her again?'

'Of course I've seen her—we work together—she's in my office.'

'Have you seen her outside work?'

'When would I have done that? I've been back here as soon as I could, to prove—'

'Lunch? I believe there is such a meal. I want to trust you.'

Henry seemed to slow.

'We did have lunch, once, last week. To finish it for definite.'

'And you didn't tell me.'

'I didn't want to upset you—you're upset enough.'

'Did you have a *nice* lunch?' May asked.

'What does that have to do with anything?'

'What did you have for lunch?'

'I can't remember.'

'Was it a restaurant, a cafe, sandwich on a park bench?'

Henry looked at her.

'You are genuinely slightly mad, you know.'

'Tell me!' shouted May, aware it might wake Felix.

'I think I had asparagus—you know, wrapped in that Italian meat. With balsamic vinegar. And then I had veal.'

'And what did she have?' asked May.

'I'm not sure.'

'It was a *nice* restaurant. You had a *nice* little lunch together, while I was up to my eyes in shit and puke and children. You can remember. What did *she* have?'

Quietly, Henry said, 'She had the same as me.'

'She had exactly the same.'

'We always had the same.'

May spoke. 'I'm good at things you don't even know about.'

Then she went into the children's room and looked from Hope to Felix. Felix lay on his back with hands alongside his face, as if surrendering. Hope was foetal, thumb in mouth.

Henry came and quietly stood beside May.

'We don't share this,' she said. 'We don't share anything. Leave this room before I scream.'

Without argument, Henry left.

May stayed almost an hour, then returned to the attic.

Bloodkill was back online, too.

'**How r u?**' Amanyana asked.

'**did my homework. can stay 10 mins maybe more. depends.**'

May looked at the on-screen clock. It was ten to ten. She knew that the Caverns of Carnage would take at least half an hour.

'**Not really enough time to go back,**' Amanyana said.

'**Well** . . . ' said Bloodkill. One of his hooves came up and scratched his chin. '**if we go fast** . . .'

Amanyana didn't hesitate—she was off towards the Caverns at a sprint. *This* time the Shriekbats wouldn't defeat her. The Skull of Anthill would be regained!

Bloodkill cantered along in her wake.

'**How old r u?**' May typed.

'dont wanna say,' Bloodkill replied. 'im not me here.'

'Me neither,' May typed. 'Sorry for asking. Homework sucks.'

'2 rite,' said Bloodkill. 'I hate it n muthafuckin exams even more.'

The two adventurers journeyed on towards the Caverns. May wondered whether she shouldn't make an excuse and go offline. But she knew that, if she did, she might not get another go at this dungeon for several days. If Bloodkill said it was all right for him to stay, then it must be. (She assumed he was a him.) Bloodkill's parents would stop him if they really didn't want him to play. Or Bloodkill's mum, if his dad wasn't around.

It took Amanyana and Bloodkill four impatient minutes to reach the Caverns.

'i tank again,' said Bloodkill. 'stay more back. say help early if u need it.'

Amanyana made a deep bow.

They entered the Cavern.

It took much longer than May expected. There were more monsters and their resistance levels were higher. At half past ten, during a lull in the action, she asked Bloodkill if he could still stay.

'yes. mums gone out. at last.'

'Really?'

'i got hours now. wanna do STD?'

STD, as May knew, stood for Scorch Tunnel Deep. It was a dungeon several levels above her own. If she completed STD, she would receive a Cloak of Deluded Vision—one of the most powerful items a sorceress could get hold of.

'I'm too squishy,' Amanyana said. 'Need more than us. One healer at least.'

'my mate mincer can asst. will call him now. start a group.'

May typed. 'Let's do this first, then see.'

'kk,' Bloodkill said. 'but u get lots x points.'

Five minutes later, the Ram-Warrior and the Sorceress were on the threshold of the inner chamber. Shriekbat Guardians came at them from all sides. Bloodkill swung his battleaxe, smiting two and three of the attackers with a single blow. Amanyana hung back, casting freeze spells to slow the ghouls down. Ever since she donned the diadem from Blood-kill's jewel box, she had noticed a real improvement in her casting power.

After five minutes of slaughter, the chamber was emptied and Amanyana was able to make her entrance. The casket containing Lord Anthill's skull was located beneath the Bat Boss' web-like throne.

'when u loot it he comes,' said Bloodkill. 'be ready.'

May checked Amanyana's enchantments, making sure she was as Strong and Soulful as she could be. Then she clicked to open the casket.

Hardly was the skull in her possession than the terrifying Shriekbat Emperor swooped down upon her. A single bite from his clawed mouth poisoned her badly. Bloodkill launched in to rescue her. Amanyana tele-ported away from the monster, then turned to fire off some spells at him. But it was no longer necessary. Mincer, a level-70 Bone Dwarf, had just entered the chamber—and with two blows of his might hammer, the boss was dead.

'yo bruv what took u?' Bloodkill asked.

'DAD WATCHING TV,' said Mincer. 'END OF FOOTIE.'

'she wants to do STD.'

'KK. HI.'

'Hi,' said May.

Once they'd gathered a group together, Scorch Tunnel Deep took them ten minutes to reach and an hour to complete. By the time Amanyana emerged—dressed in her new cloak of Deluded Vision—it was quarter past midnight. Bloodkill, Mincer, Voidmaker, Skarekrow and Mintyfreshbreath were planning to do at least one more dungeon. Before she logged off, May tried to suggest they go to bed.

'**jus drank a coke. cant sleep**,' said Bloodkill.

'CAN SLEEP AT SCHOOL,' said Mincer.

'**lol**,' replied Bloodkill, and threw his head back to laugh.

Voidmaker applauded, Skarekrow did a somersault and Mintyfresh-breath moonwalked in circles.

'MISS WARREN CAN SUCK MY COCK!!!' said Mincer.

'**if she can find it**,' said Bloodkill.

When May got into bed, she found that Henry was wearing pyjamas.

AGATHA & MAX

'Where's owls?' asked Max.

'I suppose they're in the trees,' said Agatha. 'They live in the trees.'

'Why we can't see them?'

'It's still a bit early in the evening for them to come out. They're probably still in the trees.'

'Are they in those trees?'

Agatha looked off to the left of the motorway, to where a wide rising field was bordered by a copse of horse chestnuts.

'Yes, there's probably an owl in those trees,' she said.

'Where?' asked Max.

'Well, we've gone past it now,' Agatha explained. 'So we can't see it any more.'

'But where is it?'

'Sweetie, it's behind us.'

'Will the owl chase us?'

'I don't think so,' said Agatha. 'Maxie, aren't you tired? It's past beddybyebye time.'

Max was quiet for a few moments, then, 'Do owls live in just big trees or little ones, too?'

Agatha inhaled and asked herself to be patient. On the radio the DJ was talking about Ibiza.

'Well, most owls are quite big and so they need big trees to live in, otherwise they wouldn't fit.'

'Are owls in *those* trees?'

'Those ones, no—I don't think so.'

'Spooky,' said Max.

The trees were indeed a little creepy, in full summer foliage, shadows on the near sides of their trunks.

'What animals live there?'

'Max, we already talked about this. Foxes—'

'And badgers.'

'Yes, well done. Badgers. And smaller creatures, probably, like rabbits and field mice and voles.'

'What a vole is?'

'It's like a mouse but slower and darker and, I think, fatter.'

'Mummy,' said Max, 'is Granny dead?'

'Yes,' Agatha replied, 'Granny is dead.'

'And is Granny buried in the sand?'

'In the *earth*, yes,' said Agatha, as direct as she had promised herself she would be.

'Does Granny still got her skin on?'

'Yes, she does.'

'Is sand on the beach?'

'Yes, beaches are made of sand. Most of them. The one we're going to on holiday this summer has lovely yellow sand and blue water and—'

'Did they dig the earth with a digger for Granny?'

'I don't know, Maxie. It was a while ago.'

'Did they dig the earth with a digger or a spade?'

Northbound, they went past the Hemel Hempstead turn-off—four lanes in both directions, smooth new tarmac. Agatha was doing eighty-five, but slowed down when she realized this.

'I think they used a spade.'

It was a country churchyard. Agatha couldn't picture a digger there, even a very small one. But she also found it hard to imagine a man digging out all that earth. It would take too long. They probably had used a digger.

'Maybe it was a digger,' she said.

'I have a spade,' said Max.

'You do. You have a blue spade and a red spade and you have your new superspecial gardening spade from Hope and Felix.'

'I can dig to Granny,' said Max.

'We don't have your spade with us,' Agatha said. 'We left it at home.'

'I want to dig,' said Max.

'Do you remember Granny?' Agatha asked.

'I can dig to her wooden box and open it.'

'No, that's not a good idea. Do you remember Granny?'

'Granny gave me a strawberry cake.'

'Yes, that's right.' Father's Day last year. The picnic on the beach. Her mother had visited a patisserie shop on the way through London. Agatha knew what Max would say next, and he did.

'It was *stinky*.'

'You didn't like it much, did you?'

'It tasted of worms,' said Max. 'Slimy worms.'

'I don't think you liked the cold custard.'

'Granny was trying to poison me.'

Agatha said, 'Where did that sentence come from?' She angled the rear-view mirror for a look at his eyelids. Max obviously wasn't going to sleep for another quarter of an hour, maybe longer. 'Is it in one of your pirate books?' Agatha thought it probably was, but she couldn't remember which. Poisoning wasn't in *Star Wars*.

'Poison is black and small,' said Max, definitively.

'Granny wasn't trying to poison you. That was vanilla. She was trying to give you a lovely treat.'

Agatha remembered that, in the aftermath of the *tarte aux fraises* meltdown, Max had to be carried to the pier and bought a large candyfloss.

'Granny is stinky,' said Max.

'Granny is not stinky,' said Agatha, then thought of her, buried, decomposing. 'Granny was not stinky.' She would much have preferred her mother be cremated, but the grave plot was all paid off, and the will said what it said. They would have to buy some flowers, somewhere, tomorrow morning. Perhaps the post office did chrysanthemums. She knew the service station five miles off had them, sometimes. Agatha hoped Penny had the wine open already, dinner cooked. Penny was a great cook, especially of meat.

'Granny has painted hands,' Max said.

'Yes,' said Agatha. 'That's right.' Max had always referred to her mother's nail polish as painted hands.

'Why Mummy doesn't have painted hands?'

'I don't have time for things like that, Maxie. I'm too busy with you. And they'd just get chipped. You'd smash them to pieces with your lightsaber.'

Agatha realized her mistake.

Immediately: 'Where my lightsaber is?'

'It's in the boot.'

'Can I have my lightsaber?'

Agatha explained, again, as she had at the long-ago beginning of the journey, that Max couldn't have his lightsaber because he might hit her in the eye while she was driving; at eighty miles an hour, she saw, and slowed down. 'And that would be really dangerous.'

'But can I have it, please?' Max asked.

'No,' said Agatha. 'You *can't*.'

'Why can't I have it?'

For a while, Agatha didn't respond to this question. Then, patiently, she gave the same answer again.

'I won't hit you, Mummy,' Max said. 'I *promise*.'

'Look, the lightsaber is in the boot. I can't get out and give it to you, we're driving.'

'It's boring—' said Max. 'This motorway is boring.'

'Well, why don't you just think about going to sleep, then?' She tried to stop her voice from sounding pleading, failed.

'I'm *not* tired,' said Max.

'Why in hell not?' muttered Agatha. 'Maxie, why don't you look out the window and—'

'What breaking it is?'

'What?'

'What breaking it?'

Agatha paused for a moment, then heard the lyrics of the song on the radio. Not breaking it but breaking up—breaking up, repeated over and over again, as the chorus.

'Breaking *up*,' said Agatha. 'Do you really want to know? It's when a boyfriend and a girlfriend decide not to be boyfriend and girlfriend any more.'

Max seemed to think about this.

'Do you like the song?' asked Agatha. She realized how close she'd come to being angry at him.

'Why do mummies and daddies have mummies and daddies?'

'Because,' said Agatha, 'that's how we get here. We're born because mummies have babies, and babies grow up to become more mummies.'

'And daddies,' said Max.

'Mummies and daddies, yes,' said Agatha.

'Daddies are more powerful,' said Max.

'That's not true,' said Agatha.

'Sperm,' said Max.

They had answered him very directly whenever he asked where he came from. They had described the sperm meeting the egg—and had eventually managed to find a couple of suitable clips on YouTube: one, a digital animation of the sperm's journey, and another showing cell division in a fertilized egg.

'Yes,' said Agatha, 'the daddy has the sperm and the mummy has the egg.'

'What breaking it is?'

'Breaking *up*,' said Agatha. 'It's breaking *up*. I told you. Up.'

'Up, up, up,' chanted Max. 'Up, up, up your nose. Up, up, up your bottom.'

'Stop it, please,' said Agatha.

'Up your bottom and up your nose and up your wee-hole!'

'Max, *no*,' she shouted.

'Snot up your wee-hole and bogey up your—'

'Max, shut up! I'm trying to drive. Just be quiet, please. I really can't concentrate like this.'

Agatha checked the rear-view mirror, saw the middle lane was clear, indicated and moved across, decelerating. Then she repeated the manouevre, crossing into the slow lane and reducing her speed to sixty-five miles an hour.

'I'm sorry, Max,' she said. 'But Mummy can't drive with you shouting like that. Mummy has a horrible headache. Now, why don't—'

'I kiss your head,' said Max. This was what he did when Mummy had one of her horrible headaches. Sometimes Agatha felt so 1950s. She remembered her mother, once, and only once, referring to The Curse. She remembered asking her mother what it meant, and her mother saying she would understand all in good time. Agatha did understand, much later, but not until she'd spent several years believing that her mother had somehow angered a witch. Perhaps she had. It would explain a lot.

'Thank you, darling,' said Agatha. 'Thank you.'

Max said, 'I kiss your bottom! I kiss your fanny!'

'Maxie.'

'I kiss my bottom!'

'Please, Maxie. Mummy is very tired. I'm just trying to get us there in one piece.'

'I kiss my snot bottom!'

'Max, if you don't stop this, I won't let you have your lightsaber when we get to Penny's.'

Immediately: 'I want my lightsaber.' Max was already crying. 'I want my lightsaber.'

'Stop crying, Maxie. I said, if you are a good boy, and not noisy, you can have your lightsaber. But if you shout at Mummy, you can't.'

Max let out an ululation that meant *I want, I want.*

Agatha hoped the crying would finally exhaust him, and he would sob himself to sleep. She hadn't deliberately made him cry—not as such. But she'd known that making the lightsaber threat would get to him. Denial of lightsaber privileges had been Max's main punishment for the past month. They hadn't used it that often, maybe once a week.

'I hate Mummy,' was the first thing Max said when his noise became more words than wail.

'Maxie,' said Agatha. 'I'm sorry. Calm down. You know you don't mean that.'

'I hate you,' said Max.

'If you say that, you'll make Mummy sad.'

'I want my lightsaber.'

'Max, it's *in* the *boot.*'

'I hate you.'

'You'll make Mummy sad. Maxie wouldn't like it if Mummy said I hate you to him, would you? What if Mummy said to you I hate you?'

Max went wild. He yanked at his straps. He kicked his legs against the passenger seat.

'Max, calm down. Calm *down.* Mummy loves you. I love you. But you make Mummy sad if you say bad things.'

Agatha hated how she was talking. She changed tone.

'Max, look, this would all be a lot easier if you just went to sleep.'

He was still raging, trying to climb out of the car seat.

'Don't pull your straps off. Don't pull them off!'

She reached back to grab one of them, and the car swerved onto the hard shoulder; Agatha tried to straighten it up, using only her right hand. But this took them too far across—half into the middle lane. Lights from behind got bright, quickly. She could hear brakes. Now, she had both hands on the wheel. They were fully into the middle lane. A moment of brighter lights. There was a very slight touch on the back of the car—

bumper kissing bumper. In the rear-view mirror she saw the aghast faces of a man and a woman. She pressed her foot down on the accelerator, but the car seemed to take a huge amount of time to respond. The car behind was too close, much too close, and it stayed that way for what seemed like a whole minute. We could all be dead. Then they were back to a normal distance, and were pressing their horn and flashing their headlights.

Max was safe in his seat. His mood was completely different. He knew something appalling had happened.

'Are you all right?' said Agatha.

'Fine, Mummy,' said Max, a good boy.

'Stay in your seat.'

'Yes, Mummy.'

She checked her mirror, indicated, moved across into the slow lane—slowed down, slowly.

The car which had almost hit them overtook. In the passenger seat, the woman—who had long, dark hair—was shouting at Agatha, pointing at her. Agatha kept her eyes on the car in front, but in her peripheral vision she saw the woman's angry movements. The car—an old SAAB—pulled ahead as Agatha continued to slow down. In the back window of the car, she saw a sign, 'Careful, Small Person Aboard.' Without thinking, Agatha accelerated. The SAAB was going about seventy five. Agatha gained on it, but the car in the lane in front of her was going too slowly. And Agatha *had* to find out. She waited until the SAAB had got ahead again, then pulled across behind it. She couldn't see anything in the back seat. Outside, it was dusk. The red of the brake lights silhouetted the head-rests and the heads of the man and woman. Agatha drove at a safe distance from them until she had passed the too-slow car in the slow lane. Then she indicated left and sped up once more. The next thing ahead was an articulated lorry, without a trailer, but it was already under the next bridge. Agatha had the accelerator to the floor. In ten seconds, she was alongside the SAAB. The long-haired woman was staring at her—less angry, more puzzled. Agatha kept turning her head to the right, trying to see into the back of the car. But it was too dark, the windows started too high. The woman looked beyond Agatha as the SAAB sped up. She turned to speak to the man—she'd obviously spotted Max. Then she turned back towards Agatha and, looking over her shoulder, twizzled her finger round her ear. You're mad, she mouthed. Agatha tried one last time to make out the form of a child in one of the SAAB's back seats.

'Well,' she said to Max, who was asleep.

'God,' said Agatha, as soon as she was sure May was far enough from the front door.

Paddy laughed. 'Now *that* was unexpected.'

They went back down the hall and into the kitchen, Agatha leading the way, still chuckling. Paddy finished loading the dishwasher and Agatha, once seated, finished the Rioja.

'The food really was delicious,' said Paddy.

'She must be so incredibly unhappy,' Agatha said. 'To fall for something like that. She's intelligent. It's the only . . .'

'Is it in her family?' Paddy asked.

'Not that I know of, no.'

'Some people it just gets, suddenly—The Spirit.'

'But surely she knows. She's getting divorced. Her life is in bits. A week, two weeks ago, she'd never have said all that. Wouldn't you be embarrassed?'

'They wait,' said Paddy. 'They wait until people are weak, and then they make their little suggestion.'

'She had the thing,' said Agatha, 'in the eyes. It was a bit scary. And saying that she was *happy* for what had happened—because of what it had done for her. Terrible things—'

'And the children,' said Paddy, pushing the button to run the cycle. 'They're got, too.'

'At least she says it's stopped her playing that computer game. She was completely addicted. Hours a day.'

'Is it better? Isn't this just another—'

'Prop. Yes,' Agatha said, rising.

They went through into the front room and lay down one on each of their sofas.

'He'll be . . .' said Agatha.

'Oh, he'll piss himself,' said Paddy. 'He will absolutely, I mean—*Jesus*. No mere human replacement for Henry, but Christ our Lord.'

'It might help her, now, and then she can ditch it later, when she's stronger.'

'But they'll keep her weak. That's what they do, that kind of church. Once you're in, you're in.'

'If I said anything she wouldn't listen.'

'No, she's beyond that.'

For a while they didn't speak.

'He was so stupid,' said Agatha. 'It's such a predictable thing—and she-the-girl clearly wasn't even interested in him, just flattered, or curious.'

'I don't think May is the easiest person to live with.'

'They lived together before they got married.'

'But, children. She changed.'

'Yes, she *is* more boring,' said Agatha. 'But Henry's more boring, too.'

'And sex,' Paddy said. 'No sex.'

'Do we want any more wine?' asked Agatha.

'I think so,' said Paddy. He had thought, for one moment, she was asking do we want any more children? His voice had gone somewhat overemotional.

'Sorry,' Agatha said. 'Can you—?'

Paddy went back into the kitchen, which was still fuggy from cooking and talk. There was a greater density of Jesus around their kitchen table than anywhere else in the house. From the wine rack, Paddy pulled a bottle of red—then rejected it because it had a screwtop. This was Saturday night; he was slightly drunk; he wanted a cork and a proper pop; this was a secret celebration. He and Agatha hadn't got on so well for years. The collapse of Henry and May's marriage had, by contrast, by becoming a subject, been the remaking of theirs. In such a mood, Paddy thought it would be stupid to tell Agatha about Kavita—about his near-thing fling. But thinking of continuing not-to-confess immediately made him awkward. And when he returned to Agatha, and refilled her glass, he felt extremely middle-aged. The two of them were more boring, too.

Agatha said, 'I don't think May ever really liked sex. Maybe God is much better for her. Is there anything you want to watch on television?'

'No.'

'You wouldn't have an affair, would you?'

Paddy needed to answer as quickly as possible, and with a convincing amount of honesty.

'If I fell in love. If I couldn't help myself. How do I know?'

'You're meant to say *no* just like you said about the TV. You're meant to be certain.'

'You know I'm never certain about anything.'

'But you wouldn't do what Henry did.'

'Do you want to talk about this?' Paddy asked. He couldn't any longer pretend to be comfortable lying down, so he pivoted and sat forwards, elbows on knees. 'Really?'

The wine was now for another purpose.

'I want to know that you're different from Henry.'

'Yes, I'm different. But who knows if I'm better. I have lusts.'

Lusts, though, made no impact; Agatha seemed almost capable of going to sleep. 'Why don't open relationships ever work?' she asked, suddenly clear.

'For some people they must. Gays.' Paddy wished he'd said this more tentatively.

'Not for people like us.'

'And May and Henry are people like us?' asked Paddy.

'Oh yes. We're very different but they're still more like us than anyone else is.'

'What a depressing thought.'

'I didn't think any of our friends would get divorced,' said Agatha. 'I suppose you don't, not when you're going to their weddings all the time, like we were.'

'That was exactly what I *did* think about, right through every single service. How much is this costing? How much per future year? Anyway, do you feel like taking the wine to bed?'

'Not yet.'

Without saying anything, Agatha went to check on Max.

'Fine,' she said, when she came back. Then, after a few moments, she said, 'Are you going to tell Henry—about Jesus?'

'He'll find out pretty soon. I can't see her keeping quiet about it.'

'No.'

The doorbell rang, and they knew it was probably May, back again. Because it might be a crisis—she might have been mugged—they both went to the door. May was in tears, possibly divinely inspired.

'Come in,' said Agatha and Paddy. May, they saw and heard, was hyperventilating, gasping.

'Pan,' said May, once in the hall. 'Tack.'

Paddy went to find a paper bag but they only had plastic. He brought an Ocado one into the living room, where Agatha sat with her arm around May—who was breathing into a softly crumpling brown-paper bag.

Paddy looked at her and said, 'Take your time.' Then he perched on the arm of the other sofa.

'I left—' said May.

'You haven't been attacked, have you?' Paddy asked.

May glanced up with shiny-surfaced eyes, shook her head.

'Just get your breath back first,' said Agatha. 'Paddy, could you fetch May a glass of water?'

While he was in the kitchen, Paddy heard May start to cry. He decided to wait until he was called for. After a couple of minutes, May quietened—but he could hear the two of them talking. Then Agatha came through.

'Henry's wedding ring is in our toilet,' she said. 'Can you go and get it out?'

'Down the toilet?' Paddy asked.

'She tried to flush it away.'

'Fine,' said Paddy, and got some rubber-gloves out from the cupboard beneath the sink.

The wedding ring was dead-centre in the bottom of the bowl, four or five inches of clear water above it. Paddy remembered Veronika's floater, and her embarrassment. He hadn't paid the toilet much attention since then. It was going brown with stained limescale. With the rubber-gloves on, he reached for the ring—but it kept slipping away from his fingertips. Next, he tried putting his index finger into the circle and working it up the side of the bowl. This got it out of the water, but when he tried to drop it into his other hand it bounced away. Two goes later, and with his wrists now wet, Paddy decided he needed a tool.

'Are you okay?' Agatha asked, up the stairs.

'It's a bit tricky,' he said.

From the wardrobe in the bedroom, he brought a wire clothes-hanger—and, once he'd unwound the hook and part-straightened it out, the ring was caught easily enough.

He took off the rubber-gloves and washed his hands with soap, up to the elbows. Then, with a second lot of soap, he washed the ring, though it looked perfectly clean. He dried it on the handtowel hanging from the bathroom door. This wasn't like May, this behaviour—but May downstairs wasn't usual-May. Out of simple curiosity, Paddy tried the ring—pushing it onto his right-hand ring finger. It fitted, tightly. Paddy held his hands up, side by side; the rings—plain gold bands—were almost identical; Paddy's was perhaps a touch thinner. What if he were to give May back the wrong one? Would she notice?

'Is something wrong?' called Agatha.

'I'm just cleaning it up.'

'Oh, for God's sake,' said Agatha. 'That doesn't matter. Bring it now.'

But the ring wouldn't come off; not without soap and water and tugging.

'Just a minute,' shouted Paddy.

He locked the bathroom door, then quickly lathered up his right hand.

Agatha's footsteps were on the stairs.

'Come on, she's very upset.'

With a sharp yank the ring came off—Paddy feeling his knuckle as gristle.

'Open the door,' said Agatha. 'What are you doing?'

He washed the soap suds away, once more dried the gold, unlocked the door.

Agatha held out her hand. Paddy placed the ring in her palm. Agatha, suspicious, noticed the redness of Paddy's knuckle.

'You didn't?' she asked.

'I did.'

'Always comparing cock size, aren't you? Just can't help it.'

'I was not.'

Agatha made going downstairs her answer.

'Here,' Paddy heard her say to May.

'Thank you,' said May, sounding calm. 'I'll go now.'

Coming into the living room, Paddy bumped May back a step.

'Sorry,' he said.

'Thank you for getting it,' she said.

'Why here?' he asked.

'Shut up,' Agatha said to him.

'I'll see you soon,' said May. She was hunched over with the ring in her fist.

'Stay a bit longer,' said Agatha.

'No. I want to be home,' May replied.

'I'll drive you,' said Paddy. 'I'm still under the limit.'

'You're not,' said Agatha.

'I can walk,' said May.

'I can drive you,' said Agatha.

May looked from one to the other of them.

'If Paddy will take me,' she said.

All of them, even May, seemed surprised at this.

His keys were hanging from a hook beside the front door.

'Okay,' said Agatha. 'If that's what you want.'

They were in the hall.

'I'll call you tomorrow,' said Agatha.

'Bye,' said May, who was hurrying.

The car was out the door, left and about twenty yards off. Paddy waited until they were very close before unlocking it—to do otherwise would have seemed tasteless. May got in the passenger side very quickly, as if it were raining hard.

When he'd put his seatbelt on, Paddy said, 'I won't speak if you don't want me to.'

'You think I'm stupid, don't you? You've always thought I was stupid, both of you.'

'What's this about?'

'I believe in something now, and you're so patronizing. I bet you couldn't wait till I'd gone, so you could talk about me. And when you go back, you'll talk about me all over again, in your kitchen, only this time I'll be the loonie who tried—' She stopped talking and started crying. She plucked the brown-paper bag from her handbag.

'Shall I drive or do you want to walk?' Paddy asked.

May pointed to the steering wheel and then to the road. He waited, and May repeated the gestures, more forcefully. Paddy started the car.

As they reached the end of the quiet road where Paddy and Agatha lived, May began wiping her cheeks with her fists.

'I don't know why I did it at your house,' said May. 'It was a stupid thing to do, but I'm not stupid, not like you think. And God isn't stupid.'

'Did we say or even hint that God was stupid?'

'No, you were both very restrained. I could tell you weren't being honest.'

'You know neither of us believes in anything like that.'

'But you disbelieve more than Aggie.'

Paddy was driving more slowly than usual.

'You're probably right.'

'And you did talk about me after I'd left?'

'You made quite a big announcement. We weren't going to not talk about it.'

The orange of the street lights made the semi-detached houses look warm and sinister. Young people were waiting at bus stops. It was all very September.

May asked, 'Did you laugh?'

'We were surprised.'

Paddy heard May breathe in and then waited for her to breathe out. He began to count.

'You're so smug, in your marriage. What if I called Aggie when I got out of the car? What if I called, before you could call, and told her you grabbed me or tried to rape me? How would that be?'

'She wouldn't believe you.' Paddy was sure of this, so kept calm.

'She might,' she said.

'Is that the kind of thing Jesus wants you do to?'

'Of course not,' said May. 'Don't talk like that.'

'May, you're very upset. We don't have to talk at all.'

There was no gap in front of her house. Paddy drove on a bit further, until he came to a disabled parking bay.

'If Aggie wouldn't believe me, then you could rape me and get away with it.'

'If I'd really done it, she'd be able to tell. From your voice. This is ridiculous.'

Paddy finished reversing into the space, then turned the engine off. But before he could speak, another car had driven up, and the driver— a black woman—was making angry gestures towards Paddy's windscreen. He didn't have a disabled parking permit. She did.

'All right, all right,' he said, and started the car.

'*She* would believe me,' said May. 'Mrs Steiner. I know her. If I told her you'd attacked me. I know her a bit. She hates men. And the baby-sitter would believe me.'

'Perhaps they would, and then you'd have to deal with the consequences.'

'Don't talk about me when you get home. Don't say any of this to Agatha.'

'We are your friends,' said Paddy.

'I know it sounds silly but Jesus loves me,' said May. 'Thank you for the lift.' She pushed open the passenger door and pulled herself out of the car.

Paddy watched her in the rear-view mirror, until she reached her front door. But she didn't go inside—she turned round and came back.

'Oh God,' muttered Paddy, and pressed the button to wind down the window.

'Hold out your hand,' said May. Then, when Paddy did, she pressed the wedding ring down into his palm.

Without saying anything, she turned back towards her house.

'Is this for Henry?' Paddy shouted. 'Do you want me to give it to Henry?'

May did not answer.

When Paddy arrived home, Agatha said, 'May called. She told me you asked her for the ring. If she didn't want it.'

'That's not true.'

'She said you had it, and that she wants it back. Do you have it?'

'She *gave* it to me. She's lying. In the car, she said she was going to phone you and tell you that I'd tried to rape her. She's not stable. I told her you wouldn't believe me, so she's done this instead.'

'Show me it,' said Agatha.

Paddy had the ring in his wallet, among the change. 'Why would I want Henry's ring?' he asked.

'Why did you try it on?'

'I don't know,' said Paddy. 'But I did *not* ask May for this ring. Do you believe me or not?'

The phone began to ring.

They went into the kitchen and Agatha picked up.

Paddy would hear tinny wailing.

After another minute, Agatha understood.

'She wants it back,' Agatha cupped the receiver as she spoke. 'She said she gave it to you. She wants me to bring it back. She says sorry and asks you to forgive her.'

Paddy said he did, then went to pour himself a glass of water.

'I will,' said Agatha, into the phone. 'I will.'

'You see,' said Paddy, when the call was over.

'Where are the keys?'

'By the door,' said Paddy. 'Do you want me to go?'

'She wants me,' Agatha replied.

Agatha returned home about an hour later.

'How was she?' Paddy asked.

'Fine. She doesn't want us to talk about her.'

'But this—'

'I promised her. We're not going to talk about her. At all.'

Then Paddy laughed. And Agatha laughed. Then Agatha stopped. Then Paddy stopped, then started again.

HENRY & ANYONE

(Anyone who'll listen.)

Henry told his laser printer:
    Don't fuck with me.
        Don't you *ever dare* fuck with me.
  Because
          —do you hear me?—
                    I will fuck you up.
    I will fucking fuck you up so bad—

Henry told himself:
    Nothing in the flat is on fire.

Henry told the postbox:
    Good luck, my letters.

Henry told the taxi driver:
    Yeah, two.
                    A girl and then a boy.
  Hope, she's three, and Felix who's one and a half.
    But I don't see them much right now—
        we're getting divorced.
                 Not me and them.
        My wife is divorcing me.
  She has the car.

It's my fault.
    I'm the one to blame, if you're looking to lay the blame . . .

I'll bet you're curious,
     well, you see,
         it's terrible, really,
I had a passionate affair with this beautiful young twenty-four-year-old,
  from the office
      where I work. (I'm a journalist.)
I just couldn't resist her, you know?
        She was so *fresh* and had such

  great
  skin.

  It's one of the nationals.

  Her hair was great, too, and those chances
don't come along all that often—

  Yes.

—and she went for me in a big way—
   sending me these subtle signals.
    (She thought the signals were subtle.)

  I cover the environment, mostly.
      But my wife—
         y'know how
 it is,
 some women, after kids.

        Well,
   my wife's like them, only *worse*.
   Absolutely not.
   No fucking way.
   Not up the back,
   not up the front.

I'm not even sure how Felix was

conceived.

He may in fact *be* Jesus

because the conception

must've

been

immaculate.

You're not Christian?

Bloody Christians.

My wife-soon-to-be-ex-wife has gone all

Born Again.

Do I regret it?

Of *course* I regret it.

But would I do it again?

Would I do it again

if I could have May back

on the condition

I never did it again,

ever?

Yes.

I would do it again.

Yes.

I do still love her.

Philippa.

And my wife.

I really did mess up.

I love my kids.

Henry told the young woman sitting opposite him on the train:
    Nice shoes.

Henry told the policewoman:
    I don't know this area.

Henry told the barmaid:
    Guinness, please. Pint, please.

        No, actually—
                have you started pouring it?
                                —bit heavy—
I'll have a London Pride.
                Thanks.
                Sorry.
                Thanks . . .

      Wait, I think I've got the right, um . . .

      What's it like in here?

           Bet you get really fed up of men trying to chat
you up?

      Where d'you come from?

      Originally?

Henry told the man behind the counter in the off-licence:
    I dunno, I think we've had a pretty good summer.

Henry told the voice:
    I found your card in a phone box near King's Cross.
    I want what you do.

147

What do you do?
(Is it *you*?)
I want to know what you do.

Right.
This is actually the first time I've done this.
Can you explain what happens?
Where do I go?

Not my hotel.

Okay. I'd like two.
Young ones.

No, not—just young! Just young.

Yes, she sounds fine.

Mmm, not sure.
Are there any others?

Okay, then, I'll have her, too, then.
How much is this going to cost?

I don't understand.

No, I don't want that.

Yes . . .

How about two hours?

Are they, you know, clean?
They always use condoms, don't they?

I won't require any kissing.

Henry told the call girls:
No, I'm sorry, this isn't working—
this isn't going to work.
I don't feel—

the room is too cold—this isn't . . .

I thought it might—

I'm just too embarassed.

No, I can't relax.
Thank you.
Thanks for trying.

I keep thinking of the diseases.
No offence.
I keep thinking of all the dirty cocks—
I mean, I've got this friend,
right,
has been faithful to the same woman
—*totally* faithful—
not like me
—ever since they got married, and—
and Agatha suddenly turns round
two days ago
and tells him he needs to get a
test for,

you know,

HIV—

she says it's because she slept with

(isn't that stupid?

Do you ever actually *sleep* with

men?)

—she fucked another man—

but only once,

is what she says.

And he, the man, phoned her up and said.

So they've had sex so Paddy has to get a test, too.

And they've got

kids.

He's just *destroyed.*

And why am I here?

I expect you have them all the time,

tests.

I fucking well hope you do, for our sakes—the punters.

That's what you call us, isn't it?

Tricks.

You must hate us so much.

Men.

Agatha,

God, I hope she's okay

—she's a lovely woman—

but this completely surprised me—

not that she isn't *sexual,*

but she's been so bloody fucking depressed since she had the
dead baby.

But the bastard thing is,

listen,

even if this first test is okay

they have to wait another *three fucking*

months

and take *another* test
before they can be
well, almost
a hundred per cent sure
they're okay.
And even then they're not out of the worry-woods
because,
in rare cases,
people don't get it until a year after.

You probably don't want to hear this, do you?
You'd prefer it if you could just fuck me
fuck off
and start
fucking
some other
fucker.

Would you like some of this?

Can you get drugs?

Maybe not.

Tell me, how does it compare?
Be honest?
Is it average-size?
Take a good look.

Or larger? I've always thought it was about average . . .

Go on. Be honest . . .

Oh.

Really?

Fantastic!

And do you think that, too?
(Wow.)
You're not lying, are you?

Henry told the concierge:
The *Guardian*, please.
And the *Sun*.

Henry told Freddie (on the phone):
It just wasn't happening.
Couldn't fucking get it up at all.
What a joke.
Then they told me I had the biggest penis they'd ever
seen.
Not really.
Just in the top fifty per cent.

Henry told the minibar:
You and me, we're gonna have a parteeee!!!

Henry told the television:
No.
No.
Never.
Go *away*.
And you can shut up, too.

Why?

Henry told himself:
    Oh, fuck.
    Oh, fucking Christ.
        What have I done?

Henry told Paddy (on the phone):
    I read one of those magazine articles—
        since I moved out, I've been buying men's
magazines.
    Not porn.
        Esquire. GQ.
    I get my porn on the Internet, like everyone.
        And one of them,
            GQ, I think,
        had this article on fifty things to do before you die.
        That's fifty things a *man* should have done before he
dies.

    Do you know how many of them I'd actually done?

        Guess . . . .

Four,
        and I'm almost forty—
so, some of the others left are just about physically impossible
any more.
And I'm not going to go skydiving.
    So I decided that I wanted to've done ten of the things
                before my birthday.
    That way I'd be a fifth of the man I should be—
        which,
            given the way I've been going,

I thought was pretty good going.
A fifth's about as much as anyone can hope for
of being
a man.
Two of them were easy,
fucking expensive but easy.
I have now drunk a bottle of Cristal in a jacuzzi,
and
—last Saturday—
I had tea at the Ritz.
It was on my own in the jacuzzi, by the way.
Six down, four to go.
But the next one was a bit more
difficult.
It was
Have a threesome.
Now, I know what you're thinking—
why didn't I pick something a bit easier?
Because the ones I picked *were* ones I actually *wanted* to do,
that's why.
Two women had always been a fantasy.

I knew I wasn't going to do it by picking anyone up—
not the way I look.
Most of them hate me on sight.
So
wait for it

I decided to use prostitutes.
It was just like with the Cristal—
it would cost money, but I'd get it done . . .

I know . . .

                                           Calm
down.

         Of course, condoms—

     Yes, I *know*.
         But May's *never* going to get back with me, is she?
So what does it matter if she hears?
                  You can tell her, if you want.
That'll help the divorce go swimmingly.

     She wouldn't tell *them*. They're so little.
                         Later, maybe.
By then, they'll have realized what a nutter she is.

     Do you want to hear or not?

     Oh, don't be so puritanical.

   Okay. I'll spare you.
               Suffice to say, it didn't happen.
I think I can claim to've had a threesome, according to *GQ*—
    I was *in the same bed* as them, and some stuff went on.
      But it just wasn't happening.
        I'm no porn actor,
                  I've learnt that.
                     I haven't got it.
                   Well, I've got a bit.
   They weren't *dirty*.
   Their English wasn't up to much.
     I think they were Chinese, not Japanese.
      I've never been with someone so disengaged—
      I don't mean sex.

I mean not even prepared to be in the same room as you.
I knew I could tell them anything and it wouldn't make a
difference,
    they wouldn't remember it, or understand it,
                  so I just talked at them.
    Told them everything.
      Then I got them to feel each other up a bit more,
           just to see if that would change things around,
then I got dressed and left.
                      What do you think of me
now?

    I like that.

    'Stop reading magazines.'
                  You're a good one, Paddy.

Henry told his old answerphone in his old hall in his old house:
    I wish you'd pick up.

    I don't want an argument. I just want to talk.

    You can even tell me about Jesus, if you want.

Henry told Paddy:
    I don't think I've ever told you how it happened,
                  with Philippa?
    Have I ever told you how it actually happened?
                       Sorry.
    It was interesting.
We were at a press conference in Birmingham
          —I know,
          Birmingham—
something to do with some eco-car—

and I was showing her the ropes,
    and I introduced her to someone,

                              a man.

He's married.
That's important.
    I just said, blah,

                Philippa this is Michael,
                Michael, Philippa
                    sort of thing.
                          Didn't think much of it.

    He obviously fancied her.
    Eyes all over her fucking tits.
    Then, about five minutes later, he texts me and asks if she's single.
I said Michael's married, didn't I?
        And I remember thinking,
                standing there
                reading the text,
    fucking NEC centre,

                    No, you won't have her.
                    No, you can't fucking have her.
                    She's mine.
And because of that, I had to make her mine.
And I did,
        that evening,
                in her room at the hotel,
after I lied about our train and bought her loads of drinks.
    She told me later she knew I'd lied about the train,
        and that I didn't need to've bought her the drinks.
                              But

then,
        later still,
    she told me
unless she'd been so pissed she'd never've slept with me in the first
place.
        So,

I don't know what to believe.
Probably the being-pissed version.

People are meant to tell the truth
when they're breaking up with you,

aren't they?
I've certainly given May a fuckload of truth
this past couple of months.
More than Jesus fucking has,
I tell you.

Henry told the view from the tenth floor:
Oh,
fuck ajff.

Henry told Paddy:
I hate hotels.

Henry told the photograph of Hope and Felix:
But your father
is not a *bad man.*

And Henry asked Paddy:
I did ask if *you* were all right, didn't I?

And Henry told the television:
You've always been a great actor,
no, a great *screen presence.*
No one appreciates that.
It's a really hard thing to do.
They carp—call you wooden.
The carpers.
But cheers.

Cheers to you.
I love your work
and I love you
and I salute you.

VERONIKA & ROGER-ROGER

When she meets new people, Jennifer will always wonder if they have seen it, if they have seen her.

Jennifer spends the whole day in thongs, a short jean skirt and one of about ten short-sleeve T-shirts.

Going up the staircase, she isn't afraid. It isn't seedy.

The surfers in the bar talk in a way she can't understand about things she knows aren't important—and this is just perfect.

The apartment where Jennifer is staying has a cat called Roger-Roger.

All the young women look so beautiful, lit from the left-hand side.

At the end of her last shift, as at the end of every shift before, Jennifer puts the chairs upside down on the table, sweeps the walked-in sand off the lino, pours it all into the IGA Rite-Way plastic bag and hides this behind the garbage bins.

The ones she likes best show the thing from an up-high angle, sort of a ceiling-fan point of view—down onto the bed, so you can see all the way from pillow to below-feet.

Veronika doesn't want to be Veronika, so she becomes Jennifer when she starts applying for jobs, and, as soon as she gets one, she becomes Jenny, Jen and Jens.

Everything in Australia looks as if it's half made of sand. The people, too.

Roger-Roger has been in the flat for at least a dozen generations of tenant, and the reason for his name has long been lost.

When she has finished all her other jobs, but before she goes out for a proper celebration drink with the other waitresses, Jennifer carries the plastic bag across Campbell and down to the beach.

Veronika has never been in the sea, although she knows seagulls from Prague, where they sit on the Karlovy Most.

'Maybe you should think about it a bit longer,' says Grass.

On the glass of the bathroom window, Jennifer sees some kind of bug making its way upwards.

The landlady had always insisted—if you took on the flat, you took on Roger-Roger, too.

To start with, she does lots of babysitting.

A view of a beach where people ride boards on grey water.

From the ceiling-fan angle, slimness doesn't seem to matter any more.

On the plane out of Bangkok, Veronika decides about crying that it's simple—if she doesn't want to, she doesn't have to.

Behind and above the bug is the daylight moon.

Jennifer still doesn't know why she came to Australia—unless it was simply because it was the farthest away from her mother she could get.

'Hey, Jens, we all clubbed together and got you a present.'

Roger-Roger is a black-and-white cat of middle-age with ears that show his streetfighting skills are worsening.

The young woman's breasts look very circular—that's Jennifer's first thought.

From the start, Veronika likes Australia; Veronika isn't sure about Australians, however—white Australians.

What bothers Jennifer isn't the idea of the beach disappearing—she knows that it never will.

With a slight shift backwards and to the side, Jennifer makes it look as if a giant bug is climbing across the lunar surface. This pleases her.

'We're all gonna miss you, Jens.'

In order to look younger for her job interview, Jennifer wears the best bra she can afford—one thing, at least, her mother has taught her.

And Jennifer answers: 'I love it.'

If the surfers flirt with her, it is without seriousness or hope; and so, once or twice, when she goes back to their rooms with them, they are genuinely delighted.

Jennifer still hasn't told her sister Alice where she is. Instead, she's emailed, once, from a Gmail account she set up several years before in England. And she made sure the hour she clicked send gave no clue to her time zone.

Jennifer decides she likes white Australians, they have just the right kind of reserve.

Roger-Roger, sitting beside the spider plants on the verandah, doing nothing but watching the flicking of his tail.

'My God!' she says, looking at the first.

What bothers Jennifer is the idea of just pouring the walked-in sand into the alley bins.

Jennifer much prefers being Jennifer to being Veronika.

Some of the young women, lit from the left-hand side, wear watches which they haven't taken off.

After the moon-bug lunchbreak, Jennifer goes back to the cafe full of a new happiness.

The aboriginals, Veronika has a sentimental sympathy with; they are so bad at drinking, so bad at being modern.

You can see the marks the young women's jeans have left around their sometimes doughy waists.

Jennifer decides she likes white Australians, they have just the right kind of warmth.

If she feels happy, Jennifer is still just about capable of feeling young.

No one has to be there, once the person has shown her how to set up the still camera.

'Take a look at this,' Grass says. It is very simple. He surfs. He is very young. He has a laptop. He will be genuinely delighted.

If she has children, they might one day see it. She wonders about this.

Most of all, she thinks, as she drinks more water, she will miss Roger-Roger.

When she watches it again, she feels she looks more beautiful than she knows she is.

Something is happening in this moment, eyes closed.

'My name is Pete, but everyone calls me Grass.' He is very young.

Going down the stairs, Jennifer feels proud and brave—even though she knows the guys at the bar will find it and watch, and other people will hear, and it will exist for ever.

Almost every night, she does babysitting for one young couple or another.

'Hey,' he says, the afternoon of the moon-bug break. 'Hello, you.'

By an extreme act of will, Veronika allows herself to drift.

They all seem so pleased that she can't help feeling pleased for them, the young women. As they have their orgasms, she wishes them well in their future lives.

'Come over here,' says moon-bug-afternoon surfer, when they go back to his room. 'Look at this.'

The ceiling-fan shot makes the young women look flattened out, in a good way.

'Because my ass is grass.'

As soon as she sees one, she wants to be in one.

You can feel the way her skin feels against the cotton sheets.

She doesn't even think about whether it will have any consequences. All she thinks about is what she will look like—how they will make her look, lit from the left-hand side.

This is average pleasure, made to seem extraordinary.

The room around her is darker than a room would normally be.

The woman is young, her skin is good. She wears little bracelets, beads. She has no make-up on.

'Show me another,' she tells Grass.

She knows she only needs to do it once, and to know she had done it, after that she can continue—until then she knows she will remain paralysed by the thing that has always paralysed her.

As she orgasms, Jennifer says the word *no*, and knows she will feel very sad once she stops feeling happier than ever in her life before.

$200, but that's not why.

Eyes closed, she is sharing something. It has been so long since—has she ever?—has a celebration ever been a celebration? She can hear the shutter go *ssk* when she presses the plunger at the end of the cable.

The other waitresses buy her drinks and drink her health and say *aloha* and *see you in the next life* as she walks away, waving.

'Can you help me be like her?' she asks Grass, straight away. 'I want to do it.'

The first young woman's body looks like Jennifer feels her own body would look.

The sand is more grey than yellow.

And another is what he shows her, and they look like they are interesting women, ones who do other interesting things, not just this. They look like women who Jennifer might be friends with, or who might come into the bar any day after surfing.

While she is young she will do young things.

A person comes with a still camera and a tripod—a young woman—a friendly young woman—not creepy.

Climbs the stairs to a place which is not seedy, where the sheets smell of being-washed, and she does it and while she is doing it she enjoys doing it.

Conversation in the bar afterwards: 'I admire you, you know, I really do.'

They will make her look more beautiful than she is. It will be in their interest. The still shots need to be done first. They arrange a time for a person to come.

Veronika knows she is too thin.

The young women wear watches that, in the street, they'd use to tell the time. They aren't props.

Conversation afterwards: 'You must feel so *empowered*, Jens.'

Veronika wants to be thinner.

This, she hopes, climbing the stairs, will be something different in her life.

'And another,' she tells Grass.

Jennifer wants to assure the beach, and through it the sea, that she is on their side.

Jennifer decides to cry. She goes into the kitchen, fills a glass with tap water, drinks it, then refills it.

Conversation afterwards: 'Slut.'

Grass asks: 'What do you think? D'you like it?'

Alice, her sister, hasn't replied.

Looking at her present, she still doesn't cry.

Jennifer can swim.

Their truthful waists, the young women.

Down on the beach, Jennifer tips the sand out of the plastic bag and onto the sand, along with the paper ends of sugar packets and clear plastic straw wraps.

The light falls gently on her right-hand side.

ALICE & RIK

Hello is test for see twitter message working. Hello twitter people!
5:11 PM Nov 25th from web

Because I am get married it will to be the happiest day in my life, I want share it with everyone. Hello world be happy for me!!
4:00 PM Nov 26th from web

Rik is biotechnology expert on grow plants for get high. I am erotic interpretative dancer. We are live in Praha not together yet. Soon.
4:12 PM Nov 26th from web

I have thrush yeast down there what it smell like is bread bake in piss oven, I must to get cure before soon, is not nice.
4:22 PM Nov 26th from web

Paris Hilton is have trouble but strong woman so she make trouble make more strong, also she has beauty, so beautiful hair is, my hero
4:30 PM Nov 26th from web

Rik is most sex man in world for me. He is big strng and also gentle as a perfect combo like Big mac and fries and also Choclat milkshake.
4:48 PM Nov 26th from web

Also I need more space say Rik like me tie him up! In bath! You know!! I only tell best friend Lenka this. I tell you soon story how we met

4:49 PM Nov 26th from web

BigJersey RT @can_u_feel_it #getmarried no need for the strip clubs! Give it to her and . . . recycle you money! lol

4:52 PM Nov 26th from web

I not happy this morning. This day was big drag after last nite when there were most English in the club ever. I am all over with bruises.

8:21 AM Nov 27th from ÜberTwitter

When I go sad i think about what I buy for wedding for myself. It is good way and if you have not a wedding then my advise you make it up.

8:25 AM Nov 27th from ÜberTwitter

Also when I sad I think word Rik and Rik face then make happy.

8:28 AM Nov 27th from ÜberTwitter

I hate go pharmacy they look me like I prostitute every time, they wear all the more of makeup than i ever. now for long bath with candles

3:21 PM Nov 27th from ÜberTwitter

now I go out in dress which I wear only to the club and back home when i finish. its against cold, not for sexy. In the club I be hot bitch!

7:12 PM Nov 27th from web

I like money so i like work i do. some man last nite he was very rich and i like men who is very rich becaus they make me more rich

11:21 AM Nov 28th from ÜberTwitter

when i stay all nite out it is a hard thing in next day morning and afternoon, so i go starbucks an sit try not to think of my sister there

11:24 AM Nov 28th from ÜberTwitter

i should say my sister is total bitch! she not coming to my wedding which now be soon in future, Valentine Day I is hope

11:30 AM Nov 28th from ÜberTwitter

I join group @HenTales about hen party but so far I left organize of my hen to Lenka. we not go to stripclub! maybe I should say my likes?

4:48 PM Nov 29th from web

My best hen is go with Lenka in Brno for smoke pur heroin, my first big drug. I was twnty, not so old. Lenka is divorce again but not sad.

4:52 PM Nov 29th from web

In Mcdonalds Vodickova. i have many favorite food Ii'm lovin. Most I like Big Mac of course but not green gerkin which remind of wet of cum

1:22 PM Nov 30th from ÜberTwitter

RT @Josefeenx3 #iaintafraidtosay that i'll do anything for ma man he dont got no complains like i said im a lady in the streets but a freak in the sheets;)

5:22 PM Nov 30th from web

some people tweet very wise here i think
5:31 PM Nov 30th from web

is time go faster for you now you are older than young before?
today seem like yesterday again but more boring becasue we
know yesterday
5:37 PM Nov 30th from web

My thrush yeast gone now and cunt smell like honey and taste
like money, Rik say always
5:39 PM Nov 30th from web

i love rik so so much sometimes love hit me like a truck in the
middle of the nite hours
1:17 AM Dec 1st from ÜberTwitter

RT @weddingbelle: Fresh off the runway—the hottest wedding
dress of the spring season. http://tiny-url.com/defntc
11:25 AM Dec 1st from ÜberTwitter

I love rik so so so much when i must wonder where he is, like
now, because he not call. When Rik married me i have right
know his locate.
11:36 AM Dec 1st from ÜberTwitter

My friend Martina do my manicure because she is the best in
Praha. We have big plan for make my nail beautiful for wedding.
2:31 PM Dec 1st from ÜberTwitter

Explain, martina do manicure for my left hand do I this with
other hand. Martina is cool, she has two boyfriends know about
each the other!
2:34 PM Dec 1st from ÜberTwitter

Rich man again he want me all the nite, his come from Russia so I call him Gangsta. His hotel room pay his company and he own all company.
9:37 AM Dec 2nd from ÜberTwitter

Lenka say me not call Rik, wait him call me. Always she say this and trust me baby I have divorce.
3:37 PM Dec 2nd from web

Handjobs is boring for woman, I count how many it takes of up and down before over. Best record is two.
5:29 PM Dec 2nd from web

For me blowjob is more interest because mans are appreciate good work and big please. handjob is anyone can do it, i think anwyway.
5:30 PM Dec 2nd from web

my best work is lapdance, for the Burlesque i must to have titties more bigger, and strip also maybe. I give pressure for implants on Rik
5:32 PM Dec 2nd from web

When I up close and personal with man do lapdance on him i using my eyes and lips to turn on so titties not so much important get the $£.
5:34 PM Dec 2nd from web

Rik not to call me four days. But Gangsta say now he spoke Rik today.
3:38 AM Dec 3rd from ÜberTwitter

i in Starbucks alone
11:28 AM Dec 3rd from ÜberTwitter

i tire but many drugs with Gangsta and not sleeping today i think, teeth hurt and cunt becaus of sextoy games. Gangsta hurt also i hope.
11:29 AM Dec 3rd from ÜberTwitter

I one of first custom for Starbucks here Praha franchise. I so loyal but was mistake bring here bitch sister who hate on my and my places
11:34 AM Dec 3rd from ÜberTwitter

when Starbucks first in Praha on Malostranske Namesti open I go escort businessman who tell them I singing and modeling and acting. i like.
11:38 AM Dec 3rd from ÜberTwitter

about singing is true I want sing but sound is bad of me when I get nervou. I do model with other girl or man but for sex not clothing!
11:41 AM Dec 3rd from ÜberTwitter

They ask me sing with jazzgroup in Starbucks till i say too shy even when everyone clapping. Businessman hit me later for embass him.
11:43 AM Dec 3rd from ÜberTwitter

Acting I think i be like Keera Kniteley who classic English rose and no titties no bootie. But still Rik not call :(
11:45 AM Dec 3rd from ÜberTwitter

Rik is sometimes bastard, today is bastard
4:49 PM Dec 3rd from ÜberTwitter

After big mac meal i feel just like i want feel, empty but full but also empt
4:55 PM Dec 3rd from ÜberTwitter

tonite i will not be lonely because tonites gonna be a groovy nite
4:59 PM Dec 3rd from ÜberTwitter

Gangsta just text me!
5:31 PM Dec 3rd from web

i go home get ready and no answer Rik when he call. Gangsta gave special idea i tell when i know.
5:33 PM Dec 3rd from ÜberTwitter

Gangsta phone cancell meet tonite. Rik not phone. It is Wednesday and club will be empty and i will be hot bitch and want die.
5:56 PM Dec 3rd from ÜberTwitter

As i sending tweet Rik call say sorry sorry. I weak and I answer. Rik sound like best rik of flowers and luv you all the time. Now I smile.
5:58 PM Dec 3rd from web

I feel me ugly and fat with water. I really want no go to party but we all hire for pole dancing so we go. Germans.
6:18 PM Dec 4th from web

I driving home in cab. Walking is more cold.
3:35 AM Dec 5th from ÜberTwitter

Praha street is empty and city look like in old time when i was baby girl and see big yellow light in high dark.
3:41 AM Dec 5th from ÜberTwitter

I pay no cab. One handjob for journey and every both happy. I not happy.
4:02 AM Dec 5th from ÜberTwitter

When i on period I wish for vampire man to drink me and love me, drink all of me quick so then i emtpy and go to work. Tonite blood no work.
5:11 PM Dec 5th from web

I want bath and need bath and love bath and bath love me too.
5:30 PM Dec 5th from web

my wedding dress is be long white silk with minimal style, no lace no puffs, and white shoes Lenka borrow me with tall heel for up kiss Rik.
5:01 PM Dec 6th from ÜberTwitter

In McDonalds there i feel safe, i like watch japan people eating who are so tidy and small with there mouths of delicate.
5:30 PM Dec 6th from ÜberTwitter

When I hear fantastic song I wish be singer who can singing song to people and make people felt the same feeling I is feeling hearing
5:42 PM Dec 6th from ÜberTwitter

But Alice sing sound like fanny fart in bath
5:43 PM Dec 6th from ÜberTwitter

My best song is call Kiss me by American band Sixpence no the richer because it romantic world I go and stay until stop and play again

5:45 PM Dec 6th from ÜberTwitter

After I own beautiful BlackBerry i feel not so much lonely, is always something read somebody say somewhere in world, and i talk them back

1:45 PM Dec 7th from ÜberTwitter

Friend who know my friend Jiri say someone say bitch sister is naked in porn site but he not say if she hardcore. Big news to find.

1:01 PM Dec 8th from ÜberTwitter

I call to Jiri.

1:03 PM Dec 8th from ÜberTwitter

I must to see porn of bitch sister compare my porn because she say always she hate me on this, like victim for be paid. Is she anal do?

1:18 PM Dec 8th from ÜberTwitter

Jiri not call back. Now I mail to him ask my sister picture where is? I tell to him is urgent, if she is hypocrit maybe she come my wedding.

3:33 PM Dec 8th from web

My sister is disappear September and one email for mother is all, say she alive and happy and not worry about, so big bitch, the one email!!

5:06 PM Dec 8th from web

It hard now remember sister when I like her in childhood time when we live in world of doll talking on doll big secrets
5:12 PM Dec 8th from web

Jiri friend say he speak his friend tomorrow maybe, I say now!!! Please Jiri, I need know truth on my sister.
9:34 PM Dec 8th from ÜberTwitter

Someone ask why hate you bitch sister so much? She hit my mother until hospital is must go, cut the face with a knife. OK?
11:11 PM Dec 8th from ÜberTwitter

I have sister URL! must pay money join pornsite. Jiri say is video 5 minute. I tell you it now but Rik has visacard not me so I ask on him.
1:36 AM Dec 9th from ÜberTwitter

Rik say he pay tonite, he like watch sister porn with me. We must to wait, friends of me here in twitterland.
2:54 AM Dec 9th from ÜberTwitter

I hate wait to see. I smoke too much Marlboro and cry. Call to mother.
12:04 PM Dec 9th from ÜberTwitter

Is my sister! pretty hypocrit, but she does not anal groupsex just make self cum in bed, she is more fatter and short hair I think lesbian
6:45 PM Dec 9th from web

Really is my sister? I watch again with Rik, he say yes. I think maybe. I not link because twitter angry on porn I think. I angry on her.
7:03 PM Dec 9th from web

Is her. Now she pornstar still she think she better of me becaues I dancing and men look, she touch herself in bed with camera, is better?

7:06 PM Dec 9th from web

There is girl now read a book in Starbucks and I want really not read the book but know girl idea about it because she is totally smiling

10:06 AM Dec 10th from ÜberTwitter

I hate all the books, love magazine, magazine is more true, life is picture not black white word dead

10:15 AM Dec 10th from ÜberTwitter

I call to mother, say her about bitch sister do porn. Mother is not understand and still think is me, she call me whore I call her whore.

1:01 PM Dec 10th from ÜberTwitter

Rik not come with me shop for wedding dress. I send him picture girl in shop take and he text, You are beautiful, which is just right words

2:40 PM Dec 10th from ÜberTwitter

Tonite is for Gangsta, privat. I send him picture dress too.

2:44 PM Dec 10th from ÜberTwitter

Now Rik text me he want fuck me which is not right words but is good words for me, not wedding dress

2:46 PM Dec 10th from ÜberTwitter

Gangsta like dress, he say me he like see me wearing and after not wearing. This i not do for no money.

2:19 AM Dec 11th from ÜberTwitter

RT @weddingbelle: Tip of the Day: Have your eye on a spendy piece of jewelry? Look into renting—it's cheaper & a fabulous treat to yourself!
6:15 PM Dec 11th from ÜberTwitter

SocialSync RT @xxii: The difference between style and fashion is quality ~ Giorgio Armani #quote #fashion #lifestyle
6:19 PM Dec 11th from web

Back in the club with the music go boo boo and the men eyes looking looking.
1:03 AM Dec 12th from ÜberTwitter

Sun come up beautiful today morning, pink like for girls. I think #ParisHilton much like this morning because coordinate her Chanel outfit
8:08 AM Dec 12th from ÜberTwitter

Rik say one time sunrise is for him bad time because nite is for make money and day only for sleep and wait make money
8:10 AM Dec 12th from ÜberTwitter

Gansta make offer to Rik for us get marry soon, me Rik marry, and he pay everything! He want see me marry, he say, he want see me in dress!
11:15 PM Dec 12th from ÜberTwitter

my big dream is live in Hollywood have small dogs like #ParisHilton, and Rik be film producer put me in film so I win Oscar after new breast
5:01 PM Dec 13th from web

I forget say how meet Rik, he not come club to see girl. Rik is come club test the drugs like biochemistry, club not open. I dance privat!

5:03 PM Dec 13th from web

I want be #richandfamous to make #lifestyle more easy, but dance I do is not make me famous because I having no #style.

1:11 PM Dec 14th from ÜberTwitter

Like #ParisHilton have style so #ParisHilton have #ParisHilton life, is beauty I feel of her.

1:13 PM Dec 14th from ÜberTwitter

If I famous then every I do is more good because people is pay attention and is pay money.

1:16 PM Dec 14th from ÜberTwitter

#Fashion is me most important in world because if no #Fashion I only be all day in bed, want for #Fashion make me to visit world.

5:42 PM Dec 15th from web

Is time make plan, my mother say, if wedding in February must reserve Town Hall.

1:29 PM Dec 16th from ÜberTwitter

Is big argue in my apartment about big nothing, but so depress me

6:38 PM Dec 16th from web

Rik want only stay Praha for #honeymoon, or go Ibiza for #groupsex, I want not #groupsex in middle #honeymoon

2:13 AM Dec 17th from ÜberTwitter

Lenka say me leave Rik, Rik is bad, but she want Rik I sure. Is she best friend for me like say this?

4:29 PM Dec 17th from ÜberTwitter

I ask Rik time we get marry, because I hope is valentine day or day beside valentine day

1:43 PM Dec 18th from web

Sometime Rik different, not real Rik

2:52 PM Dec 18th from web

Sometime Rik is typical typcal

2:53 PM Dec 18th from web

Today Rik hit at me, make me understand him feeling

2:54 PM Dec 18th from web

Sometime Rik is just #muthafucka

2:56 PM Dec 18th from web

You want know why i not more angry on Rik is because he is good man under bad man face, and i am knowing it. i trust heart of him.

3:22 PM Dec 18th from web

RT @ AniFernandez7 The woman cries before the wedding; the man afterward.– Polish proverb

3:33 PM Dec 18th from web

I is #feminist because sex is power and money is power and one time I piss on face of Billionaire.

3:39 PM Dec 18th from web

Here is question, I love Rik because he bad on me or because sometime he no bad on me?

2:21 AM Dec 19th from ÜberTwitter

I imagine Rik with me as old man old woman walk on Charles Bridge.

5:31 PM Dec 19th from web

Here mind happy imagine is lie. I imagine Rik fucks Martina and i kill two both with gun.

5:33 PM Dec 19th from web

I want be a good person, if I kill Rik this help me more than not kill him, I think. He impossible, he not call again, he wiht woman

5:40 PM Dec 19th from web

I want be a good person so god love me who love everybody same so why i need be good person? I wnat killl Rik.

6:01 PM Dec 19th from web

I want kill Rik, if God want me kill Rik I not be bad person when after I killed Rik. Is logic.

6:11 PM Dec 19th from web

and #HappyChristmas

6:13 PM Dec 19th from web

I not see Martina no more for manicure because of suspect she #downlow with Rik.

1:29 AM Dec 20th from ÜberTwitter

Rik he yesterday smell like Martina smell. Fish.

1:31 AM Dec 20th from ÜberTwitter

Is hard in Praha find somewhere for manicure you also get view and air because usual is all downstairs, like club. Any you got suggestion?

4:13 PM Dec 20th from web

I think depress so not to write. Nobody follow me like friend.

5:23 PM Dec 21st from web

Gangsta say terrible horrible, oh I crying

2:13 AM Dec 22nd from ÜberTwitter

Gangsta say at club he want fuck me after wedding before recepce, in that time, if I to wear my wedding dress

2:36 AM Dec 22nd from ÜberTwitter

Is offer, Gangsta say $1000 and he buy all best food and champagne for party after wedding which he pay for also

2:38 AM Dec 22nd from ÜberTwitter

Tonite I tell Rik Gangsta say me $1000 for fuck bride which is me, Rik be angry on him and say #gotohell

4:48 PM Dec 22nd from web

I think what #ParisHilton do in my life if she me. She telling me in head be strong positive and life be for you wonderful romantic

4:51 PM Dec 22nd from web

Martina call me say why i not call her? I tell to her my suspect of her with Rik. She laugh and i believe her, she honest. I think.
5:55 PM Dec 22nd from web

Rik want me fuck Gangsta because Rik say me $1000 is much of money for nothing
11:21 PM Dec 22nd from ÜberTwitter

Rik say words, money for nothing, like me is nothing woman.
11:25 PM Dec 22nd from ÜberTwitter

Can some do magic on my head, and make it full of #happy where is now hate at men and world of men? I change my head for head of pigeon!!
11:38 AM Dec 23rd from ÜberTwitter

I broke my heart to him! Idiot!
11:48 AM Dec 23rd from ÜberTwitter

This what innocent is for, be total destroy by bastard.
11:50 AM Dec 23rd from ÜberTwitter

People in Starbucks here, you not know my life is so big shit. You is lucky people, you is free
11:54 AM Dec 23rd from ÜberTwitter

I wish someone do not never say me word #love so i never know to feel such bad, for me is better live like animal who most fun is eat food
5:57 PM Dec 23rd from ÜberTwitter

Rik is total change. He come my apartment with flowers today morning. He say me Never see Gangsta again if not want. I luv him.

11:03 AM Dec 24th from ÜberTwitter

Now I feel happy.

11:07 AM Dec 24th from ÜberTwitter

#sex for day make me happy but also so becuase all day is not #sex day, some day is just sad lonely day, but after sad lonely is best #sex!

5:51 PM Dec 24th from web

BigJersey RT @Kimlanta: #ifthesexisgood ALL THE OTHER PROB-LEMS SEEM MINOR LOL

5:55 PM Dec 24th from web

I discover songs of #TaylorSwift. Is she most beautiful? More fresher than #ParisHilton but same of blond.

about 23 hours ago from web

We need more Americans in world so be better if all Europe union be turn to American and have optimism lifes we change every day, and Hummer

about 8 hours ago from ÜberTwitter

Praha is greatest city in world for high in air view of Castle and down here Vltava river and how feel your heart bang like bomb at beauty

about 8 hours ago from ÜberTwitter

I love Rik so much that some hours thinking of him hit me like tsunami and i suck out to sea middle with just me an seagulls shit on me

5 minutes ago from web

is Christmas wonderful time of year for love of two peoples, most when one called Rik and one called Alice. Happy to all you! x

2 minutes ago from web

#HappyChristmas

less than a minute ago from ÜberTwitter

'And how is it this week?'

'It?' asked Kavita.

'Whatever you take it to be.'

'*How am I this week*? Or, *How is my situation this week*?'

'You see them as different, the one from the other?'

'Or, *How is my guilt this week*? *How am I coping with my guilt this week*? Before we talk about what my guilt really is. Before we say hello to Daddy.'

'Perhaps we could do some work with your anger, before we turn to Daddy.'

A silence followed.

Kavita said, 'The more I read of Lacan, the more of a charlatan I find him.'

'Indubitably. As you've said before, on a number of occasions. At which point we have tried to both broaden and deepen the question. Why is it, we have asked, that you feel the need to attack what you suppose is my father figure? Is it because you think this approach will succeed in causing me anguish? Wrong-foot me? Would you like to force me into the same emotional position in which you place yourself?'

'No,' said Kavita. 'I'd like it to be much, much worse.'

'It?'

'Your anguish.'

'Because . . .? Because I somehow deserve it?'

Kavita said, 'Because I shouldn't be able to afford you.'

'Your family can afford me. And you are part of your family. Therefore you can afford me.' He smiled. 'I am expecting you, as a philosopher, to do a very thorough demolition on the logic of this.'

'You remind me of the very worst images of Vishnu.'

'Would you care to expand on that?'

'No,' said Kavita.

'Although,' said Kavita, smiling, 'sometimes your skin does appear to be blue.'

'You have a way of making your Symbolic-order meanings extremely clear, Dr Singh.'

'And now you punish me.'

'. . .?'

'. . .'

'. . .?'

'By calling me that.'

'I thought we had agreed—was it two weeks ago, Monday?—that I would address you in this manner, by your formal title. If you prefer, I can revert to using your first name. That seemed to be your preference for a while.'

'Try to refrain from referring to me in any way at all. By name.'

'Your silent sessions have often been as productive as your less silent ones.'

'Do you think about me when I'm not speaking? Is that something you're obliged to do, because I'm here, physically—or maybe because I'm paying?'

'Because your *family* is paying, you mean? You know I'm not going to answer that.'

'Because it isn't about *you*, is it?'

'I have my own analysis, which is ongoing.'

'I imagine you as spending most of your time crying. Do you go foetal when you cry? I think foetal would probably suit you. On the couch. Vishnu is such a big blubbing baby, underneath.'

'Do you think there's a particular reason for your aggression this morning? Are you wishing to disrupt the rhythm of our sessions, perhaps?'

'I didn't realize they had a rhythm,' said Kavita.

'Of course they do. That may be one of the reasons for your aggression. Perhaps we could explore that?'

His office was high up on the north-facing side of one of Bombay's tallest buildings. If the sky outside had been a different colour, not piss-on-cotton yellow, she might have been in Manhattan. There was no sign of India here, apart from her sari. The psychoanalyst wore an imported suit and imported shoes. Also, the artworks on the walls were from the United States—a late Barnett Newman, an early Rothko. The psychoanalyst's couch was from Europe—a steel and black leather construction located towards the echoey centre of the room. Kavita had never touched it, always sitting instead on the middle cushion of a black-leather-and-steel sofa. The psychoanalyst—face to face with her—had an Aeron office chair, usually in a reclined position, feet crossed. His left shoe twitched from side to side as he spoke, as he listened.

'Perhaps we could explore Peru?' said Kavita.

'Analytic convention requires me to ask you what particular associations Peru has for you?'

'None. But it alliterates with *perhaps*.'

'So would Patagonia, Paraguay . . .'

'Patagonia has associations.'

'And Paraguay?'

'Was something you brought up,' said Kavita.

'Have you ever been to South America?'

'That's a very pedestrian question, for a Lacanian.'

'You have never mentioned it before. Do you know South America well?'

'*Connaissez vous bien l'Amerique du Sud*? Not as well as I know North America, nor as well as North America knows me. In Peru, people are brown-skinned, as they are here. Many of them are poor.'

'But Peru could not be said to be here.'

'I have never visited Peru.'

'And have you ever visited here?'

Kavita said, 'That's the most useful thing you've said in six months.'

'Thank you. Why?'

'Oh, don't go back to being Vishnu. You know why.'

'I assume you feel you have never visited here.'

'Yes. No.'

'Meaning India? Meaning Bombay specifically?'

'Meaning this place,' said Kavita.

'Have you tried? Have you tried to visit it?'

'A few weeks ago.'

'I will wait.'

'Could I have a glass of water?'

He fetched her one.

'Could I have another glass of water?'

He fetched her another.

She drank from neither.

'A few weeks ago I made an appointment to go into Dharavi. I thought,' Kavita said, 'I would go to the worst place I could find.'

'Because here-where-you-haven't-been is the worst place?'

'I thought you weren't going to interrupt?'

'Interrupting is, in a manner of speaking, my job.'

'I thought *listening* was.'

'No, that's my vocation.'

'If you annoy me too much, I won't tell the story.'

'Perhaps that would be the most useful thing. If you want to tell me the story, what's the point in me hearing it?'

'It's not a story. It's not a dream,' said Kavita. 'It's what happened.'

'What didn't happen. When you weren't here.'

'Do you want to hear it?'

'No.'

'I went to the slum because I had arranged to meet Dr Anise, who works there. She has a clinic. She is a breast cancer specialist. A small clinic. Since I got back from Texas, I have been funding her—and, yes, I feel guilty about that, too. But not as guilty as I do about this.' Her hand gesture managed to snag the Newman but the Rothko somehow got away.

'How did the slum strike you?'

'Hard. I would have adopted at least ten of the children straight out of there, if I could. It's where the smell of the city comes from. It's why Bombay stinks.'

'You knew that already.'

'There's what you know and what you choose to stick your face in so you really know it.'

'The slum was *Real*, was it?'

'No. Even when I was there, I didn't believe in it. I thought, *After I've gone, they will tidy this away. They don't really live up that ladder, under that piece of plastic.*'

'But you still wanted to remove their children?'

Kavita found herself beginning to cry.

'I wanted to steal them all *all* away.'

'But it wasn't real. They tidy it up. At night, it doesn't even smell, and the rats don't come. People don't spend their lives walking through liquid shit in flip-flops.'

'This is my analysis, not yours.'

'I am trying to make some contribution. You were extremely distressed. You are still extremely distressed. That is understandable.'

With the handkerchief Kavita dried her cheeks, then her eyes.

'I wasn't distressed *enough*. Part of me was indifferent. Part of me was quite glad. I enjoyed being there, because I could leave. Do you know the song "Common People" by the English band Pulp?'

'Jarvis Cocker? A national treasure.'

'Yes. You know the words?'

'I know the sentiment.'

'I can always call my dad. Everybody hates the tourist.'

'Do they hate her as much as the tourist hates herself?'

'How do I know? How do I know if they are even capable of feeling anything? Things fall down there, roofs, and they crush people, babies— and then life continues. What time do they have? What time do they have for anything but eating and arguing?'

'Answer your own question.'

'They suffer as much as I do. I mean, they suffer as much as I *would*. Oh, that was a gift, wasn't it?'

'Thank you for your gift. You have never been there but *they* are *you*.'

'This is the condition of the poor, in reality,' said Kavita. 'I am *not* thinking *I am India*. I don't go round like that.' She thought of her grandmother, then thought about saying she was thinking of her grandmother.

'India as bilateral mastectomy.'

'People as cancers. I don't believe that's my image.'

'Which you just spoke aloud.'

'We walked down tunnels of trash until we came to where the clinic is. My name is written above the door, because I have given them so much money. And my picture was on the wall in the kitchen with some flowers around it. Orange flowers. Plastic.'

'What happened?'

'I asked them to take the photograph down.'

'Did they?'

'Of course. But they will have put it back up again, as soon as I left.'

'You didn't think of asking them not to?'

'They want to see me.'

'And they saw you. Was that the *what happened*?'

'I was there for an average day. And when I came back, I wrote them a cheque for everything in my bank account. My father cancelled it, of course, as soon as the bank contacted him. He allowed me to make a more sensible payment, monthly.'

'Did you experience your guilt more richly, deep in our slums?'

'I expected a lot of my visit, and I wasn't disappointed. It was as bad as I'd hoped. I didn't tell Dr Anise about myself, but she knew—she knew that's why I was interested.'

'Dr Anise is a young woman?'

'She looks about thirty-five. She's twenty-nine. I found her on the Internet. All day, she tells women they are going to die soon. They can't do operations. They give painkillers. I am going to pay for some operations.'

'How many?'

'As many as I can afford,' said Kavita. 'For the rest of my life.'

'And how do you feel about that?'

'I wish I could afford more.'

'Would you give away all your money?'

'All my family's money? No. I am desperate for us to remain rich. I know I don't exist without that—a woman without a room of one's own?'

'Would you describe your state of mind as confused?'

'The questionnaire approach? You're that desperate? Yes, I don't understand myself. But I can't pretend I want to be Jesus. I am not the right kind of doctor. You're not, either.'

'I am not a doctor. I don't pretend to be.'

'You don't heal people, either.'

'No, but I pretend to. However, I thought we'd moved on from the aggression. We can go back there, if you want. I think we should.'

Kavita said, 'At the very end of the day, Dr Anise asked to see where my breasts had been. There were four other women in the room. One nurse, one assistant, two patients who had come together, one carrying the other on her back. I did not hesitate. So many people have seen my breasts—so many people I didn't want to. And those I did want to see them didn't get to see them. I mean Paddy, specifically.'

'You are still thinking about him frequently?'

'I showed them because of what I'd seen. The women. Dr Anise looked at them very closely and said, "Exquisite. Beautiful." She purred just like a cat.'

'And this made you feel?'

'Rich.'

'Was this a significant moment for you?'

'Enough for me to tell you about it.'

'Enough for you not to tell me about it for several weeks.'

'Two months,' said Kavita.

'You said *A few weeks ago* . . .'

'I meant *Two months*.'

'You were deliberately concealing how long it had been.'

'I am not reporting to you like some spymaster.'

'How did you feel, as you exposed yourself to those women?'

'That I was not exposing myself. That I was exposing the work of a plastic surgeon—a man who got more for my operation than Dr Anise will earn in ten years.'

'Was this what you might call a "moment of truth"?'

'No, the moment of truth came when my father cancelled the cheque.'

'How do you feel, talking about this now?'

'I wish I hadn't told you. I wish your reaction had been more satisfactory.'

'I am sorry to disappoint you—yet again.'

Kavita said. 'Would you like to see where my breasts were?'

'You feel the desire to show this to me?'

'I feel you need to see, in order to understand the story I am telling you—in order to have the full facts.'

'I am not sure that would be considered appropriate. But it is very interesting that you are forcing this situation.'

'I will show you now.'

'Stop!'

He said, 'As you know, this has nothing to do with what I would like. I feel we should talk this through a great deal more before any action is taken.'

'I will not offer again.'

'That, in itself, will give us a great deal of ground to cover.'

'You said *to cover*.'

'I did.'

'You said *ground*.'

'That is what I said.'

NYKVIST & BARBIE

INT. DEPARTURES. GEORGE H. BUSH INTERCONTINENTAL AIR-
PORT, HOUSTON, TEXAS. AFTERNOON.

Size 13 (at least) Air Jordans in Titanium/Blue move
fleet-foot across the polished vinyl floor, and as we
pull back we see they are propelling a very tall, pale
man, 58: DR LOKE NYKVIST. He wears a crisp, new grey
tracksuit and a Texans baseball cap. He's pulling along
a tiny rolling case. Beneath his bright blue eyes are
telltale dark shadows. He's a man in a hurry.

We fall behind NYKVIST enough to see he's speeding
towards Security. Burly male and female SECURITY GUARDS
stand beside the empty doorway of the metal detector.

X-RAY MACHINE SCREEN.

A couple of average bags go by, containing dinky beauty
products, cameras. But as NYKVIST's tiny case scrolls
left to right the only thing that shows up on the
screen is the X-ray of a very slim, diaphanous doll.
She almost makes it to the right of the screen, but
then is stopped. Is rolled back until she is front and
centre, as if standing before us.

                                        DISSOLVE TO:

Standing before us, behind cellophane in her cardboard
box, is a BARBIE doll—but there are other BARBIES in
other boxes to her left and right, and on shelves above
and below her. They are all identical.

                                            CUT TO:

INT. DEPARTMENT STORE, HOUSTON, TEXAS. MORNING.

NYKVIST stands looking towards us, the aisle of the
store running off to infinity behind him.

Reverse angle, and we see NYKVIST dwarfed by a vast
pink wall of BARBIE dolls. They stand, blonde, smiling,
identical. NYKVIST steps forward, as if to pick one up,
but then pulls his hand back. He repeats this move with
another of the BARBIES. Clearly he is trying really
hard to choose the right one. Her? What about her?
Finally, he pounces—grabbing a BARBIE box front and
centre. Our BARBIE.

INT. SECURITY. GEORGE H. BUSH INTERCONTINENTAL AIRPORT,
HOUSTON, TEXAS. AFTERNOON.

We start hard on the back of NYKVIST's pale-haired
head, then go wide to see he is facing Security Guard
JOHNSON across a plain grey desk. Both men stand. TRAV-
ELLERS who haven't been stopped stroll past in the
background, sneaking sideways glances at NYKVIST.

> JOHNSON (O.S.)
> Could you open your bag for me, please,
> sir?

NYKVIST does nothing.

> NYKVIST
> I will miss my flight. I am already late.

NYKVIST's voice is grave and gravelly.

> JOHNSON
> Please, sir, could you just open your bag?

> NYKVIST
> It was also you last year, wasn't it? So
> you know what's in there. And you know it
> isn't a problem.

> JOHNSON
> Sir, would you like to follow me, please?

INT. SECURITY OFFICE. GEORGE H. BUSH INTERCONTINENTAL
AIRPORT, HOUSTON, TEXAS. AFTERNOON.

Sound of unzipping, and NYKVIST's case, completely
empty but for BARBIE and an eyeshade, lies exposed on
the table.

                    NYKVIST
It's for my niece. Just like last year.

                    JOHNSON
I'm sorry, sir, but I can't remember last
year.

                    NYKVIST
Her name is Ana Nykvist. You can check.
Ana Nykvist.

                    JOHNSON
It's not the doll that concerns me, sir.
It's you. What kind of man travels to Sweden with nothing but swimwear BARBIE and
these?

JOHNSON picks out the eyeshades, lets them dangle from
his thick finger.

                    NYKVIST
        I do.

Close up on NYKVIST's face—a touch of Clint Eastwood in
the way he wince-squints before—

                    NYKVIST (CONT'D)
And she's not swimwear BARBIE.

                                            CUT TO:

TITLE. White letters on black: DR NYVKIST and BARBIE

                                            CUT TO:

INT. AIRPLANE. MOVING. RUNWAY. GEORGE H. BUSH INTERCON-
TINENTAL AIRPORT, HOUSTON, TEXAS. EVENING.

In a window seat, NYKVIST has the eyeshade on and a
blanket over his body as the airplane rapidly speeds
up, tilts and takes off through murky pink twilight.

INT. SIXTHSCALE AEROPLANE. FLYING. ABOVE SIXTHSCALE
ATLANTIC OCEAN. NIGHT.

Bobbing up and down, BARBIE AIR STEWARDESS approaches
BARBIE, who sits strapped to a seat the perfect size

for her. The seats surrounding her are occupied by other BARBIES and some KENS—most wear eyeshades and appear to be asleep. As asleep as dolls can appear to be.

> AIR STEWARDESS BARBIE
> (WITH PERFECT DICTION)
> How may I help you today?

> BARBIE
> My husband is shivering. Is it possible to get another blanket for him?

> AIR STEWARDESS BARBIE
> Of course, I'll fetch one right this minute.

> BARBIE
> Thank you.

> AIR STEWARDESS BARBIE
> You're very welcome.

As AIR STEWARDESS BARBIE bobs off down the aisle, we close in on BARBIE who reaches across to a KEN-type doll of NYKVIST, who is indeed shivering. Although her stiff plastic fingers can't convincingly do this, BARBIE'S hand pulls NYKVIST'S blanket further under his chin, then pats it down.

EXT. SIXTHSCALE AIRPLANE. FLYING. ABOVE SIXTHSCALE ATLANTIC OCEAN. NIGHT.

NYKVIST'S hand holds the plane as it cruises through the starry night sky, cotton wool clouds apparently far below it.

> CUT TO:

MAP OF SWEDEN.

A graphic airplane leaving behind it a red line flies in from the left and lands at a seaside dot labelled STOCKHOLM.

INT. ARRIVALS. STOCKHOLM AIRPORT. EARLY MORNING.

As NYKVIST wheels his tiny case along, he is observed closely by an IMMIGRATION OFFICER in blue uniform.

NYKVIST is almost through when—

                    IMMIGRATION OFFICER
     Stop.

INT. SECURITY OFFICE. STOCKHOLM AIRPORT. EARLY MORNING.

NYKVIST stands and waits whilst the IMMIGRATION OFFICER
very closely examines the exterior of his tiny case.

INT. EUROPCAR STAND. STOCKHOLM AIRPORT. MORNING.

NYKVIST, unshaven and dishevelled, wheels his tiny case
up to the green-themed EUROPCAR stand. But the EUROPCAR
REP is dealing with a BUSINESSMAN. NYKVIST stretches
his long arms out wide and looks around him. NYKVIST is
thinking about what he has come here to do. He is too
tired to be embarrassed or anxious. NYKVIST scratches
the back of his head in a trademark GEORGE CLOONEY
move. An attractive BLONDE WOMAN in her forties who
is walking towards us gives him a not-at-all-coy smile
and joins the queue behind him. NYKVIST turns to look
forward.

                    BLONDE WOMAN
     God mórgon.

Her Swedish words are subtitled in English:
'Good morning.'

               NYKVIST (ONLY HALF TURNING TO HER)
     God mórgon.

From now on all dialogue is in Swedish, and all is subtitled in English.

                    BLONDE WOMAN
     Have you come far?

               NYKVIST (WITHOUT TURNING)
     America.

                    BLONDE WOMAN
     Poor you. You must be very tired.

NYKVIST doesn't reply. He waits for the EUROPCAR REP to
come free.

As they queue, we pull back very fast, panning down to the floor which dissolves to the receding tarmac of a grey road.

Slowly we climb up and over the dark blue roof of what is eventually revealed to be a PEUGOT 207. Peering through the windscreen we discover NYKVIST at the wheel. This early in the morning the road he drives is empty. But NYKVIST keeps glancing in the rear-view mirror, as if expecting he'll be followed.

We float away over a roundabout in the middle of which is a rough wooden sculpture of a dog. We rise higher, until we're directly above the 207 as it makes a right.

The 207 goes off-screen and thirty seconds later, an Acacia Green 1979 SAAB 900 GLE comes into view, turns right.

EXT. SELF-STORAGE FACILITY. STOCKHOLM. MORNING.

The 207 is parked outside a red Portakabin. Echoey acoustic clangs caused by who knows what rebound off metal surfaces.

The SAAB 900 drives up and parks. We can't see who is driving. No one gets out.

INT. SELF STORAGE FACILITY. STOCKHOLM. MORNING.

NYKVIST, his tiny case with him, unlocks a caged unit. As we follow him inside we see a wardrobe with a large suitcase on top and a spade leaning against its side.

Businesslike, NYKVIST pulls down the suitcase, puts it on the concrete floor, unzips and then opens it. The smell which escapes is not <u>exactly</u> that of mothballs, nor precisely of damp—it's more the slight sugary whiff of airlessness.

He opens the wardrobe and begins to remove clothes from inside—white cotton shirts, vests and Y-front underpants. These, he puts in the suitcase. A grey suit hangs waiting in a zip bag. This is his neutral European uniform.

EXT. SELF-STORAGE FACILITY. STOCKHOLM. MORNING.

NYKVIST comes out, still dressed in his American
clothes. He carries the suitcase in one hand and the
spade and tiny case in the other.

With a glance, NYKVIST takes in the presence of the
SAAB 900. He looks away almost as soon as he's looked,
but the sight seems to have galvanized him.

Hurriedly, NYKVIST unlocks the car boot and stows first
the suitcase then, on top of it, the spade. He shuts
the boot with a SLAM!

EXT. DARK BLUE PEUGOT 207. MOVING. MORNING.

The engine strains as NYKVIST changes a gear. The
BARBIE case is beside him, strapped into the passenger
seat. NYKVIST looks in the rear-view mirror—and sees
the SAAB 900, keeping its distance.

INT. DARK BLUE PEUGOT 207. MOVING. MORNING.

NYKVIST looks harrowed as he drives. His voiceover is
in Swedish, subtitled.

> NYKVIST (V.O.)
> Before this, nineteen years. This is year
> twenty. How many more years to go? How
> many more times?

                                              CUT TO:

The front left wheel of the 207, spinning around.

> NYKVIST (V.O.) (CONT'D)
> How many more BARBIES?

                                              CUT TO:

The 207 heads away from us between low-rise block of
flats.

Beat.

> NYKVIST (V.O.) (CONT'D)
> I have rituals, or they are maybe super-
> stitions, and I rigorously follow all of
> them.

EXT. DRIVE-IN MACDONALDS. STOCKHOLM. DAY.

The 207 rolls up to collect its huge order—bag after
bag is handed through the driver's side window.

                    NYKVIST (V.O.) (CONT'D)
          No Swedish food until it's done.

EXT. NYKVIST'S MOTHER'S APARTMENT. KIRUNA. DAY.

The 1960s low-rise is very spruce. Rain falls thickly.

                    NYKVIST (V.O.) (CONT'D)
          No visit home, until it's done.

EXT. CHURCHYARD. KIRUNA. DAY.

Heavy raindrops splash off the top of a neat gravestone
with clear lettering:

                    DR KLAS NYKVIST

                    1939—1979

                    NYKVIST (V.O.)
          No other visits, until it's done.

The sound of rainfall carries over to

INT. DEPARTMENT STORE, HOUSTON, TEXAS. MORNING.

NYKVIST stands looking towards us, the aisle of the
store running off to infinity behind him.

                    NYKVIST (V.O.)
          I always feel guilty the BARBIES aren't
          wearing more. It gets cold here. Sometimes
          very cold.

EXT. DARK BLUE PEUGOT 207. STATIONARY. MCDONALD'S CAR
PARK. MORNING.

Noise of rainfall continues as NYKVIST eats without
pleasure his French fries, one by one. Close up on his
face which is starting to seem more handsome, more
filmstarrish, with every moment the film goes on. This
actor is probably very well known, in his home country
of Denmark. He puts his mouth round the stripey straw
and sucks—slurp.

NYKVIST (V.O.)
I'm sorry, I should have introduced myself
earlier.

NYKVIST sticks another French fry in his mouth.

EXT. 207. MOVING. DAY.

The 207 drives away from us, into a flat, green but
rocky landscape. Still we hear rainfall although what
we see looks likely to prove a fine day.

NYKVIST (V.O.)
My name is LOKE NYKVIST.

MAP OF SWEDEN.

A car-graphic drives north from the Stockholm dot,
leaving a red line behind it. It is heading towards the
words 'ARCTIC CIRCLE'. Sound of rainfall stops abruptly
before

NYKVIST (V.O.)
I cut off women's breasts.

INT. 207. MOVING. DAY.

The 207 emerges from beneath a bridge, and as it does
so a clatter of raindrops hits the roof. We see the
windscreen, going washy before the wipers clear it—
washy, clear. Then we turn to look at NYKVIST, grimly
driving.

EXT. 207. MOVING. DAY.

In the middle distance we see the 207 enter the
screen, going left to right, along a long flat horizon.
Immediately above the 207 is the kind of small, vindic-
tive, pursuing cloud that you get in Warner Brothers'
cartoons—the kind that only rains on one character. But
NYKVIST's personal digitally rendered cloud looks completely natural, not cartoonish. It hovers directly
over the 207, raining hard until we hear

NYKVIST (V.O.)
That is all I have to say at this present
moment.

At which point the cloud stops dead and the 207, escaping from under it, keeps going—no longer rained on.

Beat.

> NYKVIST (V.O.) (CONT'D)
> I doubt I will have anything else to add later.

Beat.

> NYKVIST (V.O.) (CONT'D)
> But I might.

EXT. FOREST ROAD. DAY.

The 207 enters from the left, pulls over to the side of the road, stops, and NYKVIST hurries out—towards us—into the trees, where we are hiding with the B-Unit, waiting for him.

EXT. FOREST CLEARING. DAY.

NYKVIST, far enough away from the road not to be seen, quickly selects a tree, unzips his fly as he canters up to it and begins to piss, hard. We hear him sigh as a strong gush of urine hits pinewood. The flow goes on quite a while. We're almost getting impatient, cramped.

NYKVIST finishes, relieved, but immediately—as we watch his face, which reveals this—he begins to feel his prostate heating up until it's like he's riding a tiny unicycle that has just caught fire. This is what it is to be a man in your late fifties, even an apparently healthy man. The realization of this could be said to dawn upon him at the exact moment we dive in for a close-up of the pupil of his left eye.

We cut to the spinning driver's side wheel of the 207, then draw back until we can see NYKVIST, face screwed up in pain, making the epic journey from the left of the screen to the right. As we draw closer and closer to him the landscape behind his profile changes from the real thing to a back projection with heavily satu-rated colours. Suddenly a life-size BARBIE pitches for-ward into view, turns her head and says (in English)

           BARBIE (BUT HER LIPS DON'T MOVE
                 WHEN SHE SPEAKS)
He's thinking about me, right now. That's
another of his superstitions. He has to
think about me as much as possible, all
the time he's driving up.

We get closer to BARBIE, leaving NYKVIST behind.

               BARBIE (CONT'D)
He's imagining me as a real woman. That's
why I'm here. That's my reason. A real
woman with a real woman's body.

Now we pull back to driving-NYKVIST, but he's now a
lifesize KEN version of himself. He ignores us.

EXT. SIXTHSCALE 207. MOVING. SIXTHSCALE ROAD. DAY.

NYKVIST's hand pushes the dark blue car containing him
and BARBIE north, and as it travels it paints the road
behind it bright red—with real wet, sploshy paint.

               BARBIE (V.O.)
I've been here nineteen times before. Not
me actually. Earlier versions of me. Slim-
mer waist. Bigger tits. Same smile. Nineteen times. Different hire cars. Same
road. Same lonesome Swedish landscape.
Same Doctor Nykvist.

Fade to white. When it's completely white

            BARBIE (V.O.) (CONT'D)
I like him, even though he is kind of a
serial killer.

INT. 207. MOVING. DUSK.

Close up on the face of the KEN version of NYKVIST,
deadpan. Behind him, the back projection of the landscape slowly melds back into the real thing.

EXT. ALPINE STYLE MOTEL OR EQUIVALENT. EVENING.

The 207 pulls in at the reception.

INT. ALPINE STYLE MOTEL OR EQUIVALENT. EVENING.

NYKVIST walks along the corridor, carrying tiny case
and suitcase. The spade must be in the boot of the car.

He reaches his room, 103, and unlocks the door. Pushes
through and finds himself in

INT. A VAST SELF-STORAGE FACILITY. DAY FOR NIGHT.

With the room door behind him, NYKVIST is standing
before an epically vast wall of human-size BARBIES, two
hundred of them all stacked up. Suddenly, they all
start to move—mostly to beat their palms or fists
against the cellophane which separates them from the
world. But they don't cry out. Apart from the thumping
echoing through the cavernous space, they don't make a
sound.

Then all of a sudden the surrounding walls fall away
and a terrified NYKVIST is exposed in the middle of an
infinite open white plane. His body seems to dissolve
and be pulled wispily away in every direction, until
it's just a thin layer of mist.

INT. MOTEL ROOM. NIGHT.

Hard on NYKVIST's darkened face. He is asleep. As we
pull back we see life-size BARBIE in the double bed
next to him. She is turned sideways, looking at NYKVIST
in a way that seems tender. Her plastic breasts are
exposed. They have no nipples. The bed is surrounded by
a thin layer of mist.

EXT. SIXTHSCALE MOTEL OR EQUIVALENT. MORNING.

NYKVIST's hand reaches in and removes the roof. Inside
we see sixthscale NYKVIST in bed alone. Suddenly, in
stop-motion animation, he sits up and looks to his
side—where BARBIE no longer lies, but only a sixthscale
tiny case.

EXT. MOTEL OR EQUIVALENT. MORNING.

NYKVIST leans against the side of the 207, eating a
cold McDonald's cheeseburger and cold French fries. He

is extremely pained by this. Partly because they are disgusting but mostly because they remind him of the previous times he's made this journey. He takes a sip from a completely flat extra-large Coke. Gurgle-krrr. Finishes it. Stows the extra large cup and burger-related trash back in the brown-paper bag, which he places back in the boot. Gets into the driver's seat of the 207.

EXT. EMPTY ROAD. MORNING.

The 207 drives towards a hitchhiker—a YOUNG BOY dressed in a distinctive grey school uniform with a knapsack on his back, his thumb out over the road.

INT. 207. MORNING.

NYKVIST glances across at the YOUNG BOY but does not stop. The car drives on for a while, until the YOUNG BOY is out of sight. At which point ANOTHER YOUNG BOY, absolutely identical to the first, comes into view. There has been no cut or edit between the YOUNG BOY and ANOTHER YOUNG BOY. NYKVIST stares incredulous at ANOTHER YOUNG BOY. He drives on for a while, then slows the car and and looks in the rear-view. He can only see ANOTHER YOUNG BOY, trudging along the dewy-grassy verge of the road.

EXT. 207. MORNING.

The car three-point turns and heads back past ANOTHER YOUNG BOY.

INT. 207. MORNING.

NYKVIST looks out at ANOTHER YOUNG BOY, then ahead down the road—where, after a minute, the YOUNG BOY comes into view. NYKVIST is amazed.

EXT. 207. MORNING.

The car pulls up alongside the YOUNG BOY, who, after speaking to NYKVIST for a moment, opens the back door and gets in.

INT.207. MORNING.

NYKVIST drives, the YOUNG BOY behind him, until they reach ANOTHER YOUNG BOY—who has already turned round and is waiting for the car to stop.

ANOTHER YOUNG BOY, wordlessly, gets in. NYKVIST drives off. He glances in the rear-view mirror, checking out the twins—left, right. They have not acknowledged one another.

But NYKVIST has not been going for more than half a minute before the school gates come into view, and YOUNG BOY and ANOTHER YOUNG BOY reach forwards to tap him on the left shoulder.

EXT. 207. MORNING.

The car stops and the two BOYS get out. Faintly, we hear them say thank you, then they turn towards the school. No other children are in sight.

The car waits until they have gone up the steps and in—then it starts off again.

MAP OF SWEDEN.

The red line travels inexorably northwards.

EXT. ANOTHER MOTEL OR EQUIVALENT. EVENING.

207 parked outside. Empty SAAB 900 is alongside it.

EXT. ANOTHER MOTEL OR EQUIVALENT. MORNING.

As before, NYKVIST sniffs his cold, rancid burger before chowing down. His face is a picture of disgust.

We pull back to see the SAAB 900 is right next to him, unoccupied. NYKVIST looks up at the windows of the motel, and some parted curtains fall back into place.

EXT. 207. MOVING. DAY.

Seen from high the 207 drives along an exposed main road, then makes a right turn down a single-lane track.

NYKVIST (V.O.)
I should tell you this is Treriksroset.
Here is where the borders meet of Sweden,
Norway and Finland. Treriksroset means
'three-country cairn'. That is all.

INT. 207. SINGLE-LANE TRACK. MOVING. DAY.

NYKVIST looks anxiously in the rear-view mirror, and
sees the SAAB 900. He speeds up.

EXT. 207. CAIRN. DAY.

NYKVIST gets out of the car, carrying the tiny case. He
goes round to the boot, opens it and gets out the
spade. Meanwhile, the SAAB 900 has arrived and parked
next to the 207. Still we can't see who is driving it.

Hard on NYKVIST, who has arrived at his destination. He
takes a breath and then walks forwards. The landscape
is as beautiful as something so entirely desolate can
be. Beautiful like Nico from the Velvet Underground,
who was German.

The air smells icy as NYKVIST moves forwards through
it. He remembers this particular scent and associates
it with what he is about to do. It will be such a
relief. For a moment, he thinks about the desk in his
office in Houston. We can see this very clearly in his
blue eyes. Some music would probably be appropriate.

NYKVIST keeps walking for a length of shot that only a
European art movie with a name-director would tolerate
—until he arrives at where he has been headed all
along. A row of oblong mounds in the ground. The latest
one fairly clear, the next more overgrown, the next
hardly visible, etc.

Paranoid as always, he looks behind him. We do not see
what he sees, but he seems to smile.

Placing the tiny case to one side, NYKVIST begins very
seriously to dig. He chops the blade of the spade down
into the flinty earth, carving out chunks. These he
carefully lines up to his left.

We cut to watch him from behind. A cheap horror-movie handheld point-of-view shot. We hear gravelly foot-steps. We get closer and closer.

NYKVIST finishes digging and sticks the spade in the ground off to his right. Then he bends down and unzips the tiny case for the first time. BARBIE is there in her box. He looks at her sadly for a while, then turns to us as we approach.

And we cut to a wider view—of the BLONDE WOMAN from Stockholm Airport as she walks up to NYKVIST, her sensible boots crunching. She moves until she stands opposite NYKVIST. They face one another over the oblong hole in the ground—a BARBIE-size grave.

Wordlessly, NYKVIST passes the BARBIE over to the BLONDE WOMAN.

BLONDE WOMAN

Thank you, LOKE.

NYKVIST begins to undress, taking off his American sneakers, socks, tracksuit, T-shirt and finally jockeys. He stands naked in the snappy Swedish air, closes his eyes and breathes in. Opens his eyes. Then he neatly places all the clothes into the grave.

NYKVIST holds out his hands and the BLONDE WOMAN ritually passes BARBIE back to him. NYKVIST places BARBIE tenderly down in the BARBIE-grave.

NYKVIST picks up the spade and, with the spade, a divot of turf. He holds this over BARBIE. A long pause. He looks off into the distance, where he sees the YOUNG BOY and ANOTHER YOUNG BOY standing watching him.

NYKVIST throws aside the spade, reaches down and picks BARBIE out of the grave. He brushes the dirt off the box and then hands BARBIE over to the BLONDE WOMAN.

BLONDE WOMAN (SHOCKED) (CONT'D)

What? Really?

NYKVIST looks round to see how the BOYS have reacted, but they are gone. He didn't really expect them to stay.

NYKVIST reaches across the hole and takes hold of the
BLONDE WOMAN's right hand. He straightens her index and
middle finger, bends the rest inward. His mouth opens
and NYKVIST inserts the two fingers, all the way to the
back of his throat. NYKVIST gags, forces himself forwards. Understanding now, the BLONDE WOMAN jabs her
fingers a couple of times.

NYKVIST pulls back as he starts to vomit—and vomit and
vomit. All the food of the last couple of days gushes
down into the hole. BLONDE WOMAN steps back, smiling.

NYKVIST finishes. Steps back. Wipes his mouth with the
back of his hand.

                         NYKVIST
          Thank you, ANA.

Taking up the spade, NYKVIST proceeds to fill in the
hole, watched by ANA, the BLONDE WOMAN, cradling BARBIE
in her arms, as we pull further and further away.

FILM ENDS.

JOSEPH & EMMANUEL

Joseph had been waiting and waiting on Dolly Wagon, and finally he got his Orthodox Jew—black fedora, grey beard, grey cagoule, brown hiking boots.

'Well done,' said Joseph, meaning the 378 metres above sea level.

'The view, is it worth it?' asked the Jew, a breath for each pair of words. He must be over seventy. Seventy-five, even.

'Most people seem to think so.'

'The book said this, and I believe the book—most times.'

Joseph almost cried out in delight; he knew what the book was.

The Jew seated himself on the concrete base of the cairn and did not look up. 'You wear—' he said. 'Such clothes you wear.'

As Joseph—very dark-skinned—was never exactly going to fit in, he had made the tactical decision to stick out as far as possible, in as many ways as possible. He was dressed in a tweed jacket and kilt (with sporran); unusual enough, but to go even further, the fabric of both, by House of Holland, included lime green, turquoise, lemon yellow and purple. His socks, by contrast, were grass green, accessorized with dark green kilt hose—and, so as to create another conversational opener, upon his feet were a pair of the most expensive hiking boots on the market: Asolos.

'The kilt is very practical,' said Joseph, expecting the usual follow-ups from the Jew: Where are your bagpipes? Are you a *true* Scotsman? You mean you're not Scottish at all? If you're not Scottish, why are you wearing a kilt? Why is it so brightly coloured? Which clan?

The Jew asked nothing, just rasped, then spat.

Joseph rarely encountered aggressive racism; instead it was amused, bemused or terrified racism. People actually seemed to think, dressed as he was, standing where he was, that he might still intend to mug them—simply because mugging was what young black men did. (Joseph was thirty-three years old. His first-class degree in anthropology came from Sussex University.) People—women *and* men—were also afraid of rape; the kilt suggested this to them just as much as the colour of his skin. But, generally, his study group had proven highly cooperative. Five in six ramblers were prepared to stop, talk to him—gradually relaxing. Two out of three were happy to give him the four minutes it took to fill out the form. A tenth of them, the friendliest or loneliest, were eager to accept his card and meet him later for a more in-depth interview.

'I wasn't made for such heights,' the Jew said. 'Better for me is under the ground.'

'You seem fit enough,' said Joseph. 'Lots of men your age couldn't make it up here.'

'I died twice, down below. Only stupidity brought me back from paradise. This is surely the last time.' The Jew lifted his weighty gaze to the jagged horizon. 'It could be worse,' he said. 'But then, certainly my eyesight could be better. This is natural stuff. No one's messed with this. No one's messed this up.'

'No,' said Joseph. 'That's why I like it.'

'Emmanuel Steiner,' said the Jew, holding his right hand up above his head, as if a good boy in a classroom.

Joseph realized he was meant to shake it, but it had already fallen back onto the knee.

'*My* name is Steiner, Joseph Steiner,' he said. 'It's true. I have my driving licence with me.'

Emmanuel looked straight at him through waterlogged eyes. 'So you are my cousin?'

This confused Joseph.

'Is that such a bad joke?' asked Emmanuel. 'I don't know any more. You're a black man with my name. This probably means I and mine did you harm. I'm supposed to be white, aren't I? But I can't be bothered so much any more. If you are offended, I apologize. There, my breath is back—and I use it for foolishness.'

'My family is from Ghana,' said Joseph.

Emmanuel stood up and walked towards the drop. 'How you get here from there?'

'British Airways.' It was an old response which had never been all that funny.

'There are Steiners in Africa, there making black boys? You're too black.'

'My surname was a thank you to someone. A teacher in a school. They're not the same thing for us, names—not identities.'

'Identities I know. As a Steiner and not an Kohein, I know. I am glad someone was worth gratitude. How's business, Mr Steiner? You look like you're eating.'

'I'm doing very well, thank you.'

'You look rich.'

'Mining,' said Joseph. 'My father.'

'Gold?'

'Gold,' said Joseph, though these days it was more bauxite.

'That's a clipboard. You want ask me if I have a storecard? I want to buy a lake, a hill?'

'It's a form. I'd like to ask you about fell-walking. I'm an anthropologist.'

Emmanuel looked at Joseph's eyes, his own eyes starting to dry.

'Now this, this is interesting. But why the clothes?'

Joseph explained.

'Give me the form,' said Emmanuel.

'I prefer to ask the questions myself,' Joseph replied. He was excited by the older man's roughness, it seemed to promise honesty.

'I will write, and save you some trouble,' Emmanuel said, and reached for the clipboard and pen. Joseph handed over his signifiers. Emmanuel began to print his answers. 'This is interesting,' he said. 'You get many Jews?'

'A few. Retired couples. Sometimes they've changed their names.'

'No one like me. I am unique. "The Rabbi Rambler".' He looked at Joseph. 'Believe me, I am no rabbi. But I got the nickname.'

'I'll leave you for a minute.'

'You want I should put my address? Why?'

The old man had looked to the end of the form—which was self-explanatory: If you do not mind me contacting you, in order to arrange a more in-depth interview about your walking habits, please use the boxes below—address, telephone number and email.

'If I tell you too much about what it's about, then your answers won't be any use to me.'

Emmanuel's eyes went right, left, right. 'Who's watching?'

'My research is into walkers who follow the Wainwright paths—the book, books.'

'He was a mensch,' said Emmanuel. 'So much fresh air in those lungs, his brain's thoughts must be worth something. And you wear clothes so bright. Is this scientific?'

'No. It's warm.' Joseph didn't want to become defensive. 'I would be very grateful if we could conduct a full interview. I can come to wherever you are. You may check out my references in advance.'

'I don't mistrust you,' said Emmanuel. 'My address is this—' He wrote. 'The others here, the electronic, I don't personally have. The telephone is with my neighbour but he takes messages except, you know, shabbat.'

He handed the clipboard back to Joseph.

'Send me a letter first. I want your handwriting in front of me. And you can stay for lunch? Bring me an unscientific gift. I like vodka—not Russian. Anything but Russian. And now I will descend. Tell me this view was worth the agony.'

For a moment, Joseph could see the dust on the brim of Emmanuel's fedora, then he could only see the hat, receding.

'It's the most beautiful view in the country,' Joseph said, firmly.

'I believe you,' said Emmanuel, without looking back. 'Anthropology is no real science.'

A letter sent became a letter received—containing a date and time.

Joseph stood outside the house in Stoke Newington, a bottle of Wyborowa in one hand, a jar of pickled cucumbers in the other. Solving the problem, he pressed the doorbell with his elbow. It was a month since the encounter in the Lakes, and the weather was much worse. So as to be recognizable, Joseph had dressed exactly as before—but beneath an overcoat.

'Cousin,' said Emmanuel, when the door was fully open. 'Step inside.'

The ground-floor flat felt overheated, even to Joseph.

'Thank you,' said Emmanuel, receiving the gifts. 'These, I can't eat. They kill me like knives. This, too, but it brings anaesthetic with it. Follow me. I will deposit the pickles at the centre. If you came, you would be a hero with the men—for at least a half an hour. The nurses, they would hate you.'

Joseph was glad to find Emmanuel talkative. Either he had grown two inches or Joseph had misjudged him on the hilltop.

'Do you mind if I—'

'You are a good impression of an Englishman,' said Emmanuel. 'Better than me. Put it where you want.'

Joseph set the silver recorder down on a coffee table, then pointed the black microphone towards an empty armchair with books all around it. The characters on the spines were Hebrew.

'You want lemon tea, coffee?'

'Coffee, please. Black. No sugar.'

'Black,' said Emmanuel. 'Bad for the stomach, good for the soul.'

In five minutes, he returned. The coffee was very hot and very good—far better than the armchair, or anything else in the flat. Emmanuel drank coffee, too.

'The stomach is almost as important as the soul,' Emmanuel said. 'At my age. At my age.'

'You look well,' said Joseph.

'The walk was my last, definitely. Enough. I am relieved.'

Joseph, while the coffee was being made, had found on the shelves a full set of soft-spined Wainwrights. He worried that he was becoming too excited. The digital recorder had been running for a couple of minutes.

'May I ask, what started you fell-walking?'

'I hate sport. I need exercise. I need something to make me breathe, without thrashing a football. Cities are now where Jews live, but when I was younger I wanted to force some variety upon myself. So I thought of the countryside and high places, to get more value out of the walking. On the way, one day, I see a woman and she is looking into a beautiful book with a beautiful picture of what was right in front of us. I politely demanded what is it? It was Wainwright three. The Central Fells. I ordered the set, when I got home, from a bookshop. They were no disappointment. This was 1979. There they are.'

Joseph had been born in 1979, but he did not mention it.

'You follow the walks?' he asked.

'They got out of date. Roads are more busy.'

'But you do follow them?'

'I try to see what is left. The rubbing away the land when you walk, one of such crowds, it makes you feel guilty.'

'Have you done many of the walks?'

'One hundred and ten. The full two hundred and fourteen—too many for me. I was forty when I started.'

For the next half hour, Joseph got Emmanuel to tell him about the hills he had climbed, the times he had followed the books and so been led astray. This was the crux of Joseph's research. He had some theories about the structural formation of religious beliefs; the very earliest days, when doctrine begins to override the evidence of the senses. He had studied Bobo Ashanti Rastafarians, fans of *Star Wars* and Elvis Presley, members of the Nation of Islam. But it was Wainwright walkers, he believed, who were the clearest example. They followed their holy book even when they knew, in advance, that it was likely to lead them astray. Joseph was particularly interested in those path followers who also held more developed religious beliefs. Which was why he'd been so delighted to see

Emmanuel approaching. He already had all the Christians he needed (from Lutherans to Catholics, though fewer Catholics—they weren't so outdoorsy). He had five Buddhists, seven Sikhs, three Muslims. But an Orthodox Jew was his Holy Grail.

'You think this foolish?' Emmanuel finally asked.

'No,' said Joseph.

'But you have amused distance from it?'

'I started walking before I started my PhD.'

'And your reasons?'

'I wanted to know where I was—and to go places people wouldn't expect me to go. It's like a white man being at a Ghanaian wedding.'

'You are not married?'

'No.'

Emmanuel coughed for a while, then asked, 'You are really homosexual?'

'No,' said Joseph. 'I'm bisexual.'

'But more often the men or the women?'

'More often the men. But more of the time with the women.'

'Until they find out about the men,' said Emmanuel.

That made Joseph laugh.

'You sure you're not a rabbi?'

'I'm a comedian.'

Joseph couldn't tell whether this was a true statement or not.

'I don't understand it with the men,' said Emmanuel. 'Surely there is too much competition over the biggest—mine or yours?'

'It's only an issue if you make it one.'

'Such a very modern answer. But the whites, they like the experience of a black boy?'

Already Joseph was thinking about whether he really had to transcribe every word of this interview.

'We have a certain reputation.'

Emmanuel took a sip of coffee that went on and on until the cup was emptied. Then he said, 'I am still a virgin.'

Joseph had nothing he could say.

'Do I regret this? I still don't know. I am certain I could not live with a woman, particularly the kind of woman I would have to live with. I do not like women. They pretend to be clean. I like being my own kind of animal. I don't need to pretend. The hills are a trip out from the cave.'

'It's a very nice cave.'

'It's a dump, but then these days the synagogue is also a dump.'

A door opened off the hall, and another Jewish man rushed through into the lounge. He was holding the bridge of his nose but streaks of bright red were appearing on the white of his shirt.

'Oh God,' said Joseph, not standing up. 'I'm very bad with blood.' Already his feet felt dizzy.

'Stop picking it,' shouted Emmanuel. 'Stop picking it and I will have decent linen for once!'

'Hello there,' said the other Jew.

'Hello,' said Joseph.

'Please,' said the man.

Emmanuel pulled out his handkerchief, which was unevenly pink, and handed it over.

'This is Isaac, who is a fool and a burden to his friends.'

'I will go and lie down,' said Isaac.

'It's over the books,' said Emmanuel—and a few drops had fallen on some covers.

'Goodbye,' said Isaac.

'Do not lie down,' said Emmanuel. 'Go to the sink and wait for it to stop.' He added something guttural in a language Joseph guessed was Yiddish.

'He is a good friend,' said Isaac, pointing towards Emmanuel with his free hand. 'He is very patient.'

'Until today,' said Emmanuel.

Isaac went back into the other room.

'Here we have a Kohein,' said Emmanuel, who suddenly seemed exhausted. 'What can you do?'

Joseph shut his eyes and began to hum. He could feel how close he was to fainting; he could feel how close fainting was to him. 'Sorry,' he said, and concentrated on getting inside the tune. He wasn't sure whether it was something he'd made up or not.

When Joseph opened his eyes, a few improved minutes later, Emmanuel's head had lolled to the side and his eyes were shut.

Joseph knew he should leave. He had asked all the standard questions; he had enough.

A phone began to ring, quite near by. Someone answered it, and Joseph recognized Isaac's voice. At first, he couldn't hear what he was saying—not until he began to shout.

'Mince, not mints,' he cried. 'Mince. Mince! No, not mints. Mince. Lamb mince made of lambs. You got that? For cooking, not eating. You got that down? All right. Goodbye.'

Joseph stood up. Inside the sofa, a spring sang.

'Let's eat,' said Emmanuel.

JOHN AND AGATHA

Before I really knew what I was doing, John writes, I'd hired the car with mirrored glass windows all around, driven down from London (slightly murky evening), feeling like some Essex twat, and parked in a space right in front of her address.

I was well prepared to lay siege, not: on the passenger seat (guilt guilt) were two packs of mini-Scotch Eggs, salt'n'vinegar crisps, a Yorkie, and two cans of ginger beer.

Okay, I had not thought ahead, only—I *had* bought a 2l bottle of water and emptied it out at the petrol station, so I had something to piss into.

Let's not be untruthful—I didn't just feel like a stalker, I *was* a fucking stalker.

The car was a Subaru of some sort—high up driving position, but didn't smell fresh. It smelt roughly like I myself did, even before I got in it.

And so I sat there, what a wally, what a plonker, hoping Agatha wasn't on holiday—who goes on holiday in October?

The nice mid-terrace standard-Victorian-layout house had one upstairs light on; it was after eleven: not on holiday, unless they had one of those light turner-on-and-offs, for fooling burglars.

At this point, I should record, I was absolutely certain I wasn't going to speak to Agatha, or apologize to her husband, or start crying in front of their sweet little long-haired child (I was pretty sure I remembered her mentioning a boy).

The purpose of this mission was to see her movements and skin and hair—to see that she continued, independent of my few wankbank memories and my wack imagination.

I remember the fuck, obviously. And her lack of awkwardness afterwards, though I was schoolboy-gauche. (Foolishly wanting that second fuck that was never gonna come.)

I could've found a B&B and set the alarm on my iPhone, made myself comfy, but I wanted to play at Stakeout, I suppose.

So, I set the alarm on my iPhone for 7 a.m., reclined the driver's seat as much as I could, hunkered down with a Scotch Egg and guilt guilt.

Slept maybe three and a half hours, four hours in total.

Middle of the night, when the light upstairs had been off for hours, I walked around the block.

It wasn't freezing. You could bear the cold until you couldn't. I was in one of my grey flannel T-shirts.

I saw a taxi arrive two doors along, and a neat Asian man—suit and tie—came out and gave a large suitcase to the cabbie and then went to sit with his briefcase in the back.

Heathrow or Gatwick, and why didn't you book it for a more civilized hour?

A nice house in a nice street, and this must be how you pay for it.

Accountant.

Sunrise turned the rear-view mirror pink.

I hadn't written anything like since the Monday before like last. That was a cunting book review. I had been googling—I had been on the laptop . . .

And I had found Agatha, because she was easy to search: I knew her surname (she'd written it on her story, which I secretly photocopied) and where she lived . . .

At my desk, I had looked at her house, clicking the arrows to approach it and pass it. The hedge outside meant I couldn't see anything inside but the top of the light-shade hanging from the front-room ceiling. I printed this out, and it was on my corkboard when I began to assemble my mission.

Details.

I was going to write my guilt guilt.

I found out what the house cost when she and her husband bought it, and got a couple of instant quotes for what it might be worth now.

I tried to find photos of her, friended other students from that course, but none of them seemed to be in contact with her. (She didn't really like any of them, apart from the older woman.)

This was when I began to have spying and being-caught fantasies.

I just wanted to see what she looked like.

Naked, says the voice.

No, I just wanted to check how much of my remembering her had been my inventing her.

This was a cover-up—this is a family I may have screwed, killed.

I wanted to see them in their day-to-day life; I think I felt I needed to force myself to feel the full reality of them—to make myself cry with guilt guilt.

In this at least I was successful; I feel the boy from the inside now. (That sounds so wrong.) I feel *being* the boy.

The dawning realization of the cover-up happened with the dawn: It was the child I wanted to see, more than Agatha—though I did want to see her. Naked.

Would I be able to tell? Would she look catastrophically distressed? Or ill? Would there be any signs on the boy? Plasters on his face to protect cuts she might touch.

I had been anticipating the school run, and it happened.

The boy came down the path, pursued by a voice I recognized as Agatha's—despite it sounding muffled from inside the Subaru.

The boy couldn't have been sentimentalized any more. Blond hair in long bangs, blue sweatshirt, crumpled maroon jeans, those trainers with lights in the heels that flash with each step.

I had my notebook on the steering wheel; I looked hard, ready to start.

The first but not the last shock was that she'd changed her hair colour. I didn't think it was another woman; I did think it was another Agatha—a twin of some sort.

On the writing course, I'd assumed and then confirmed she was a natural redhead—gentle, not twangy bright. Now, and I was a bit horrified by this, her hair was dyed black black (a sign?)—the kind of sheenless black that packets of hair dye deliver. This blackness altered Agatha entirely, as she came towards me, putting her skin *quite literally* in a different light.

Agatha was more fleshy than I remembered—not fatter, but her flesh looked more like flesh. Her face looked raw, like hands that have done too much washing up or (even better) butcher's hands.

'Agatha looks,' I wrote, 'too human.'

I have never seen anyone look less like a ghost.

Even if I hadn't been thinking about the virus, I would have been reminded of blood in arteries and veins. She was mottled, but with annoyance not freckles.

'I want two,' said the boy.

Agatha asked him a question, then another question. The questions both began, 'Have you got . . . ?'

Her nose was thinner than I remembered (I was trying to find her plainly attractive), more like the beak of a bird (look up later: hawk?).

But Agatha's movements, turning the corner, reassured me—they were beautifully characteristic. Her wrist moving past her thigh at that precise angle.

Around the corner, onto the pavement, away from me, after the boy—I turn to look over my shoulder—her slightly pigeon-toed walk along the street (indie-band lead-singer level, not Japanese schoolgirl). She holds her head proudly, as well she might. No sign of illness or catastrophic depression. (The bad news is old—a few weeks. This is just a routine school run.)

They walk. They don't get into a car.

I want her to hold his hand—for that to be the cue for me to cry.

I like working from life.

On a scale of one to creepy, how bad is this?

Let's not be dishonest, I didn't just feel like a stalker, I was a stalker.

This is what I've come to, I thought, and then wrote, sitting outside my intimate stranger's house.

I should write more about the boy, but there weren't so many details to note. He is cute—he's a son I'd like to have.

What do I want here? I want to kickstart Agatha into fiction.

The fantasy is, she reads herself in my book, recognizes herself, contacts me. (Perhaps furiously.)

What do I want? At least something is happening. At least I'm not just having another lie-in before turning the laptop on.

(Fury would be an acceptable reaction.)

If I were writing a screenplay, which thank fuck I am not, I wouldn't have any choice but to do parts of this scene in slow motion—otherwise the moment of her walking past would, from start to finish, be no longer than a moment. However, it wasn't slow motion at all—because my greedy perceptions were more than a match for her speed.

Agatha doesn't have any of the sublime glamour of slow motion, as she walks past: she is as she is, she goes as she goes.

I wish her calves were a little less heavy; I wish her bum were a little more there.

On her feet are black Converse trainers with white rubber edging.

She is wearing—I am disappointed—black jeans; at least they are skinny.

Her arse looks soggy as she walks away.

I was careful not to make any noise as I turned round to kneel on the front seat.

Still, the car must have shifted slightly—she didn't notice, not that I noticed.

Skinny jeans—is that a change? Down on the writing course she never wore anything tight-fitting.

Her top took me a while to make out. Dark, not unstructured, merely shapeless: a leather jacket, the kind a student would've worn in the 1980s—out-of-date cut.

It looks like a from-the-attic resurrection. I am guessing this is comfort clothing.

I knew I should not get out of the car.

My thought bubble at this moment would have read: 'I need to see her walk.'

In another kind of cartoon, it would have been 'Arse—check the arse.'

Agatha and boy were already being hidden by cars. If I wanted to keep them in sight for longer, I would have to get out.

I had not cried but I did think I had accumulated enough guilt guilt for a cry later.

They were out of sight, and I thought it was over—until she came back in twenty or thirty minutes' time.

I began to wait.

They weren't getting in a car. They were walking.

Several minutes of note taking, perhaps three or four.

Then I imagined getting out of the Subaru to follow them and being confronted by the husband, then the husband was there, running along the road with a blue backpack with the Batman logo.

The husband ran.

He had left the front door open.

I had one of those plot-flashes. I immediately imagined going in and hiding somewhere in the house, the cellar probably, and then hoping I could wait until everyone had gone out—but finding out that Paddy was on study leave or holiday or reading week, and working from home, and never leaving the place; I saw sixteen hours in the cellar, hearing bedtime, hearing beeping, until they were safely sleeping, creeping out, setting off a downstairs alarm . . . Alternatively, sixteen hours trapped, and finding a bottle to urinate into—engine oil. Or phoning the emergency services, bomb threat, to evacuate the street. (But they'd trace my mobile. Find me. Fine me.) Getting caught by the husband in pyjamas, the naked husband, while trying to creep out. The confrontation—trying to explain. Silly arse.

This seemed interesting, so I got out of the car—I did get out of the car.

The husband—a long way off down the street, settled into a jog, and then round the corner at the end.

It seemed more interesting than doing nothing, so I continue.

This is what I do, fool that I am: I run into the house, into the kitchen, grab something at random from a white ceramic jar of stirring utensils to the left of the cooker—something that, as I sprint back down the hall (husband coming) feels slightly damp.

I give the front door an instinctive pull as I came past.

Too late, I try to stop it—too fast I am going. Their front door swings and swings towards me, and swings clunk-shut.

'Bollocking fuck,' I say.

In the car again, uncaught, and the something has resolved itself into a wooden spoon with one curved and one straight edge.

'Bollocking bollocking bollocking fuck.'

I knew, even before I closed the car door (don't slam), that I will have to return whatever it is.

I have to return the spoon.

It's not even symbolism, a wooden spoon (although I suppose strictly it is), it's just fucking obvious that I'm a big L in front of the forehead.

It's obvious that a man randomly stealing opportunist thieving stirring utensils is a loser.

No one saw me—I look around—no one seems to have seen me.

Not unless it was between curtains, through blinds, and they're already trying to get through to the police.

I have the wooden spoon.

It could have been worse, I suppose. It could have been the spatula.

A wooden spoon just made me a loser, a spatula would have made me a ridiculous twat.

I did think about the damp spoon going into Agatha's mouth, as she tasted that morning's porridge.

I did not touch it to my lips or my cock.

Coming out of the house, I had closed the bloody door—an instinct, the habit of going out of my own flat.

I sat, spoon in lap.

The husband returned.

Without keys, it turned out.

I watched him approach in the side mirror. Dead man walking? He was everyday-dressed—slippers on, green jumper and blue jeans, no socks.

No keys.

Many men would have hared off down the street again, catch up with wife and get keys.

I would.

The husband instead sat down on the doorstep and began to do what looked very much to me like mulling or thinking. He heel-toed his slippers off, and sat there barefoot.

It was not a cold but not a warm morning.

The husband put his knuckle to his chin and his eyes began to move around the paving stones between me and him. Then he looked straight at me, looked at himself reflected in this strange-ugly car's windows. Then he looked at the ground again. He seemed very philosophical about the whole incident. The son's school must be very close. Agatha must be coming back soon.

I thought about getting out of the car, and the conversation that might follow: 'Hello, mate—here's your wooden spoon back—sorry—and by the way, I was the one fucked your missus. All right? Take it easy.'

That might be interesting.

I look at the man I might have killed with the virus I might have given him.

He looks content.

It's too much of a picture to be real: me in the car, with my losses; him, content on his doorstep.

I look at a man I might have killed.

It's too fucking perfect, isn't it? If only he'd said *fuck* before sitting down, like I would've done.

I realize this is a bit serial killer.

I have done bad things, but not enough of them to make it truly satisfying.

I look at him, gangly, innocent, and could stop writing now. It would be an end.

Agatha returns.

I think, in perfection, she would have sat beside him—they would have looked at each other in the mirrored side windows behind which, me and my envy.

She comes back; there's hardly a reaction from her. Just waits for him to stand up, then hands him the keys from—I didn't see—her pocket.

The door is opened, they go in, the door is closed.

I drive to Beachy Head and do not throw the spoon off.

Is Agatha about to cook something and find her favourite wooden spoon is missing?

(Blame the boy.)

I could dress it up as a Welsh widow before I post it back through their letterbox—I could take it to Wales.

On Beachy Head, I decided to post it back through their letterbox at two in the morning.

I give in, in the car park near Beachy Head, and kiss the damp spoon and begin to cry.

The thought of the boy's trainers with their lights is what allows me to cry.

'Oh fuck,' I say, 'what have I done? What the fuck have I done?'

I drive back—this is going too fast—what's stealing a spoon to making a fucking orphan?

I park outside, knock on the door, bottle it, run off and hide up another garden path, sneak back to the car, wait in the car, wait until 2 a.m., put the spoon through the letterbox, drive home, write this.

I have guilt guilt and the worst heartburn of my life, and I can't tell them apart.

I knock on the door. Agatha answers. 'Hello,' I say, 'please don't tell your husband I stole your spoon.'

I hand it back to her.

'I came to spy on you.'

Paddy comes out of the kitchen, holding a cup of coffee.

'Are you okay?' I ask. 'Did you get tested? I need to know.'

(This is a bad scene. I can't use this.)

'Did he get tested?' I ask.

Agatha did get tested.

She's negative.

But she needs to be tested again, in a month's time.

Then she will know for certain.

I cried—I did cry.

Paddy invited me in, even though he saw the spoon.

No, I didn't want to come in.

We stood in the doorway, them inside, me on the step.

I let it out, all of it.

I kept saying sorry for the spoon, as if that mattered.

I kept saying, 'Your son is so beautiful.'

Self-portrait with Tennent's Super

The cheekbones.

Welcome home, Yaminah!

With sisters.

A nice man — Yahya.

A nice wedding

My baby

Some joy.

Worse and Worse

Family photograph

John turned his back on the bathroom mirror, hiked up his plain white T-shirt and twisted round for another look.

The spot was more than ready to be squeezed, it ached to be squeezed, but as he was currently unusually dismayingly single, he had no one to squeeze it for him—and he couldn't reach, himself.

Or he *could* reach it, and could probably have a good go at picking it. That wouldn't do, however. Not for John; not for the spot.

The spot needed a particular approach—two firm forefingers on either side, an intense, focused pressure. Merely to nailsquirt it sideways himself would be a travesty.

In his relationships, intimacy had always quickly developed to a point where the girl or woman noticed the spot—it was prominent enough that John never had to prompt. They had all of them soon and gladly helped relieve the circle of infuriating pressure—and, thereafter, had repeated this mercy at intervals of roughly six months (if they'd stuck around that long). In winter, the spot would go after an extremely hot bath; in summer, after a spell of humid weather—or halfway through the beach holiday. It was something that, as a couple, he and she, whoever she was, would come to look forward to. Because, when John's spot went, the results were extraordinary: a column of puss half an inch long would burst out of a hole the size of the ball on a ballpoint pen. The girlfriend would scoop it up on her nail, and bring it round to where John—saying 'Come on, come on'—could make his inspection. The top part, the brown carrot, would look dried out where it had been on the surface; beneath that, the stuff gradually became lighter in hue and more egg-custard-like in texture, almost lacy with expansion; the final bit would be watery squelch and the start of bleeding.

Vanessa (May 1988–January 1993, June 1993–November 1994) had called it 'the buboe', in reference to the Black Death. Sally (June

1995–December 1995) referred to it with awe as 'Spot of Spots'. Zanny (September 1995–March 2003) nicknamed it 'Old Faithful', after the geyser they saw together in Yellowstone. Others had followed: unimaginative Hermione (summer of 2002) 'Versuvius'; cosy Rosie (New Year 2002–June 2006) 'crème brulée'; Yaminah-the-autobiographical-cartoonist-from-Tehran (February 2003–June 2006, June 2007–February 2008) 'Splurge'. And of course Ophélia (April 2004–February 2008: married June 2006; divorced February 2008), who had spoken of it only as 'my sacred duty'.

On one occasion, a one-night-stand girl (Nikki-from-publicity, 18–19 March, 2008) had popped it ('this') without even asking— leaving him the anxiety that wife-Ophélia would suddenly take it upon herself to examine his back, and find the spot severely reduced, and discover this latest unfaithfulness. To make things worse, Nikki had wiped the puss on the sheets before displaying it to him.

The last one, Agatha, hadn't noticed it; he hadn't taken off his top. But Agatha was not a possibility. She had stated, on their last night at the farm, that she never wanted to see or hear from him again. John had been hurt by this, but even more hurt by her adding that she was never going to read any of his books.

John pulled down his T-shirt, went back to his desk and tried to write, but couldn't. He was now hyperaware of the spot. He was aware of nothing beyond the spot. He felt as if he had an RAF roundel upon his back, like a Mod's parka. The area round the bullseye, red, was warmer, harder and ached as if someone had prodded him there with an angry forefinger; the next circle, white, tingled with the contrast between it and red; the surrounding blue circle felt no different to normal— making John wish all his back could feel that way.

It was September 21st, and the summer had been hot. John knew that the spot would take little more than a feminine touch on either side to yield up its load. But he wanted it done properly.

He left his computer and went down to the street, for coffee and a think.

Doppio espresso, and he could always try to pick up the barista— with whom he had been on-off flirting since July. She—Gadar—was short, Armenian, with dark hairs growing across her forearms. Once, this detail would have repulsed John, but since forty he had found himself able to get turned on by just about anything. He even, from time to time, experimented with thoughts of the ugliest women he came across. What, for instance, if I put her—sixteen stone—in a pig mask and insisted on fucking her from behind? Or her—warty—would she be so grateful that she'd do absolutely anything, however depraved?

As he sat on one of the window-facing stools, John thought about visiting a Turkish masseur. They, he believed, as part of the service, sometimes cleared out blocked pores—efficiently, with dirt-free nails, perhaps without even mentioning it. But that would have been like going to a prostitute for sex. John thought about going to a prostitute not-for-sex, just to empty the spot. No. Wrong. Although he was sure he wanted a woman to do the honours, for the thing to be right it had to be a woman he knew, a woman who knew what it meant, a woman to take pleasure. That left only the Armenian, his little black book and his exes.

John envisaged the scenario: date, coffee, sex, post-sex chat (keep them sweet) and oh, before you go to sleep, would you just mind having a go at . . .

These days, he wasn't sure he would even get to coffee.

Pretending to be fetching some sugar, John returned to the counter and checked the Armenian's fingernails—bitten all the way back.

'Have a nice day,' she said, assuming he was leaving.

'And you,' he replied, though he knew her shift wouldn't end for another six hours.

His feet took him outside.

Back in his flat, John went through his little black book, which was little, black and had the words LITTLE BLACK BOOK embossed on the cover.

It didn't take him long to realize that a trawl down a single page was pretty much like remembering the fates of Henry VIII's wives—if, for *divorced* you meant *divorced and therefore mental*, and for *beheaded* you meant *lost her head and therefore mental*, and for *died* you meant just that.

John dialled Rosie, who seemed the least mental and the likeliest to agree—but he hung up before it started ringing. He'd been married once, to Ophélia, and that meant something. And seeing how he wanted the squeezing to mean something, Ophélia was the only option. Rosie might *do* it, and she might pretend to understand, she might even try to understand, but Ophélia had been the most enthusiastic of his collaborators. It was among the reasons he'd married her—though it was only now that he realized this.

Sometimes, she had speculated on the nature of the spot.

'I did ask the doctor to take a look at it,' he'd said.

'And what did he say?'

'He said it was just a very deep pore.'

'So, it can't be treated and it's not going to go away?'

'No.'

'Most excellent,' she said.

Ophélia was from Lisbon, via Greece. Her father sold tin cans to companies who dealt with fruit and fish. On retirement, he had moved to Tel Aviv—leaving Ophélia's mother in an Athens graveyard. This last had happened two months before John met Ophélia, at a reading. She had approached him, at the end, to get a book signed—already charmed. He had noticed her from the stage; she was exactly his type: Mediterranean, Semitic, stacked. He even liked the two moles on the bottom of her chin—where they couldn't exactly be called beauty spots. When she stood up, he saw she was taller than him. But that didn't put him off. For the first five years, he let himself think he wasn't intimidated by it.

Their most memorable squeeze had been midway through a stay at a friend's villa in Tuscany. There was a terraced swimming pool with a low wall looking out across a valley towards a rail track and a dual carriageway. They had tried the day before, expecting eruption, and nothing had come. Now, with no one else around, and him just out of the water, Ophélia had insisted on another go. Perhaps it was because he was so relaxed—perhaps the previous attempt had loosened things up: the spot brought forth more than ever before; it made John salivate to remember—that distinct combination of pukiness and yearning. As soon as it was done, he wished it would refill so she could do it again. The sun went down behind the hills opposite, golden. In many ways, it was a perfect moment—one of the true high points of their marriage. Then he remembered, it must have been before that.

Although they were quite friendly, for a couple who'd been divorced in court, John hadn't spoken to Ophélia since March, and hadn't had contact since receiving a birthday card in August. He knew her number; she had kept the house—because of his infidelities and minor fame, the divorce had worked out like that.

Instead of dialling, he went down again to the cafe—but the Armenian wasn't there, and when he asked after her, he found out that her boyfriend (word emphasized by the male Italian barista) had broken his hand so she'd had to leave early.

Back in the flat once more: 'Ophélia, hello. It's John.' She didn't ask straight out what it was he wanted; he knew she knew there was something. 'Can we meet?'

'You never want to meet.'

'Well, I want to meet now. There's something I need to explain. Don't worry, I'm not still in love with you or anything.'

'And you're not dying of cancer.'

'And I don't need to move back in. No, I'm perfectly healthy.'

'Touch wood,' she said. 'Okay. I can do—' The short walk to the calender beside the fridge. '—Saturday.'

'How about tomorrow?'

'It's urgent, then.'

'Sort of.'

She went away and came back.

'If you meet me outside the dentist at three, I can see you for three quarters of an hour.'

'Your usual dentist?'

'You know, the dentist with the pickle.' It was a private reference, which after a moment he got.

John was there early. Not early enough to see her go in but almost. He leant back against a shop window and thought of the best way to introduce the subject. Humorous, probably: 'Ophélia, I would like to remind you of something important . . .'

'Yes, John?'

'Your sacred duty . . .'

That, she would get. She would also think him unusually odd, and perhaps a little creepy.

So, when she came out, he first of all greeted her neutrally—then said, 'Fuck, you're pregnant.' Ophélia was forty-one. They had been trying for a baby for the last three years, minus six pre-divorce months, of their marriage. 'You're—Congratulations.'

They were kissing on the second cheek when she said, 'I'm having triplets.' He pulled back. 'IVF—what can I say? Sometimes it works *just* a little too well.'

John gave her a triplets look, then laughed. 'Oh, Spencer, Spencer, you poor bastard.'

Spencer was her second husband—a lawyer specializing in corporate-debt restructing, black.

'Try not to be so smug,' said Ophélia. 'We're very happy.'

They had started to walk, though John couldn't go as fast as his excitement wanted him to. Ophélia was moving with a gait midway between a glide and a waddle.

'Can I . . .?' asked John, and reached across—round—to take her bag. Ophélia gave it up without comment.

'In here,' she said, almost immediately. It was an Italian restaurant. John had anticipated going to a sushi place further along the same road, but that wasn't happening.

'Filling?' he asked, after they were seated, then pointed at his teeth to clarify.

'Just a check-up. I don't need anything done, they said. You get it all free when you're like I am.'

There were only two other tables occupied, both by male-female couples. Perhaps they would think he and Ophélia were a couple, too. But perhaps they weren't couples.

'Congratulations, again.'

'You've already fucked it up with the delight, John. I know you can't wait to tell your mates of your narrow escape.'

The waiter cruised by their table but her last words sent him away again.

'No,' she said, louder, 'I'd like spaghetti bolognese and some garlic bread to start.'

The waiter returned.

'Same for me,' said John. 'Without the bread. We can share.'

'No, we can't.'

'Okay, bread for me, too. And a glass of house red.'

'Bastard.'

'Right,' said John, remembering Ophélia's use of this word during the later stages of their divorce. Sometimes she'd phoned him up to say nothing more. 'Just still water. Tap water. A jug. Please.'

The waiter walked off towards the till. John was about to speak when he heard the waiter yell into the kitchen, 'Champagne, table six.' John wasn't sure if Ophélia had caught this, too. But when he looked at her, she sniggered.

'I like it here,' she said.

They had chosen a booth along the left hand wall. He was facing towards the entrance, she could see the till and bar.

'Do you know what you're having, yet?' asked John.

'I'm having spaghetti bolognese and garlic bread,' said Ophélia, deadpan in her old lovely way. 'I'm having three girls, if they all survive. It's nothing unusual. Won't even make the local paper, unless it's on Christmas day—that's our due date.'

John counted forwards: Ophélia was big already, by Christmas . . . And now he remembered the crap-months of trying to conceive. He had a particularly clear image of having, immediately after sex, been required to take Ophélia's legs, one on each shoulder, and hoist her pelvis in the air—supposedly to help the sperm swim more rapidly towards her egg. He felt the weight on his back; he saw again her wet, engorged cuntlips, wattle-like flaps.

'Really,' he said, emotional, 'that's great. You wanted—'

'I wanted two. Not twins. Though, given the time restraints, I'd have settled for twins. I have four months left of life before . . .' Her hands flew apart, mimicking a large explosion leaving nothing behind—nothing but her enlarged breasts in a bra several sizes up from her usual.

'Well, you look well,' said John.

'They are fucking enormous, aren't they? Ridiculous.'

'I wasn't looking.'

'You're male, straight, you can't help it.'

'But I divorced those breasts.'

'These breasts divorced you—remember?'

It was true—he tipped his head to the other side.

'Are you going back to work afterwards?'

'Who knows? We're planning on having a live-in nanny. I may go psycho-mum—not let anyone near.'

'Why didn't you tell me before?'

This was the first time Ophélia had had to think.

'At first, superstition. Then, later, more superstition.'

'But you agreed to meet.'

'Because *you* called *me*—and I didn't tell you, you just noticed.'

'Of course I noticed.'

'But I didn't tell you.'

John was remembering more and more: unexplained detours while Ophélia drove; days she refused to eat anything before the sun went down; four copies of *Wuthering Heights* in the bookshelf and six in the airing cupboard. 'So, why?' Ophélia asked, but John was still thinking of their marriage. It had just for a moment resolved into one distinct entity, but then had fragmented into the usual incommensurables. 'Why are we here?'

'Your sacred duty,' said John, from his confusion. 'Sorry—I mean, I'd like to ask if you—'

Ophélia assessed him.

'No current girlfriend, then?'

John had once told her about the spot's previous nicknames. They had had an unfortunate period (August–September 2004) of total honesty.

'No.'

'What happened to Samantha?'

'She binned me.'

'Need I ask . . .?'

'You needn't.'

'You're never going to learn, are you?'

'Some women would accept—'

'Exactly. You're never going to learn.'

'Will you do it?' John asked.

'Let me have a look.'

'Not here.'

'Why not? You don't know any of these people.'

'If you see it, you'll probably want to do it straight away.'

John was aware those people might overhear.

'Promise. I won't.'

He looked around, then leant towards her. She leant her cleavage towards him.

'Meet me at the loos,' he said.

'But I went at the dentist's.'

'Come on.'

One minute later, he was in the Ladies; Ophélia had refused to enter the Gents.

'Wow,' she said.

'Is it bad?' he asked.

'The worst,' she said. 'It's sort of poking out.'

She ran the pad of her finger across it; John heard himself groan. 'No. Don't.'

'Why not? It's ready.'

'Someone might interrupt. I want to look at it.'

'The inspection?' She remembered.

'It needs time. Meet me somewhere.' He tried to pull down his jumper. Ophélia still held it bunched up round his neck.

'Funny how it hasn't gone away,' she said.

'I feel sick with it,' said John.

'You must be desperate,' said Ophélia. 'To have to ask me.'

He did not reply, and after a second she must have realized there was a degree of banter he could no longer share.

'I will,' she said. 'I'll do it. Go back. I need to pee.'

The waiter saw John come out of the Ladies, but the look he gave John suggested he'd also seen him go in.

Ophélia returned. They ate without mentioning the spot.

Outside, afterwards, Ophélia said, 'I'm not coming to your flat.'

John heard superstition.

'All right,' he said, 'I'll get a hotel room.'

'Fine,' Ophélia said, faster than he expected. 'It'll have to be the middle of the day. We need to look as suspicious as possible.'

'Saturday?'

'Okay. Text me the details. I can be away for a couple of hours, and I'll need to return with serious shopping. I don't go out these days unless I've got a good reason.'

'I'm not paying you.'

'No, but I'd still like a present.'

He bought her the most expensive skin products he could find, and waited in a scalding bath in room 37 of a chain hotel.

'I'll be Mr Jones,' he had texted.

'Much more original than Mr Smith,' she had texted back.

Ophélia was late enough to make him think she wouldn't come.

When she knocked on the door, he shouted, 'It's open.'

Ophélia came into the bathroom, dumped her bag and made straight for the toilet. She didn't say anything until she'd finished peeing. 'Not taking any chances, then,' she said.

'It's ready,' he said. 'I'll get out.'

He'd put a towel where he could reach it, on the floor, but she picked it up and handed it to him. He purposely hadn't covered his penis, when she walked in—and he knew she had looked.

'I'll wait in the bedroom,' Ophélia said, and it was these words that made John start to go hard.

She closed the door behind her, as if a naked ex-husband standing up were different to a naked ex-husband lying down.

He got out, appalled by his sudden erection, pulled the plug and called, 'I'll just be a minute.'

Ophélia hadn't flushed. He sat down on the warm seat, above the fragrant water, and wished he'd wanked before she got there. But she'd have smelt that.

Two minutes later, she said, 'Stagefright?'

His clothes were on one of the twin beds. She would be sitting with them. The bath had been a stupid idea, but he couldn't resist. He didn't want to have to do this again.

John stood up, still semi-hard, and wrapped the towel tightly around his waist.

As soon as he was out of the bathroom, Ophélia, eyes at cock-height, said, 'Oh, hello you.'

'I'm sorry,' he said. 'It happened. Nothing to do with me.'

'Lie on your front,' Ophélia said. 'Here.' She was on the clothes-empty bed.

The word *here* and the pat-pat which followed were not without sexual content—or so John sensed.

'I haven't let Spencer near me since the test,' said Ophélia. 'It's another thing.'

John understood—a thing like not visiting him at his flat, like *Wuthering Heights*.

'Oooh,' said Ophélia. 'It's so—'

John was on his front, so he knew she could only mean the spot. This was what he'd wanted. Ophélia *knew*. She wasn't Rosie or a prostitute or rushing. There was a year and a half of specialness, all built up. Her speech would make the moment. He felt her hands resting on his shoulderblades. 'It never looked like this.'

'We never let it get this bad,' said John.

'Why didn't you call me before?'

'I thought I'd meet someone.'

'Are you ready?'

'A little longer.'

She left her hands where they were.

John's cock was doing its best to flip him over onto his side. He closed his eyes and breathed in, not meaning to smell Ophélia as purely as he did. Her scent was different—fuller, heavier.

'Don't perve out,' she said.

John laughed.

'I'm ready,' he said. 'Try to do it all in one go. I don't want it broken.'

Ophélia slapped the back of his leg. 'Don't tell me anything,' she said. 'This is my sacred duty, remember.'

For a moment, he thought she was about to start. But then he felt her weight on the mattress beside him—she was climbing onto his back. The old way. The best angle.

When she came to rest, her pelvis was on his thighs. He wasn't sure he could take her weight without asking her to move—which would be insulting.

'Now,' she said, shifting forwards until she was bearable. 'Come on.'

Her fingers touched his skin to left and right of the yearning point. Pressure was applied, force flowing straight down her forearms. 'Oh yes,' she said. 'Yes, here it comes.' She pushed into him for what seemed like a very long time. Already his back felt lightened. 'Oh my God. Oh, fucking hell.'

'Let me see,' he said. 'Is it out?'

'What if I didn't let you look?'

'You bitch. Come on.'

A heavy silence above and behind him.

'Don't ever call me a bitch.'

He went still. Her resettled weight forced him into the springs.

'I'm sorry. You have all the power now. Please, can I see?'

He twisted his head to the right, and her thumbnail came into unfocussed vision—a white line running down it.

'Further away,' he said. 'My eyes—'

She moved it to focal distance and a little beyond.

Tuscany was outdone.

John's mouth filled with spit. 'Thank you,' he said, his cheek half-buried in the pillow. 'Just hold still—where I can see it.'

He closed his eyes. He was feeling her weight, their weight.

'Forgive me, Father, for I have sinned. And I'm not a Catholic. I'm sorry about that. But I still call you *Father*, don't I?'

'Whatever you find yourself most comfortable with.'

His voice, thrillingly for May, was Irish profound. She had heard it during Mass but it sounded even richer up-close. Just perfect, for what she wanted.

Also, the Priest had looked right—although she'd sat throughout at the very back. He was famine-gaunt and had lush grey hair cut very short.

'Father—yes, that feels okay—Father, I'd like to do confession. Am I allowed to? I go to a completely different kind of a church, and I haven't been going very long. I'm pretty sure you would disapprove.'

'Oh, you'd be surprised. That's a Christian Church? It's Jesus Christ they worship there, is it?'

'Very much so.'

He made tasting sounds of contentment—as if he were a dog settling down on a sofa.

'And what is it, then, that you wish to confess?'

May found she was weeping. The moment, which it had taken all her bravery to contrive, was too much.

The Priest couldn't not hear.

'Take *all* the time you require,' he said.

May used breathing techniques learnt for delivering Hope. She wasn't worried about keeping others waiting—she had waited until everyone else had confessed, then gone in herself.

'What it is is, I've lost my faith,' she said. 'Or, I've lost my faith in the thing I thought was my faith—I don't think it was ever real, what I felt. I think someone caught me at a moment of weakness, and did exactly what they wanted with me. They preyed on me.'

'That sounds very distressing. Do you feel able to tell me about it?'

May sobbed again, and thought of the thousands of women who had cried as she was crying, sitting where she was sitting.

'Is it a sin to lose your faith?'

The Priest's answer didn't come immediately, and when it did it felt to May like some inner adjustment had been made. This silly woman here needed the correct response; much depended upon it—so the Priest must feel.

'If you lose your faith, you are more likely *to* sin,' he said. 'But it's an illusion, *always*, that faith has vanished completely. Not when you've made that initial acquaintance with God. In my experience, limited though it may be, He is there whenever He is needed, and through many persons. He doesn't just appear and then disappear from people's lives. His is the most constant presence.'

'This church I go to is very full-on. They expect miracles every week.'

'Ah,' said the Priest. He was, she thought, pretending to be beginning to understand.

'I don't feel what they feel. I feel—mainly I feel embarrassed. It's much easier for me to believe in God cosily tucked up in here rather than there, singing rubbish pop songs that aren't proper hymns.'

The Priest allowed himself what sounded like a rivalrous chuckle.

'But I sense the pop songs aren't at the root of the problem . . .'

'I believe enough to be worried,' said May. 'I believe enough to believe that losing my faith is very dangerous. One of the big things that got me, at first, about the whole Christianity lark was—it was the fact of hell. I wanted a hell to exist so that I could be sure my husband would go there. I was certain that *I* wouldn't be going there because *I've* never done anything nearly as bad as him.'

'Husbands are always the worst sinners, aren't they?' May wasn't strictly sure the Priest should be saying this. And perhaps he felt the same way, too, because he followed this by adding, 'From the point of view of the wives, anyway. And the so-called ex-wives.'

'I suppose you want to know what he did.'

'Not if you don't want to tell me. He isn't here—you are. It's you that I'm talking to about.'

'He completely cocked up our family, that's what he did. He slept with someone else. I expect you get this all the time. I expect you don't hear much else.'

The Priest let quiet waiting be an answer. Then, when she didn't say anything, he said, 'And this hurt you very deeply, didn't it?'

'Of course it fucking did,' said May, forgetting.

The Priest laughed.

'I'm sorry,' he said. 'I am a little weary. The usual sayings won't do, I can tell. You're very intelligent. Far more intelligent than I am. That may be part of your problem. Would you like to go for a coffee? As you're not Catholic, this doesn't have to be quite so formal.'

May looked around her. The confessional was like a Victorian attempt at a Photo-Me booth: the velvet curtain, leaving her lower half uncovered. Instead of a camera lens, an ugly-patterned wooden grille. When she tried to see through it, she could make out fleshtones but no features.

'No,' she said. 'I want to be hidden. That's why I came here. I can talk to anyone like that, with coffee. I don't want to be able to see you while I speak. And I certainly don't want anyone to eavesdrop. I need to try this out. See if it's for me.'

The Priest could not prevent his sigh from being audible. He really *had* wanted that coffee. May felt bad for not allowing him to end his day.

'I could go and get you a cappuccino,' she said. 'Bring one back, and we could keep going. There's a place just round the corner.'

'No,' he said.

'I didn't mean to swear. I know I shouldn't.'

'Your lack of respect is refreshing.'

'But will send me to hell.'

'I hear a lot of unexpected language here. That's what this contraption's for, partly. You say you are worried most of all about your loss of faith.'

'I'm worried I can't believe any more because I've been given the wrong Jesus. I don't want a God who's quite so chummy. I never fancied friendly boys, only standoffish types—the ones who seemed destined never to acknowledge that I existed. By making them fancy me, I made them admit that I was there. It was just like that with Henry.'

'Jesus isn't a boyfriend,' said the Priest.

'But I had *such* a crush on him, and now it's gone. That's what I'm saying—now I want something properly grown-up, but I don't believe in it any more.'

'If you wish to begin attending this church, you would be more than welcome. Our relationship with Jesus, as you would expect, isn't quite so presumptuous. But that's not me trying to say their Jesus is inferior—He takes all forms, when necessary. In this modern world, it's important to come at people in a way they understand.'

'But not to change completely,' said May. 'You haven't sold out. You're nasty when you need to be, if it means you're still consistent. You believe gays go to hell.'

'That isn't—'

'Okay, you believe buggery is a sin.'

'Sodomy, yes, is a sinful activity,' said the Priest. 'But those who are contrite are not condemned.'

'Contrite on a regular basis.'

'We are in danger of straying from the subject.'

'Not really, you know, but I'll let you get away with that. My friend Julie came round for a quiet evening, dinner, and by the end of it . . .'

May flashed on Julie—how appalled she would be by this whole thing: the Priest, the mock-confession. There were so many things about Julie she couldn't say here. Like how important it was that Julie had managed to keep her faith without losing her fashion sense—this loss was something May had always been massively anxious about, should she be converted herself. And for a few weeks, it had seemed that, with Julie as her model, she could become Christian without accepting naff knitwear into her life. Julie dressed well, better than almost all May's friends, better than May herself, maybe, and without even a hint of prudishness or overpracticality. May had even seen her fancy-dressed in fishnet stockings and a basque. Julie did not come down on stray comments with disapproval. She could joke, smoke, bitch. She even blasphemed, saying *Oh God* without seeming to realize it. But, along with this, May had always known—ever since university—that Julie attended church and that, for her, attending church meant much more than just attending church.

'What happened?' asked the Priest. 'Tell me, from start to finish, as you experienced it.'

May remembered the opening, and how it had happened. While they ate, she had spoken about Henry non-stop for more than an hour. 'I feel so destroyed,' she had ended up saying, not for the first time.

'May,' Julie had said, taking her hand across the dinner table. 'You don't have to do this, it may seem a little strange, but I would really like you to try saying a short prayer with me—just to see how it feels. This may not feel like the right place to you. You probably associate Jesus with going to church and being bored by sermons. But if you'll only just let yourself feel Him, He's a real living presence anywhere you want Him to be. I feel Jesus very strongly at this moment. I know He loves you and wants to come into your life. He realizes why you've been resisting Him. It doesn't matter at all.'

May looked at the collars of Julie's shirt—black silk embroidered with two tiny white chrysanthemums.

'I'm not sure,' May remembered saying.

Julie spoke on, in a hypnotherapy voice. Some of her phrases seemed to have come directly from instructional DVDs, but enough of what she said was recognizable as something May's intelligent friend would say.

There were plenty of things Julie wasn't saying, however, and it was partly these which held May back. Around the corner, in about half an hour, she could sense tears and hugs and joy and love. Although it would be nice, she was glad she wasn't in it just yet. She was embarrassed by the anticipation of her moment of opening just as, she knew, she would be embarrassed whenever she remembered it—unless all the promises held true, and she really *was* totally changed. But how embarrassing that would be for everyone else.

Speaking to the Priest, May tried to explain this without seeming disrespectful of anyone involved—Julie, the Priest himself, Jesus, God.

'And you prayed with her? Wasn't that a good thing?' the Priest asked.

'It felt like it, at the time.'

From the kitchen they had moved into the living room and gone down on their knees. An hour later, it had happened.

'You see,' Julie said, her face nothing but smile. 'He was there all along—guiding you, loving you. Oh, I'm so happy for you. Whatever happens now, you'll be able to remember this. I hope it will give you strength. Once you've felt the power of Jesus' love, it's impossible to resist. Oh, thank you, Jesus—thank you, Lord.'

Julie had several times switched from addressing her to addressing God, sometimes within the same sentence—because, May now realized, they really were one and the same thing. It didn't matter who you were speaking to, you were always at the same time speaking to God. This was terrifying but also delicious. Prayer wasn't just prayer, prayer was everything. You could give thanks in every moment you existed.

'It sounds to me like a genuine encounter,' said the Priest, his voice becoming for one little instant American.

'Even then, even in the middle of it, I doubted,' said May.

She remembered one of the pauses between prayer. They had started and stopped any number of times, after the breakthrough. She had had questions.

'Were you waiting for me?' May asked. 'Is that why you were always my friend—you wanted me for a Christian?'

'No, of course not,' said Julie. 'How can you say that? I'm your friend because we're friends—not for any ulterior motive.'

'But you thought there was a chance you might get me. I mean, I can see how it is—everyone at your church will give you maximum respect if you bring me in.'

'I thought that you were unhappy,' Julie said. 'And because Jesus brings me such great comfort, I knew He would be able to help you, too—if you would only let Him. It's Jesus, not me, that's making you feel all that you're feeling. I don't have any power at all, individually, no one does, not even the greatest leader—it all comes through Him.'

'I don't blame you,' May said. 'Not now you've done it. I can see why I'd want to do it, too. But wasn't I your number one target as soon as Henry did what he did? You go to courses and away on weekends. They tell you to look out for a moment of weakness, don't they?'

'I would prefer to see it as a moment of need or, even better, a moment of openness.'

'But I feel weak rather than open,' said May.

'But isn't that exactly how being open feels? It's not pleasant—something is about to change, and possibly radically. *Everything* is about to change.'

'You were glad,' said May.

'If I can bring a soul to Christ,' said Julie, 'of course I rejoice.'

'You were glad I was miserable.'

'I'm a Christian, May. I believe people need Christ, even people who don't want Him and refuse to be open to Him.'

'There are so many people.'

'Christ's love is the biggest secret in the world, even though we spend all our time trying to tell people about it.'

The Priest behind the grille was bored; May could sense his impatience.

'I haven't felt anything like that since,' she said.

'And perhaps you never will,' said the Priest. 'There's only one first time for anything. But that doesn't mean that, as time passes, you won't experience a deeper communion.'

After midnight, May had excused herself and gone upstairs to see Hope and Felix. They looked to her as beautiful as the first time she had got them home from hospital—not the moment they were born; then, in the delivery room, they'd looked like blotchy, scum-coated aliens. Unnecessarily, she bent over their beds and stroked the hair off their faces. Hope flinched; Felix turned over on his other side. She was glad she had given them such positive names. She had made them with God. Henry had been involved but not fifty per cent. God was their real father, just as He was hers.

May wanted to be alone with her glow—to feel the feeling of her feelings. She would be grateful, perhaps really *eternally*, to Julie, for what she had brought her, but right this moment she wanted her to leave. There were a number of things she needed to say to God privately, now that she was sure He really did exist.

When she went downstairs, Julie was standing in the hall, coat on. 'If you want me to stay,' Julie said, 'then I will. But I thought you might want some time, just to pray by yourself. I'll come round tomorrow morning.' She looked at her watch. 'Later this morning. You look wonderful. So radiant.'

'Yes,' said the Priest, when May finished speaking. 'There is good reason for faith—you've seen that. The nearness you felt, in prayer, was real.'

'It wasn't,' said May. 'I just wanted some way of getting back at Henry. I've gone through lots of different phases, since he moved out. This was just one of them. It felt different but it wasn't. I'm a total mess.'

She thought for a moment of Bloodkill. Once she'd discovered he was a schoolboy, she'd been unable to keep playing with him. But before she could transfer her character to another realm, Bloodkill had deleted himself. This had made her cry for half an hour, she didn't quite know why. The Internet seemed to be creating new forms of grief.

'If you were Catholic,' said the Priest, 'I would give you penance. You don't know the Hail Mary, I expect?'

'No,' said May.

'But you know the Lord's Prayer,' the Priest said.

'I do.'

'In fact,' he said, 'on consideration, I don't think there's anything you need do penance for. Not from what you've related. We all have times of doubt. It's not easy to maintain that high level—'

'Do you?' May asked. 'Do you ever have days when you don't believe at all—when you just go through the motions, dead?'

'My faith is challenged. But ultimately I believe those challenges are sent by God, and that He assists me in meeting them.'

May said, 'You didn't answer my question.'

'I tried,' said the Priest.

'If you can't admit that sometimes you think it's all a load of rubbish then I can't believe in you.'

'Whether you believe in me personally is quite beside the point.'

'Tell me you sometimes don't believe in God and I'll go away and try to believe in Him.'

She could hear the Priest's breathing, louder and raspier than before.

'I would prefer it if you would simply come back,' he said. 'I myself will not be here, but there will be someone—a very good man—who will be able to guide you.'

'I'm giving you one more chance,' said May, then waited.

'God exists,' said the Priest, finally. 'God truly does exist.'

'Thank you for your time,' said May, and pushed aside the curtain. 'Goodbye.'

The Priest arrived in Starbucks not five minutes after May. The place was busy, and she was still waiting at the service counter for her non-skinny latte. He joined the order queue, head bowed, and did not look up. He was checking his texts. It took May a small moment to realize that so long as she didn't speak, he would never know he already knew her.

'Latte,' announced the barista.

May took it without saying thank you—something she would never normally have done.

A couple climbed down from two stools in the front window, and May was quick to take one of their places. She still had an hour before the nanny expected her back. From her bag, she pulled out a novel. There had been an exceptionally brutal double murder in Trömso. An alcoholic detective whose wife had just left him was under intense pressure from his commanding officer to get results, fast. His only lead was—

'Excuse me but would this seat be taken?'

May shook her head at the Priest, then made an inviting gesture with her hand—rather this than try to put on a funny accent.

'Thank you,' he said.

May opened her book as the Priest dialled a number.

'Yes, just finished now,' he said. 'The last of the last. Went on for a little while longer than expected.' He listened. 'No. No celebrating yet, Mother—not till they force it upon me. Aren't you—' May could hear the tin-tin of a replying voice, female. 'Yes, I expect that I shall miss it.' Tssk. 'No, not that. I'll be seeing you in a week. Thursday, mother. Thursday afternoon. I'll take a taxi. It's fine. I'll take a taxi. God bless you.'

He closed the phone, shucked the lid off his cup, began to sugar his tea.

'I'm sorry,' said May, before she realized she was about to speak.

The Priest looked at her—no recognition yet.

'If I'd've known I was your last one ever, I would've tried harder.'

'Ah,' he said, and nodded. 'No matter.'

'And now you'll always remember that you failed with me.'

'Actually, I have a very good bad memory,' he said. 'I would probably have forgotten entirely, had you not chosen to remind me of it.' Then, after a characteristic pause, 'Was it that bad?'

'I thought you did very well,' said May. 'I'm a difficult case. You probably don't get much feedback.'

'I get the best kind of feedback there is.'

May didn't know what the Priest meant, until—just a little camp—he lifted his eyes heavenward.

'Are you at mandatory retirement age?' May asked.

'If you'll excuse me,' the Priest said, shifting himself off the stool.

'I will try,' said May. 'With, you know. And not because of you.'

'Good,' said the Priest, pressing the lid back on his tea. 'God bless you, my child.'

Which, she realized, was all she'd wanted all along.

MAX & DYLAN

Max hears Mummy—Mummy shouted, *Where's the gun you usually take to school?*

Max knows that he isn't going to nursery today because today is at the weekend, and he was a very lucky boy because he is going for a fantastic superspecial playdate at Dylan's house, the first ever at Dylan's house, and Dylan was his friend at nursery, but there are two Dylans at nursery—the other was Dylan F and the other was Dylan P, that's funny, it's not, that's funny.

Max hears Daddy said, *Is it in his book bag?*

Max hears Mummy shouted from upstairs, *His book bag is where it always is—why don't you look in it?*

Max hears, *It's not there, I looked* and *It is, you just don't know how to look.*

Max sees Daddy went into the playroom and then came back with a lightsaber hidden behind his back but which Max secretly did see him picked up and he said, *Look, Max, forget the gun, why don't you take your lightsaber instead?* Max sees the lightsaber as it came out of Obi-Wan Kenobi's box in his hut on Tatooine. Max hears, *You can be Jedi Knights with Dylan.*

Luke Skywalker finds himself saying, *I want the gun*, although he grabs the lightsaber that Obi-Wan was holding out towards him even though it isn't a gun.

Max hears Mummy shouted, *Can you remember where you put it?*

Max, can you remember where you put it? said Daddy, then walked away.

Luke Skywalker can't remember the gun, and his mother is dead, and there is a Snow Monster in the hall whose arm needs to be cut off.

Max hears his Daddy from the clothes hooks near the kitchen shouted, *It's not in his book bag!*—Daddy who isn't Darth Vader or Anakin Skywalker either, but who sometimes was, when Luke asks.

Luke-as-Max says to Daddy, *You be Snow Monster. Make me upside down!*

Max-as-Luke hears Mummy coming downstairs with his spare clothes packed in his Thomas the Tank Engine wheelie-bag saying, *We haven't got time for that now, Sweetie.*

Luke whirls round and thrusts his lightsaber out towards this new threat.

Luke hears, *Don't do that, Max. You almost hit me.*

Luke says, *I'm Luke*, and imagines Mummy's arm falling to the snow after he cuts it off with his blue lightsaber that Obi-Wan Kenobi gives him because it was his father's, who was the best pilot in the galaxy, but later is Darth Vader because he was seduced by the Dark Side, and Luke doesn't want to think about the Emperor who had been Darth Sidious but was too scary now to think about.

Max-as-Luke says to Daddy, *Tell me a story where I'm Luke Skywalker.*

Max's hears Mummy said as she bent down to him, *Did you lend your gun to anyone yesterday?*

Max shouts to Daddy, *Tell me a story!*

Max hears Mummy asked Daddy, *Do you think he did? Have you seen it since then?*

Max rhythms, *Story! Story! Story!*

Max, Max hears Mummy said.

Max hears from Daddy, *He'll just have to go without it, if we can't find it.*

Max, put your Crocs on—the first time I ask, said Mummy. *Please.*

Max says, *I want to be Luke Skywalker in a story.*

Max hears Daddy promise, *When we get in the car.*

Luke insists, *The Millenium Falcon!*

Luke-as-Max hears, *When we get in the Millennium Falcon, I'll do you a story as soon as we get in the Millennium Falcon—and the sooner you put your Crocs on the sooner we'll get in the Millennium Falcon.*

Max's Crocs are blue and have two superhero button-charms poking through the holes on top—Batman and Spiderman. Max did get dressed earlier in clean-from-the-drawer stripey underpants, khaki shorts and a not-T-shirt Ben 10 top with Ben 10 holding out his arm with the watch-like Omnitrix on it. Max often likes to stop in the street, as he walks, to make sure Batman and Spiderman are the right way up, facing him.

Max hears Daddy's hands clapped and Daddy said, *Let's go*, and *Let's roll*. Max realizes as they move to the door that Mummy had opened wide that his Daddy means go and roll with Daddy only and not go with Daddy and Mummy together.

Max says, *No*, and throws the lightsaber at the wall.

Max, said Mummy, *if you do that you'll break it.*

Max hears from Daddy, *And take chunks out of the paintwork.*

Max hears Mummy said, *Like there aren't any chunks out already.*

Max knows that Daddy is saying, *If you do that again, I will take the lightsaber away from you. Do you understand?*

Max says, *Yes.*

Max is told, *Kiss Mummy.*

Max says to Mummy, *I don't want to play at the weekend. I want to stay here and play.*

Max can't hear what Mummy said into his ear as she is cuddling him kneeling down on the doorstep because his ears don't work because he is crying although it was good to cry sometimes and not just what babies and girls did, because it let out tension.

Max stands in front of Dylan's house as Dylan's Mummy opened the door and is different and Dylan is there but he isn't the other Dylan.

Max says, *He's the wrong one.*

Max hears wrong-Dylan say, *Hello, Max.*

Max hears wrong-Dylan's Mummy said, *Well done, Dyl.*

Max repeats, *He's the wrong one.*

Max knows he is about to transform into crying-Max but there is nothing he can do to stop crying-Max taking total control. Max's new body feels like a heaving animal-thing he needs to try to learn to ride while riding it while it heaves. Max's breathing only happens between sobs so sometimes his sobs are so intense it doesn't happen at all.

Max looks at wrong-Dylan and realizes how much he loves the other Dylan who isn't wrong-Dylan. Max sees this Dylan has dark hair but the other Dylan says he has five guns.

Max hears from Daddy, *I'm sorry about this.*

Max hears wrong-Dylan's Mummy said, *That's quite all right.*

Max, said Daddy, who is whispering and had pulled Max up close to the hedge, *this is the Dylan you wanted to see. I made sure. This is Dylan F, so this is where you're playing this afternoon.*

Max says, *This is Dylan pee, because Dylan P did no pee in his pants but Dylan F did a big pee in his pants so he turned into Dylan pee.*

Max is told, *No, this is Dylan F. Now, start to behave. I know you've had a bit of a surprise but you'll have a great time with Dylan.*

Max is brought back to the doorstep and his arm hurts at the top from Daddy's holding but Max still says, *No, I hate him. I want to stab his face off.*

Max, Max hears Daddy said, loud, *say sorry.*

Max says, *No.*

Max sees wrong-Dylan's Mummy was laughing.

Max's Daddy spoke close to Max and said, *Say sorry.*

Max says, *I want to stab his face off so his face falls on the floor*!

Max is spoken to by the wrong-Dylan's Mummy coming down from her tall and up-close to his face, *Max, why don't you come in? We've got some chocolate cake for teatime. And Dylan has been so looking forward to seeing you.*

Max senses that Dylan's Mummy thought she talked in a way boys like, but she really didn't.

Max stares at a blurry, pulsing wrong-Dylan who looks as if he is about to transform into crying-wrong-Dylan. Max knows he has the power to make this happen. Max also suspects he can make wrong-Dylan's Mummy into another creature, perhaps not crying-Mummy but easily angry-Mummy or sad-you-feel-that-Mummy. Max is curious of his power which he feels himself moving towards using and the movement begins to terrify him, because he knows what has happened when he's gone in this powerful direction before. Max doesn't want to feel the punished-feeling which comes after moving with the feeling of power-feeling.

Max says, *Is it nice chocolate cake?*

Max hears wrong-Dylan's Mummy said, *Well, I certainly hope it is— I made it myself.*

Max says, *I want to see it* and hears Daddy said, *Max you really are—*

Max hears wrong-Dylan's Mummy said, *Wait here,* and then she was going back into the house which smells of funny but doesn't smell of pee and it's Dylan pee's house so it should.

Max sees the cake coming down the hall with Smarties on it which he can't count because he can't count but which he sees there are a lot of, which is good.

Max says, when the cake is held under his nose, *Can I taste it?*

Max hears Daddy said, *You are unbelievable. My Dad would have given you a clip round the ear by now.*

Max says to wrong-Dylan, *Do you have a bedroom?*

Max sees wrong-Dylan nodding.

Max goes into the smelling house, and behind him he hears wrong-Dylan's Mummy said, *They're really just little savages, aren't they?* and Daddy said, *I would say he's not normally like this, if I thought you'd believe me,* but then Max is too up-the-stairs to hear.

Max walks into wrong-Dylan's bedroom and wants it immediately because of the posters which are so many of them and superhero that they make wrong-Dylan transform into Dylan-I-want-to-play-with or even Dylan-maybe-he-won't-want-to-play-with-me-now.

Max goes up to the toy drawers which are see-through-ghosty-plastic of shapes behind and pulls one out to find wooden rail tracks which were exciting a year before.

Max says, *We have a box for animals and monsters and some people too.*

Max watches as Dylan pulls out another drawer in which the red Tiger Ranger lay on top of Boba Fett and also a small Blue Power Ranger from Jungle Fury.

Max grabs Boba Fett in case Dylan wants it, then Max says, *Your bedroom is the same size as mine,* and Dylan says, *I can come to your bedroom next time and borrow some toys. Do you have a metal bed? I have a wooden bed* and Max tells Dylan all about his new cover with dinosaurs on it, *But I wanted Ben 10 and they got me the wrong one,* and then Max feeling the heat that comes when he says lies says, *My daddy buys me everything I want but sometimes he gets it wrong and I have to shout.*

Max hears Dylan saying, *Your dad has a very hairy face.*

Max says, *It's a poo-poo face,* and this cooks up another kind of heat inside him, but he's moving too fast to stop and examine the scorch of it.

Max pushes Boba Fett towards Dylan's face and Dylan steps back and goes into a Power Ranger stance, legs apart, arms crossed, hands fisted. Max hears Dylan when he makes crackling-interference noises in his mouth like a lightsaber in *A New Hope.*

Max pushes Boba Fett forwards a couple of times more.

Max says, *I have a sister but she is dead and she wasn't even born,* and adds, *I'm taller than you.*

Max hears Dylan say, *My mum has a baby in her tummy but I mustn't tell anyone because it's a secret baby until it's a safe baby,* and Dylan adds, *It might be a boy, if it's a boy.*

Max says, *Boys are more power than girls, aren't they?*

Max watches as Dylan does the stance and the crackling again, and this time Max joins in, and they do it side by side for a while with an infinite number of imagined girls being threatened and frightened away on the non-boy side of the bedroom.

Max sees Dylan kick the air and Max is quick to copy him.

Max hears Daddy said, *You boys seem to be getting on*, and his face was up in the open door, poo-poo face.

Max says, *Poo-poo face*, and Dylan says it, too.

Max hears Daddy said something complicated he, Max, doesn't understand—and then Daddy said, *So I've been invited for tea, too, although you've disgraced us entirely. So I've been sent to fetch you two— what are you being? Jedi Knights?*

Dylan says, *Let's kill him.*

AGATHA AND PADDY

'Tell me again *just* why I am making a fucking halo.'

Paddy's finger bled into toilet tissue.

'Because you are his father and you love him and I am making the mince pies.'

'It's not meant to be a fucking Christian school, is it? But they don't do half so much fucking handicraft nonsense over Eid or Ramadan.'

'Then fucking move him to another fucking school, if you want. You can drive him, every morning.'

'I'm sorry,' said Paddy, about to go back upstairs. 'I just wanted to let off.'

'Dump,' Agatha said. 'You wanted to dump—and you have.'

'But think of the environmental impact. All this tinsel, every year. Miles of it. Coathangers that could see me out.'

'Complain,' said Agatha. 'But you won't. You never do.'

'I complained about . . .'

Paddy stood for a moment, thinking about Marx, kitchens and Miss Heaton, Max's class teacher.

'Overall, I'm fairly happy with the school,' declared Paddy. 'It's Christmas I hate.'

'Do you?' Agatha said. 'You don't.'

'I hate spending money on plastic crap.'

'So do I,' said Agatha. 'But to Max these are real things. They're adventures waiting to happen. Brothers.'

'Adventure should be in the head.'

'And you didn't have toys?'

'Not as many—and the ones I had, I played with for a lot longer. They became characters.'

'You're turning into the rabbi again,' said Agatha. 'You're making up some kind of deprived childhood you never had, just so you can make a point with it—and force it on a completely different child.'

'He's going to disappear into computer games pretty quickly. How are you going to feel about that? At least I climbed a tree once in a while.'

'If Max climbs outside those stairs, you tell him off. The banisters.' Agatha realized she was even tireder than she'd thought.

'I encourage him to be physical whenever I can.' Paddy leant side-ways against the doorframe. 'But I do—I am aware—tell him to stop doing things too much of the time.' Only three Christmas cards had arrived so far, and they made the mantelpiece look pathetic. 'It's because I don't want him breaking things. Then I realize what I'm really telling him is that the things, our possessions, are more important than he is. But it's an instinct capitalism taught me, via my parents. I'd *like* to demonstrate the opposite—show him this is all trash compared to what I feel for him. But I can't burn the house down to prove a point. You wouldn't let me.'

'Is your finger still bleeding?'

'No,' said Paddy, before taking a look. 'Not much.'

'Let me see,' said Agatha.

Paddy wanted her to wince and say, 'Ooh, nasty,' but she said, 'That's not bad.'

He returned to the doorway. 'Are you going to respond?' he asked.

'Bring the stuff downstairs,' said Agatha. 'Finish it here.'

'There's already tinsel all over my floor,' Paddy said. 'I don't need to trash this place too.'

Agatha made her point, his point, with a pause.

'Okay,' said Paddy, and five minutes later was back with the hair-band, coathanger pieces, pliers, tinsel, Superglue.

'Don't complain about bits on the stairs,' he said. 'You asked me to come. It just moults. I can't help it.'

'When he used to go round to girls' houses to play,' said Agatha, 'there was always glitter between the floorboards.'

Paddy thought, pursued.

'Are you going to respond?'

'I've stopped blaming myself for not being perfect. As long as we fuck Max up in a productive way, so he's not just lazy and happy, we'll have done our job. It won't be finished, though. We'll die feeling it's way too early, but he'll be a little relieved—and if we get to see grandchildren, we'll see what of us he pushes on them.'

Paddy twisted the coathanger wire with the pliers—more carefully than before, upstairs.

'Is that coherent?' he said. 'Isn't that just mild defeatism?'

'We react,' said Agatha. 'We say things quickly to him, because we need to say something. We don't think about whether one thing is consistent with another.'

Agatha remembered the almost-car-crash on the M1—owls.

'I try to.'

'We tell him to be quiet all the time, yet we encourage him to express himself freely.'

'Freely can be quietly.'

'For a boy? No. Freedom is energy, mess, violence. No one saying no.'

This was the fullest conversation they'd had in weeks. Paddy wanted to go upstairs again—he was afraid they would end up speaking about what they hadn't been speaking about. Yet, for the moment, they were both keeping the subject to Max and Max only—plus general philosophy of life.

'You're right,' said Paddy. 'But Max would burn down the house, just to see how it looked—just to say it was cool.' Agatha thought of how cool was now a value for Max, along with wicked and sexy. 'Would really good parents—truly psychologically healthy—wouldn't they let him do that?'

'Where would he sleep that evening?'

'We could go to a hotel. Start again.'

'It's not good for children to be absolute rulers.'

'It's not good for them to think wallpaper is more important than they are.'

'If you stop them drawing on the walls, they just do it on pieces of paper instead. There's nothing wrong with that.'

Were they talking about her unfaithfulness? Neither of them was exactly sure—which probably meant they were.

'But houses—they are *for* children. Houses aren't kings. Max might discover something by being able to draw huge drawings and live with them.'

'Or watch his toys burning.'

'I think I'm saying,' said Paddy, 'that it's all on fire anyway. We live in it and pretend it's not burning, but boys know that's what it's doing. That's why—'

'And girls don't?'

'—boys are so fierce and fiery.'

'Girls?' Agatha asked.

'Different,' said Paddy. 'Ice palaces. Or mermaids under the sea. Flying. The princess stuff means something, so does the glitter.'

'So a brother and sister live in fire and ice, at the same time, in the same house, and don't know it.'

'And even if they did, they wouldn't behave any differently. I don't think it matters what children know and don't know. They exist in states and react to those states.'

'Let's say we allowed Max to realize his dream—your dream for him—and burn this place down. You're saying it wouldn't have an effect?'

'Exactly. It's the *not* burning it that has the effect—does the damage.'

Agatha's mug was empty. She was too tired to make tea but might manage a hot water bottle later.

Agatha stated where they were: 'All boys are traumatized by living in burning buildings that never burn down.'

'Obviously, some actually do.'

'And their boys grow up psychologically more healthy . . .'

'No,' said Paddy. 'Immensely damaged, because all the other boys can't forgive them for what they've been able to do, live the dream—so they punish them again and again.'

'What about after the Great Fire of London? Were all the boys healthy then?'

'We have no possible way of knowing,' said Paddy. 'But if you follow my logic, they must have been devastated by it.'

'Because?'

'Think about it.'

Agatha tried. The front room smelt of the mince pies that had cooled in the kitchen. Paddy was winding tinsel round and round the halo's metal ring. 'Because there weren't any houses left for their sons to burn?'

'No,' said Paddy.

'Oh, the girls,' said Agatha. 'All the mermaids weren't happy.'

'Because . . .'

'Don't patronize me,' Agatha said. 'I get it.'

'For the girls, it was the opposite—'

'I get it.'

They sat.

Already it was too late, and it would soon be much too late. After that, another half hour would make no difference—tomorrow would be trashed anyway. There would be shouting to get food into Max and Max into clothes.

'Which is why,' said Paddy, 'we won't be putting a box of matches in Max's Christmas stocking—although he would think that was the best present ever.'

'Some people would think this is a weird conversation.'

'They would,' agreed Paddy, trying to make a point of his agreement, after the dangerous *don't patronize me*. 'But they would silently have concurred not to give their son matches, and the same conversation would implicitly have taken place.'

'We're just so stupid we have to say these things out loud.'

'We take pleasure in saying them. We have time.'

Agatha felt their house around them, the dark outside and, southwards, the whole beginning of the sea.

'It's your job,' she said.

'It's my vocation, too.'

They were finally arrived.

'I didn't burn anything,' said Agatha. 'I fucked someone trivial.'

'I accept that.'

Paddy, too, was aware of the house—the exact extent of their mortgage.

'Intellectually,' Paddy added.

Paddy was also aware of their marriage, as if it were an object.

'It may happen again,' Agatha said. 'But I don't think it will. If you want to try it, it would be hypocritical of me not to say okay.'

'Once.'

'No. More than that, if that's what you needed. It's not the number of times, it's the fact.'

Agatha very gently became terrified; Paddy might already have stolen what she was now offering as gift.

'I've watched Henry,' said Paddy. 'I don't think I do want anything.'

'The Indian woman?'

'No.'

'You would like to hit me.'

'No, I would *have* liked to hit you.'

'Now what?'

'I suppose I'd like you to hit yourself.'

'Really, though, to kill myself?'

'No.'

'Disfigure the face?'

'Just feel the impact—the type of wound isn't important. No wound's fine. The pain.'

Agatha didn't slap herself, although Paddy could see her considering it.

In the video Paddy was taking of the carol service, Max's halo could be seen but not his face.

Agatha could tell from the occasional raised arm that Max was doing some of the actions.

His halo was the best one by far.

When they reached the first *Everyone will sing*, Agatha got to her feet, as did Paddy (putting away the camera)—'Hark the Herald'—but by the end of the first verse, still less than half the parents, grandparents and carers had stood up; so Paddy, embarrassed, but also feeling some kind of point was being made, sat down again—Agatha, though, sang louder than necessary, to make the sitting others feel guilty, and Paddy soon got to his feet.

'Haven't they ever been to church?' Agatha asked.

'No,' said Paddy, having meant to say yes. He wanted a good reason to sit down, then found he had beside him a good reason to remain standing.

He knew Agatha was remembering their wedding.

Agatha heard him singing loudly, badly, and him not minding.

Their wedding had not been in church.